A Giraffe Thing

Jo Bavington-Jones

A Giraffe Thing

Published by The Conrad Press in the United Kingdom 2021

Tel: +44(0)1227 472 874
www.theconradpress.com
info@theconradpress.com

ISBN 978-1-913567-91-0

Copyright © Jo Bavington-Jones, 2021

Typesetting and Cover Design by: Charlotte Mouncey, www.bookstyle.co.uk
The Conrad Press logo was designed by Maria Priestley.

Printed and bound in Great Britain by Clays Ltd, Elcograf S.p.A.

For Graham.
A shining lamp while he lived.
A brilliant star forever.

For each ecstatic instant
We must an anguish pay
In keen and quivering ratio
To the ecstasy.

For each beloved hour
Sharp pittances of years,
Bitter contested farthings
And coffers heaped with tears.

Emily Dickinson

Chapter 1

Teenage Kicks

I was just fourteen when you gave me the giraffe. Do you remember? You'd walked me home from school and we stood on my front doorstep, awkward and unsure of what to do next. I probably flicked my long, straight brown hair nervously over my shoulders and lowered the gaze of my green eyes to the floor.

You were seventeen and in the Lower Sixth. I was so flattered to be the object of your attention; being noticed by an older boy made me feel important, grown up. I didn't stop to wonder if I was attracted to you. I knew I liked you a lot. You seemed so tall, so finished. Do you know what I mean? To a naïve fourteen-year-old girl, you seemed so adult.

It was my first kiss. Did I ever tell you that? I think I must have done. I know it was little more than a peck on the lips, but it was still my first. I didn't like it very much, if I'm honest. It was kind of wet. But I still liked you. And I was still so damn flattered.

And then, before you said goodbye, you rummaged in the pocket of your black school blazer and produced a conker, a rubber band and a small plastic giraffe that was kind of chewed and a bit ink-stained.

'It's the only thing I have that I can give you,' you said, having decided the best of the three finds was the giraffe. You looked slightly apologetic as you held out your hand with the tatty looking creature in it.

'Thank you,' I said, blushing no doubt, as I took the small plastic figure and smiled at you. It might as well have been a diamond.

You smiled back. I remember thinking what a nice smile you had, how it made your blue eyes crinkle at the corners. And that crazy mop of dark blonde hair, always messy because you were constantly running your fingers through it.

'He's called Narbadingi. The giraffe,' you told me.

'Narbadingi,' I repeated, laughing at the wonderfully nonsense-sounding name.

'Look after him.'

'I will. I promise.'

And I kept that promise. Thirty-six years later, Narbadingi is still with me, in a shoe box full of letters and cards and mementoes; echoes of you, of us. That shoebox has been my constant companion, my prized possession; it has moved house with me many times, gradually filling up over the years, but always with me. It has survived the failure of two marriages, times when I have lost everything. Narbadingi's shoebox has inhabited many a loft and been concealed at the back of many a wardrobe; the one possession I could never let go.

Do you remember how we started? How we first met? I was wearing my stepfather's pyjamas. I vividly recall how long it took me to pluck up the courage to ask my weird, distant stepfather if I could borrow them. He and I didn't have the sort of relationship where I would normally ask him anything, let alone if I could borrow his nightwear. That's how much I wanted to go to the party though. They were ugly brown stripy things, and they smelt funny, but they didn't put you off. You were wearing pyjamas too, of course, but at least they were your own.

We were at a party in someone's cellar, weren't we – your school science partner and my older sister's boyfriend? My sister was pissed off that I was there I think, but I didn't care. I wanted to hang out with the older, cooler kids. I'd persuaded my friend, Annabelle, to come along. I wasn't brave enough to come alone.

'Hello, aren't you Laura's sister?' you'd said, smiling at me.

I probably went red when you spoke to me, gauche and shy as I was. 'Er... yes... Louise. This is my friend, Annabelle. You're Phil's friend, aren't you?' Phil was my sister's boyfriend. It was his pyjama party.

'Yep. Martin. It's nice to meet you, Louise. And you, Annabelle.'

'Nice to meet you too.' I'm sure I was still blushing. I would've been grateful we were in a dimly lit cellar.

'Would you like a drink?'

A moment of worry, I remember. Did you mean alcohol? Would you think I was just a silly young girl if I refused? I wanted you to think I was cool.

'Yes, please,' I heard myself saying.

You disappeared for a minute. Annabelle nudged me. 'Is he getting us alcohol?'

'I don't know. Don't worry – you don't have to drink it if it is. I'll drink it for you.' What was I thinking? It was just so important that you didn't dismiss us, me.

7

'Here you go,' you said, handing us two white plastic cups. 'Hope Coke is okay?'

'Oh, yes, fine,' I said, trying not to let the relief show in my voice. 'Thanks.'

'You're welcome.' You were nice to us.

There was a record player in the corner of the room and Phil was in charge of the music. I remember what was playing when we had that first drink together. It was Soft Cell's 'Tainted Love'. I still think of you and that night whenever I hear it. It takes me straight back to that summer of 1981, the summer you came into my life. I had no idea then, of course, what you would come to mean to me and the impact you were to have on my life.

Chapter 2

First Kiss

That was the summer I started keeping a diary, triggered perhaps by that pivotal first, unremarkable, wet kiss. Had I been expecting fireworks? I wonder. I still have my diary from 1981, guarded by a certain giraffe in a red shoe box. It's one of those five-year ones with a little brassy lock on the side.

12th September, 1981

Oh my god! He kissed me. Martin kissed me. Yay! I didn't like it. Boo! I wanted to like it because I really like him, but it was just a bit wet and I was glad it was over quickly. I thought I'd feel something other than yuck. Disappointed. I still really like him though, and he IS in the Lower Sixth, so… Anyway, he gave me this little plastic giraffe called Narbadingi. SO SWEET! It looks as though he's chewed it a bit and his fountain pen must leak because it has ink stains on it too. I think maybe he kept it in his pencil case sometimes. I don't care though, I love it! I might let him kiss me again, but I'm not sure yet.

I'm re-reading that entry on this my fiftieth birthday. I'm living on my own now and the shoebox has been kept under my bed for the last couple of years. I guess the occasion of marking my half-century has made me feel nostalgic for my youth. And yours. And what might have been.

Am I happy? Depends which day you ask me, I suppose. Am I happy today as I sit on my bed surrounded by your letters, the envelopes making a 3D decoupage of the patchwork squares of the quilt my late Godmother made me? It's the first time I've revisited the contents of the box properly. It was always unnecessary or too painful before. Over the years, I simply lifted the lid a fraction to slip in any new missive. Your letters always triggered high emotion. Or desperately low. But always extreme. Never anything in between.

I'm looking through the history of us, smiling at mis-addressed envelopes from the times when you couldn't quite remember my address; apologies to postmen, descriptions of where they should find me. I can remember feeling a warm glow when an envelope addressed in your lovely scrawl plopped onto the doormat. How I cherished the words you wrote and smiled at the funny little cartoon pictures you drew. I ran my fingers across the places you signed your name with kisses. You, my quirky, wondrous friend, you never failed to make me smile. And cry. I smiled smiles wide enough to light up a room, and cried enough tears in which to drown. Never anything in between.

I'm supposed to be getting ready for a family dinner to celebrate my half-century. I'm really not sure I want to commemorate this milestone. I think maybe I just want to wallow for a while, alone with my thoughts and my memories. Just a little bit longer flicking through this catalogue of us, then I will get dressed in the teal blue dress hanging on the wardrobe door. As I riffle through a packet of letters released from a blue ribbon, an old birthday card falls out. Naturally there's a giraffe on it, as there is on many of the cards and postcards contained in the shoebox. It was always giraffes with us, wasn't it? A giraffe thing. If you'd sent me a card today, would it have had a giraffe on it? Or the number fifty? I think I'd be ageless in your eyes, still that fourteen-year-old girl you walked home from school so many years, a lifetime, ago. You always did bring out the romantic in me. The romantic fool.

I'm drifting now, thoughts of you filling my head. I realise my hand is clenched, my fingernails digging into my palm. I uncurl my fingers and he's there, Narbadingi, still just the same as he was thirty-six years ago. Still a little chewed, still a little stained, but unaltered by time. I turn to look at my reflection in the wardrobe mirror and half expect to see the fourteen-year-old girl I used to be looking back at me. Maybe there's a little of her left in the sparkle of the green eyes now framed by laughter lines, but the brown hair is streaked with grey, the cheekbones not so well defined.

I don't want that middle-aged woman in the mirror to be me. I turn away. Right now, I want to be fourteen again, with my life spread before me like a great feast. Give me back the pain and angst, the heartbreak and heaven. I want to feel all of it again. I want to feel so alive that it feels like I might burst. I want the drama and the boredom, the fear and the excitement. To do it better. To do it differently.

I pick up the diary, still open on the bed, face down at the first entry. I want it to transport me, a time machine to the bedroom of my fourteen-year-old self.

Chapter 3

Prince Charming

13ᵗʰ September 1981

Couldn't believe my eyes when I came out of school today – he was there, waiting for me! I was so embarrassed. All my friends saw him. I think they were secretly impressed though, with him being in the sixth form. I kind of wish his hair wasn't so crazy though and he was a bit better looking. That sounds awful, doesn't it? Makes me sound a bit shallow. I'm not! Not really. It's just people judge, don't they? Anyway, he wanted to walk me home again, so I said yes. He carried my bag. I was really grateful because my chemistry book is sooo heavy. We talked about school and stuff. He's super brainy – doing maths and sciences 'A' Levels. I told him I'm better at English and French. And geography. I didn't know whether or not to hold his hand while we walked, so I didn't, and he didn't try to hold mine. But our hands kept sort of brushing up against each other. I really like him, but I still don't think I fancy him. I told him I keep Narbadingi in my pencil case, but it's OK because my pen doesn't leak. I showed him to Annabelle. I think she's a bit jealous.

I close my eyes and I'm there. In the bedroom of my teen-aged self, sitting at the table I use as a desk, writing in my diary. There's a tape playing – it's the Top 40 recorded from the radio last Sunday. 'Prince Charming' by Adam & the Ants is number one. I rewind it to my favourite track, listening to the squeal of the mechanism as it goes, pressing stop and play multiple times until I hear Godley & Creme's 'Under Your Thumb' start up.

I look around the room. The memory is vivid. Two single beds with purple candlewick bedspreads, the hated things concealed under cheap fur fabric throws from the Sunday market, and cuddly toys accumulated over the years. The beige and cream wallpaper I didn't choose is all but hidden under posters. I'm in a phase of liking all things astrological and there are four giant posters depicting earth, air, fire and water. The water one is directly over my bed, placed there because I found out I am a water sign: Scorpio. Back to the table, the writing.

When we got to my house, I felt a bit awkward again. I didn't know what to do. I didn't really want Martin to kiss me again. But I didn't want to hurt his feelings either. I ended up asking if he wanted to come in for a drink. He said yes. I knew I had to warn him about the house. I knew I wouldn't be able to take him upstairs to my room where it's always tidy, so I had to warn him. I told him the house is really, really untidy and that my mum isn't very good at tidying up. And that she never throws anything away. I hate how embarrassing my house is. All my friends' houses are really nice and really tidy. I really HATE my life sometimes.

I still remember how much I hated taking people into my house for the first time back then. Apologising as my friends looked around the lounge for a place to sit. Do you remember? How every surface was piled high with 'stuff'? You had to move a pile before you could sit down anywhere. And piles would suddenly reach tipping point and just collapse, where they'd be pushed to one side, making way for a new pile of 'stuff'. Sometimes I tried to sort out the piles, to tidy them into some sort of order, to throw out months' old newspapers and magazines. But the order never lasted long. It just made way for new piles. More 'stuff'. It was pointless and disheartening, so eventually I just stopped trying, seeking refuge in my room.

But you didn't seem to mind the untidiness. You just shuffled into a space on the sofa and seemed happy to be in my house. I think I got two glasses of orange squash and felt grateful you didn't try to find a clear corner on the coffee table on which to rest your glass. You just held on to it. You met my mum that day for the first time too. You thought she was lovely and I think she liked you too. She asked you questions about school and your family. I wanted her to leave us alone, not embarrass me, but you chatted away to her seemingly completely at ease.

Everyone liked my mum. I suppose it's only to us that our parents are embarrassing when we're young. It's only hindsight that reveals to us just how amazing they really are, were. You told my mum you lived with your mum and older sister. I just sat and listened and let the conversation happen, not joining in, willing my mum to get on with whatever she'd been doing, and leave us in peace. Willing her not to say anything to embarrass me in front of this boy I'd kissed. This boy I liked so much but didn't want to kiss again.

She finally stopped asking you questions and left the room. And then I didn't know what to say; how to fill the silence. I felt small and shy. You sat and smiled at me. You seemed content just to be with me, in my messy house. You were always happy to be with me, weren't you?

Chapter 4

Shine On You Crazy Diamond

It's getting late now, and I can't put off getting ready for my birthday dinner. I'd much rather stay home alone, getting lost in my memories and pretending for a bit longer that all these years haven't passed. It's probably just as well I have to go out though. I imagine I'd only become maudlin if I carried on any further down memory lane.

I suppose it's simply this anniversary of my birth that's making me so nostalgic; feeling my age and mortality weighing heavily on me. I don't feel fifty. At least I don't think I do. Of course, I don't really know how fifty is supposed to feel. Does everyone get a little morose about this particular number? The big five-oh. It's a long way from fourteen, and I'm really not sure how I got here. Certainly, I didn't take the best route to get here. My life has not gone to plan thus far. If I even had a plan. I suppose I mean if I had had a plan, this wouldn't have been it. I would've taken the fairy tale path through the rose garden, instead of the nettle-strewn track I seem to have been on most of my life.

It hasn't all been nettles, of course. There have been roses along the way but, as fast as I found them, they shrivelled and turned black. I sometimes wonder what I would tell my fourteen-year-old self if I could offer her advice. Would I tell her to do it all differently? To be brave and grab life with both hands, to grasp the nettle and the thorny stem, and never let go? To never *settle* for second best. To believe she can do anything, be anything. To live and to love with great passion, be fearless and take risks. To never give up looking for the fairy tale, for her Prince Charming. For anything else just leads to… well… to this. This fifty-year-old woman sitting on her bed surrounded by memories and shattered dreams. To feelings of failure and dissatisfaction; regret and longing. Yep. Maudlin. Knew it. Need to snap out of it and put on the teal dress and the fake smile, be the happy-go-lucky Louise everyone expects.

As I run the straighteners through my still long brown hair, the light catches on the strands of grey, little flashes that remind me I am growing old. Once, not so long ago, I would have yanked them out in disgust, not ready to accept their presence. But now, there are too many to pull out. I have, reluctantly, to accept them or to start dyeing my hair. I'm not ready for either option really, but I'm resistant to the idea of covering up the red and gold flashes in my chestnut-coloured locks. I can hold off a little longer, I think. Be in denial a little longer. My hairstyle now is not so different to that of my fourteen-year-old incarnation. I have come full circle, via perms and highlights and downright blonde times, back to the naturally straight brown tresses of my youth. Was it a conscious decision, I wonder? I don't know. I think you'd approve.

With my hair now a mirrored sheet down my back, I turn my attention to my face, tracing the lines with my fingertips; the laughter lines in the corners of my eyes, souvenirs of the good times - the frown lines of my forehead, indelible reminders of the bad. The deepest lines on my face are the two furrows between my brows. They are really all I see now when I look in the mirror. I sometimes wonder whether I should get my fringe cut back in, give the lines a curtain to hide behind. I have spent far too much money on lotions and potions that promise to conceal them and even watched YouTube videos on how to get rid of them. You'd laugh if I told you some of the things I've done to try and reduce or remove them. But, like the grey hairs, they're apparently here to stay. I'm just not ready to embrace them.

As I go to work on concealing the ravages that time has wrought on my face, I can't help but recall the fresh, unlined face of my youth. I suppose it was wasted on me then. I didn't know what I had, or how I would regret losing it, and I took it for granted. I should have revelled in it, relished it, nurtured it. What's that saying? Youth is wasted on the young? It's true. And hindsight is a bitch. A sigh escapes my lips as I apply concealer to some sun damage on my cheeks. Would you still love this face? I wonder. Would you still see the face of the girl you fell in love with? You were in love with me all those years ago, weren't you? I don't think I really understood what that meant back then. I was too young, too naïve, too insensitive. I think maybe I acted badly towards you. I didn't mean to. I just didn't understand the depth of your feelings, or how my behaviour impacted on you. I'm sorry for that. I never wanted to cause you pain.

My face is finished. I still see all the lines, they're just a little softer now. I slip the dress over my head and smooth its lines down over my body, over the extra curves which the years have given me, like unwanted gifts. As I examine my reflection in the full-length mirror, I come to the conclusion that I look okay. For my age. Yep, not bad for an old bird. That's what I say to myself. Maybe I'm being too hard on myself, but I am full of regret and nostalgia for my youth today. For my youth, and perhaps yours.

What might life have been like if we'd made a go of it? I wonder. Could we have been happy? Would the laughter lines have outdone the worry ones? But we didn't, did we? So it's pointless wondering. I made my life choices, you made yours and now we're reduced to a whole heap of memories. Those memories are currently scattered on the bed behind me, thirty-six-years' worth reduced to a pile of paper and card. And one small plastic giraffe, which I slip into my coat pocket before leaving the house.

Chapter 5

We Are Family

As I drive the fifteen or so minutes to the restaurant, thoughts of you are still jangling around my head. Apparently you have no intention of leaving any time soon. I guess that's okay. We were always comfortable together, weren't we? After that initial teenage awkwardness, we became easy together. Easy and oh so very complicated, I think with a sigh that seems to originate from the very depths of me. We shared an easiness I've never found with anyone since. Not really. And certainly not with my family. Another sigh escapes as I think about the evening ahead.

My family. Where to begin? It's complicated. It's dysfunctional. It's a whole other book. A series of books. A Britannica. I suppose you don't need an encyclopaedic knowledge of my family, though, so I'll just give you the rough guide.

We're all seated around the table in the restaurant now. Italian. My sister Laura's choice. Not my favourite, but… anyway, here we all are. I'm sitting at the head of the table, and opposite me sits my father, examining the wine list over the top of his glasses, deciding for everyone what they would like to drink. I take a few moments to really look at him. He's aging well, actually. At seventy-five, his hair is not yet completely grey, and he looks tanned from a recent golfing trip to Portugal. He makes me think of a judge, holding court, presiding over the woman he was once married to, and the grown up children he sired. It's easier to just accept his decisions than to object. He wouldn't listen anyway.

To my left sits my mother. My messy, marvellous, embarrassing mum. At seventy-two, her hair is decidedly salt and pepper, but not all grey either. Good hair genes. Something to be grateful for, I think, running my fingers through my own brown tresses. Mum is wearing her usual eclectic style of outfit; purple velvet wide-legged trousers, pink blouse and a cardigan of every colour imaginable. I got a glimpse of her footwear earlier. I think she might actually be wearing slippers.

To my right sits my sister Laura. You can tell we're sisters somehow, even though we don't really look alike. Maybe it's the same chestnut-brown hair. At fifty-three, Laura has even fewer grey hairs than me. Laura is the quiet one, always has been. Sometimes I think she resents me. Maybe even dislikes me. In this, Dad's court, I'm the jester, the clown - the one who makes everyone laugh, the life and soul. I think it pisses Laura off. But I didn't choose this role. It just kind of happened. And I've been doing it for so long now, I can't be any other way. Everyone expects me to be bright and funny, sometimes even a little too loud perhaps. I just want everyone to be happy. They think I'm always happy.

Dad's voice fills the air, loud and a little pompous. He's ordering wine for the table. Mum tuts.

'I see your father hasn't changed then?' she says in my direction. 'Still as bossy as ever.'

I just smile. I don't want this to turn into a family drama.

Laura, however, is happy to agree with Mum.

'Absolutely. Pompous old fart. I don't even like red wine. Gives me a headache. No point trying to tell him though – he never bloody listens.'

'He never did. Too full of his own importance,' Mum adds, happy to have an ally.

I don't want to take sides. I just want everyone to get on. Can't they put their differences aside? Just once? For me, on my birthday. Can't I just have one night off from being the peacekeeper, the glue?

'Why don't you order a glass of white then, Laura?' I say to my sister in an attempt to mollify her and defuse things before they escalate.

She harrumphs. 'No, no, don't want to be a nuisance.'

'You're not a nuisance. You don't have to go along with what Dad says. Shall we order a bottle of white? You and Mum could share it.' I don't really like red or white wine, and am only planning to have one small glass of whatever is put in front of me anyway. I only really like rosé, but I won't say anything, of course. Not being a martyr so much as just keeping the peace. I've learnt to pick my battles. They are few and far between.

But Laura won't budge. She's fine-tuned playing the martyr over the years, and there's no point trying to dissuade her now. I save my energy and look across the table to Laura's husband, Nigel, who's sitting diagonally opposite her. Like the rest of us, Nigel is carrying a little extra weight around his middle, and his grey hair is thinning above a kind, bespectacled face. I like Nigel, and we get on really well; more of a brother than an in-law. He's quiet, like Laura, but with none of her air of dissatisfaction and resentment. Nigel is calm, kind and considerate,

22

and I often think how lucky Laura is to have him. Sometimes, though, I wonder if he is actually happy. Sometimes, I think I see a flash of sadness in his eyes. At this moment, he's discussing the menu with their son, Richard, who's nodding at whatever his father is saying.

Richard is seventeen and doing his 'A' Levels. I can't help but remember you as I watch him now. He has the same dark blonde hair and the same studious expression to his face. He has his father's calm and kind nature, and none of his mother's bitterness.

Sitting by her grandfather, the only one of us who doesn't seem to mind his pomposity, his bossiness, is my daughter, Libby. My smart, funny, beautiful girl. My heart swells with a whole raft of emotions as I look at her now. She's squeezing her grandfather's hand and laughing at whatever he's saying. There are no words to adequately express the boundless depth of love for my child. People say she looks like me, but I think she is much more beautiful. I suppose our colouring's the same and she has my height, but she is a better human being than I. She's the best part of me, without a doubt, and I'm so very proud of her. Libby's in her second year of university, studying Psychology at Sheffield. I remember joking with her when she chose the subject that our family would provide her with a great deal of research material.

There's an empty seat at the table. It should be occupied by my half-brother, Charlie, my dad's son from his second marriage. I guess I'm not really surprised Charlie's a no-show. He's unreliable at the best of times. And impossible at the worst. The eternal optimist in me had tried hard to believe that he would turn up, for me, on this special birthday, after everything I've done for him. I've been giving him the benefit of the doubt for so long, perhaps it's time I accepted he really is a selfish sod, and to lower my expectations. Thinking of Charlie makes me sad. I find myself slipping my hand into the pocket of my coat, where it hangs on the back of my chair, and closing my fingers around the small, plastic talisman resting there.

Turning my attention back to the people present, I tune into the conversation between my mother and sister. They're talking about Charlie.

'I see the prodigal son has decided not to grace us with his presence,' Laura says, a disapproving look on her face.

Mum purses her lips as if something distasteful has crossed them. 'Waste of space, that one. If you ask me, it's a good thing he's not here. He'd've found a way to ruin it, I'm sure.'

Laura nods her agreement. A part of me agrees with them too, but I still don't want to acknowledge it aloud. I still want to hold onto some glimmer of hope that my errant brother can find his way back to us. I still want to remain loyal.

'He'd probably have turned up drunk and been loud and pompous like your father,' Mum continues.

'No doubt. Chip off the old block. He's definitely his father's son. I dread to think how much money he's chucked down his throat or up his nose,' Laura agrees.

She's right, sadly. Charlie is a wayward soul. But why do they have to be so bitchy? Does it make them feel better about themselves, about their own lives? I take a sip from the glass of red wine that has appeared in front of me, and it's my turn to purse my lips. Awful stuff, but I need something to take the edge off in order to survive the evening. I momentarily regret my decision to drive; right now a few gins would be extremely welcome. I take a deep breath and attempt to break up the conversation taking place across me.

'So, Laura, how's Richard getting on at school? Still on for straight As?'

It works. Even Laura's dislike of our brother can't withstand the mention of her own boy. 'Yes. He's doing brilliantly. Got his father's brains, thankfully,' she replies with an air of false modesty I'm clearly supposed to pick up on. I do so, dutifully.

'Nonsense. He gets his brains from both of you. You shouldn't be so modest.'

Laura simpers a little and takes a glug of her own red wine, not seeming to mind the taste in the least. 'I suppose you're right. I should take some of the credit after all.'

'Such a good boy.' This from Mum, who dotes on both her grandchildren. 'And Libby, of course, such a sweet girl.'

Laura picks up her cue. 'Yes, of course. How is Libby? Still enjoying university?'

'Yes, thankfully, she loves it. I miss her terribly though.'

'Well, yes, of course, but we must be unselfish where our children are concerned, mustn't we?' Laura says. I try to ignore her patronising tone and just smile and nod. I can't help wondering, though, what made Laura the way she is today.

I turn my attention to the menu and start a discussion about the choices on it. Safer ground, surely?

'So, what do you fancy, Mum?'

'I really don't know. I don't have much of an appetite in the evening now. It all looks a bit heavy.'

God, why can't she ever be positive about anything? I grit my teeth. 'Just order whatever takes your fancy and eat as much as you can manage. Or how about a starter instead? I'm sure they'd do you one as a main.' I'm willing her to say the right thing, just for once, for me, for my birthday.

'I'd much rather have gone out at lunchtime. I won't sleep a wink if I eat a big dinner. I'll be tossing and turning all night, I'm sure.'

Inside, I'm screaming, willing her to just shut up. What was she always telling us as kids? If you can't say something nice, don't say anything? When did that stop being a thing? Why can't she just pretend for once? Pretend she's not bitter and regretful and even a little bit spiteful. Let's all tell the little white lies that make life bearable. Let's not always say the things we're thinking, the things that may, wittingly or not, hurt the ones closest to us. I could tell Laura I hate her dress or that the shape of her glasses is totally unflattering to her face; or I could tell Mum her cardigan is hideous and should be burned. But I wouldn't, of course, because those things would upset them, would dent their confidence and would serve no-one. And so, the little white lies are told to keep everyone happy and ignorantly blissful. Lately, though, I seem to be the only one really trying to keep up the pretence.

Chapter 6

Hello, I Love You

I've survived the evening, just, and am driving home once more. I've dropped Libby off at her dad's, Alan's, house so she has a chance for a quick catch up before heading straight back to Sheffield in the morning. I'm pleased that Alan will at least get to see her briefly; he adores her and has been a great father. He wasn't a terrible husband, either. He just wasn't you, Marty, and I didn't love him, hard as I tried. Alan came into my life when I was lonely and vulnerable, and I thought he could glue me back together. Wishful thinking. Eventually, I had to stop pretending, and get out.

I normally hate coming back to my empty house, but tonight I'm grateful to be alone. The strain of an evening with my family has left me wound up like the bowl of spaghetti they'd placed in front of Mum earlier, which she'd devoured with relish before moaning once more she wouldn't sleep a wink. I hadn't bothered to remark that she didn't need to eat it all. It wasn't worth the breath or the confrontation.

Closing my front door behind me, I heave a sigh of relief, dropping my keys on the hall table as I head to the kitchen to make a cup of herbal tea. I need something to soothe my frayed nerves and reduce my undoubtedly inflated blood pressure to something nearer normal. I know, I know, a big meal is supposed to lower your blood pressure, but you haven't eaten pasta with my family, and the salmon, asparagus and fusilli is sitting heavy.

I've still got my coat on as I head into the lounge, switching on a lamp before settling into my favourite armchair and kicking off my shoes. It feels good to be home and alone with my thoughts once more. You haven't been far from my thoughts all evening, Marty, simply pushed to one side a little while I got through the meal. I pull you back to the fore once more. Hello you. Old friend. I've missed you.

I lean back in the chair, careful not to spill the mug of steaming chamomile, closing my eyes and picturing you in my mind's eye. You're eighteen in the picture. I'm nearly fifteen. We've been friends for some months now, I guess. Just friends, nothing more. Did I know you wanted more? Yes, of course I did. I must have. But I just wanted you as my friend. Did I hurt you back then? Did I lead you on? I think I must have done, but I don't think it was intentional. I liked having you in my life. But I also loved the feeling of power that came with knowing you wanted me. Maybe even loved me a little bit. I was just a silly little girl, really, though. I didn't know how my actions affected you. I'm sorry if I was thoughtless and tactless.

I realise I've still got my coat on and it's making me too hot, so I put my mug on the side and head to the hall to hang it up. I look up the stairs and remember the diary I was reading earlier and jog up the stairs to get it. Settling myself into the armchair once more, I open the diary at random.

Ugh! Mock end of year exams are soon.

What's the point of mocks anyway? I tried out for the netball team today. I don't even want to be in the netball team, but Annabelle didn't want to go on her own. Only went and got picked though, didn't I? And Annabelle didn't, so now she's angry at me, which really isn't fair, is it? She asked me to go. It's not my fault she didn't get picked. Apparently I shouldn't have tried so hard! Oh my God. Really?! And now I have to do netball practice every Friday after school. And after I let her come out with me and Martin last weekend. He's passed his driving test and got a car now, which is really cool. The driving test. Not the car. The car is definitely NOT cool. But it's better than nothing. He took us to a really nice little pub out in the middle of nowhere called 'The Black Pig'. They didn't ask how old we were. We weren't drinking alcohol anyway. I do like being with Martin. I wish I fancied him too, but I just don't. He is NOT fanciable. He's funny though and makes me laugh. I didn't want another drink and he kept asking me what I wanted, so I said a glass of ice cubes and he only went and got me one! He's so nice. If only he looked like Paul Harris. I fancy him something rotten, but I don't think he even knows I exist...

I look up from the page. You were nice. I don't think I could appreciate the value of 'nice' back then though. I thought it was all about what was on the outside. And back then, the outside of Paul Harris was much more appealing. Brown hair, soulful brown eyes and good-looking as hell; he was the object of my teenaged crush that year. Do you remember him? He was a couple of years below you at school, so you might not have known him. Or did I tactlessly tell you all about him? God, I probably did. I'm so sorry. I have no idea why you persisted in liking me back then.

Paul Harris. I haven't thought about him for a very long time. I was nuts about him as I remember. He was the object of much yearning and angst, all horribly out of proportion, I'm sure. I genuinely thought my heart was broken when he rejected me. I suppose it should have given me some empathy towards you. Maybe it did. Maybe I chose to ignore the way I knew you felt about me. It was just easier that way.

I remember the first time I laid eyes on Paul. I'd started hanging out with a few boys from the fifth year and the landlord of our local pub let us use a quiet little back room where we'd drink Woodpecker cider before going back to Guy Harrington's house to listen to Jean Michel Jarre records. And one night, there he was when I walked in: Paul Harris, the best looking boy I'd ever seen, wearing a long dark coat over dark jeans and shirt, devastatingly handsome, his dark hair flopping over his eyes, with just a slight air of moodiness. I'm sure I blushed when we made eye contact as Guy introduced us. He didn't say much at all, but later that night he started writing on beer mats and flicking them across the table to me. I remember exactly what he wrote and the way it made me feel.

Hello I love you won't you tell me your name
Hello I love you won't you tell me your name

He must have written it half a dozen times. I knew it was a line from The Doors' song. He just seemed so cool and kind of aloof, but here he was sending me these messages. It wasn't just the cider that went to my head that night. It was the start of an infatuation for me. We walked back to Guy's house arm in arm and I was much higher than cloud nine when he kissed me. It was the first kiss that ever gave me a real indication of what kissing could be with the right person. It was the polar opposite of our first kiss, Martin. I think it was also the start of me pulling away from you, and from our friendship.

Chapter 7

Crush

I finally pull myself out of the reverie and up the stairs to bed at about one a.m. I'm weary to my core and can barely summon the energy to get undressed, and let my clothes fall to the floor in a heap to be dealt with tomorrow. Today, really. But later. Much later.

The bed is still strewn with the remnants of us. I simply push them to one side to make enough room to crawl under the duvet. Switching off the bedside lamp with a sigh, I settle myself into a position for sleep, tucking my long hair away from my face and closing my eyes. As exhausted as I am, I fear that sleep will elude me. There's no point chasing after it; I never win. I just have to accept it will stop running when it's good and ready. Until then, I let my thoughts drift.

They drift inevitably to Paul Harris, who has taken your seat, temporarily I'm sure, on my train of memories. He's only in my life for a stop or two, but he usurps you, and everyone else, for a few short months. In a lifetime, Paul is but an instant, but back then he was timeless and infinite. He and I started to hang out together from time to time, going to the same house parties and sometimes hooking up. Paul was my introduction to snogging and I couldn't get enough of him. But he remained aloof and somehow unavailable. He told me he wasn't really over his ex. I hated her, whoever she was. She kept him from me, and from what I was convinced we could be. I was kidding myself, of course. He showed just enough interest to keep me hanging, wanting more, but he didn't really want me.

I don't think we really had much contact during the Paul-time, did we? You probably would have felt used, and I wouldn't have blamed you. The pinnacle of my relationship with Paul was when he offered to take me out on my birthday. I was so happy and excited; I thought maybe he did want me after all. I can remember every detail of that evening, and I have a photograph taken by my sister before he arrived to take me out. I look so happy: stupidly, naively, hopefully happy. But there was no hope and my heart finally couldn't take any more. It was the heartbreak only a foolish teenager can experience: world-ending and earth-shattering. I can vividly remember getting on a double-decker bus going anywhere, and sitting upstairs willing it to crash. Stupid, I know. But back then it felt like my meaningless life was over.

And then, just as suddenly as I had fallen for Paul, I was over him. No rhyme or reason, just done. It felt so good. Even better when he realised he didn't have that power over me anymore and he didn't like it. Taking back the control was a valuable lesson for me, and I enjoyed the feeling of power. He was, in the end, just a short chapter in my book.

With Paul out of my head and my heart, you crept back in. I realised I missed your friendship, but I didn't know if I had the right to that friendship any more after treating you so shoddily. I hadn't yet learned you would never withdraw your friendship, however much time or distance elapsed between us.

Turning over in bed with a sigh, I realise sleep is still streaks ahead of me, and I reach for the lamp next to me. Plumping up the pillows, I pull myself up and take up the diary I was reading from earlier that evening.

7th November 1982

Oh my God! It feels sooooo good to be over Paul-Bloody-Harris! Weird how it happened though – absolutely LOVED spending my birthday with him, and hanging out in my bedroom afterwards was A-MAY-ZING! I think I just got worn out with him not really wanting me as his girlfriend. I think I might – only might – have slept with him that night if he'd asked me to. He didn't though, so it doesn't matter. He behaved like a gentleman and I think I'm glad now we didn't have sex. I'm glad he didn't use me or really lead me on. I'd have felt really crap if that had happened. I really do want a boyfriend though. And I really do want to see Martin again. I've missed his stoopid face! Maybe I'll phone him tomorrow…

Did I phone you? I don't remember. It was so long ago. So much has happened since then. So many memories. So much more heartbreak.

Chapter 8

Pure Shores

I wake the next morning feeling groggy and kind of hungover. It can't be from alcohol, as I barely touched my glass of red wine. As I roll over in bed to check the time, something falls onto the floor: it's the diary I was reading last night. I must've finally drifted off still holding it, still remembering. It's early – I can't have slept for more than a few hours – and I conclude the way I'm feeling is from a lack of sleep and maybe an excess of nostalgia.

As I lie in bed I'm relieved I had the foresight to book the day off work. The thought of dealing with other people's problems all day is not a pleasant one. Forgive me, you don't know what I do: I'm a manager in the NHS dealing with complaints. Yep. I know. What was I thinking? I had some idealistic notion back when I applied; something about making a difference. Pah! What a fool I was thinking that! But making foolish decisions is something I'm pretty accomplished at, isn't it? They make sense at the time. Usually.

One decision that does make sense right now is to make coffee, so I throw off the duvet and swing my legs out of bed. They ache. In fact, my whole body aches. For no reason. I'm noticing it more and more; general aches and pains, stiffness in my joints and tightness in my muscles. Is this what getting older, what being fifty, feels like? I'm not ready for this middle-age, or whatever you want to call it. I still have a lifetime of regrets to make up for, things to do I should've done when I was twenty. Thirty. Forty, even. Is it too late now? I don't want to think about it – it's more than I can bear. Padding across the bedroom, I take my robe from its hook on the back of the bedroom door and shrug into it, pulling my long hair free as I do so. The thought that maybe I'm too old for long hair flashes into my mind. Another thing I don't want to think about, so I banish the thought, for now at least.

I head downstairs, opening curtains and blinds as I go, and taking mental snapshots of my house and my belongings as I pass. I have photographs grouped on the wall in the hall. There's one of me taken many years ago in Cornwall. I look so happy. I was happy. Utterly, completely, blissfully happy. You took that photograph. So long ago. In another lifetime. I sigh, and continue into the kitchen, going through the motions of making coffee, unconsciously, letting my mind drift once more back to you. I'm not ready to think about Cornwall. Not yet, at least. But I do want to think about you still. You. The path not taken.

With a mug of coffee in hand, I head back upstairs and climb into bed, bunching the pillows up and making myself comfortable for another trip down memory lane. You're there, waiting for me, with that lopsided grin and that messy mop of hair. I close my eyes and let my mind wander towards you. I reach out and you take my hand, pulling me into a time warp.

It's late September, 1983, and we're on the beach in Folkestone, the one called 'The Warren', throwing stones out to sea and dodging the foamy white waves as the tide comes in. I can hear laughter. Yours and mine, jumbled together with the sound of the sea, a happy harmony. I'm smiling, then and now. It's so easy being with you. And safe, somehow. I can believe you will always be there for me, will never hurt me. That you have no expectation of me, other than to be in my company. You never pressured me to be more than friends, even though I knew you wanted more. Should I have let you go? I wonder. Was I always leading you on? Just a bit, perhaps? I think I knew even then, at the tender age of fifteen, that I enjoyed the feeling of power being wanted by a man gave me.

I open my eyes to take a glug of coffee before it grows too cold, quickly closing them once more to return to you. It was the last time I saw you before you went off to university. You didn't seem nervous at all, just excited at the adventure that lay ahead. You would be studying physics at Nottingham. I didn't really mind that you were going away. We'd promised to write to one another and, anyway, I'd met someone. I don't think I told you then, did I? I don't think I wanted to spoil our last day together. Maybe it would be our last ever day together.

We're sitting on the beach now, on a bank of pebbles a short distance from the sea, breathless from our exertions. I can picture the scene perfectly in my mind's eye. And I can recall your words:

'You know I'll always be here for you, Lou? Don't you? Wherever I am, no matter how much time passes… you only have to reach out for me and I'll be there. Always. That's my promise to you.'

And I knew you meant it, even if I didn't know then how it made me feel. I think it was a jumble sale of emotions, and

I didn't try to sort through them. I just squeezed your hand, looked you in the eyes, and smiled a thank you, before jumping up and running off down the beach. Maybe the intensity of the moment scared me. I don't know. I could feel an unfathomable depth to your words I didn't know how to navigate. So I didn't try. Back then I was too young and too stupid to really understand and appreciate how incredibly special a man you were. And, anyway, my mind and heart were very much elsewhere by then.

Chapter 9

Bonkers

I've finished my coffee now and am wondering what to do with my day. Family obligations have been met with my birthday dinner, and Libby will be back at university once more, so there are no dutiful visits needed. I could go shopping or see if any of my friends are around for a catch-up, but today feels like a day for solitude, for reminiscing and drinking too much coffee.

With no one to please but myself, I don't even bother showering before dressing in comfy joggers and jumper. Running a brush through my hair, I fix it up in a messy bun. With my face washed and teeth cleaned, I start to head down to the lounge. Pausing at the top of the stairs as an afterthought strikes, I return to the bedroom and gather up the contents of the shoebox still strewn on the unslept-on side of the bed, shovelling them back in and scooping up the box to take with me. In a few minutes, I'm settled on the sofa, another mug of coffee steaming on the table next to me and a pile of your letters in my hands. They're the letters you wrote to me from university.

I examine the postmarks, trying to find the earliest letter. They're mainly marked 1984, and it's hard to make out all the actual dates. I choose one at random and take out the pages, smiling at the sight of your wonderful, familiar scrawl. I used to joke you should have been a doctor with that writing, didn't I? Your letters always made me smile – before I'd even opened them sometimes as I chuckled at the drawings on the envelope. They probably made the postmen smile too.

Even the sender's address at the top right hand corner of the page raises a chuckle:

Hovel 2,
3rd Shack on the Left
DUNGFORD

My Dear Lou,

Kindly accept my most humblest, grovellingist apologies for not writing to you sooner but, well, you know wot camels are like at this time of year, and they've really given me the hump. No, really, I've been working so hard that I haven't had time. Hmmm. I think I like the one about the camels better. If I'd told you I'd had a breakdown after my Nigerian girlfriend sawed off both legs in a fit of manic depression after coming to terms with her rampant lesbianism, chronic dandruff, piles, acne, psychotic mother (who stoned the local vicar to death with her home-baked fairy cakes) and her tendency to spontaneously detonate in public conveniences, would you believe me? Good.

Hope your hiccups are better now. I had the same old trouble last week, but at least it didn't grow out of my forehead this time, and the ointment Dr. Groper gave me works wonders.

We had a Krimbles test today (so much for the Festering Season) and Muggins here almost managed to attempt part of one of the questions in section A.

"Given the eigenvector of the harmonic oscillator has the following form,

Ua = ½ (temperature of rice pudding/average drizzle intensity 1873)

deduce the existence of Algepan Body Rub and show Mrs Edith Binliner lives at 84 Gasworks Avenue, Croydon." Ho hum. Who wanted to do fizzix anyway?

Maybe our lecturers put me off.

Do you want to wallpaper our front room this Krimbles to further your decorating experience? Wot do you mean no? It'll weaken your strongpoint... er ... I mean strengthen your weak point... be worthwhile... time well-spent... benefit to the community... blah blah blah... drains in Eastry...blah blah... totally unfounded... drivel drivel... bloody hell, I don't want to do it.

I realise I'm laughing now, as I must have done then, as I read your crazy, wonderful, nonsensical words. Your letters were always like that. Back then, anyway. I often wondered what it must be like in your head, to be able to pour forth such original ramblings. I'm trying to remember what my letters to you would have been like... but I can't. They must have been dull, pedestrian in comparison. I'm sure I would have tried to be funny and original – hiccups, for goodness sake! – but I know my words must have been pale next to the explosion of colour you sent me. I wonder where my letters to you are. Are they stored in a dust-laden box in an attic, safe from prying eyes? Or did you burn them long ago, in a hot fit of pique, a moment of anger? If I know you at all, I'm sure you would have kept them. Even when you must have hated me, I still don't believe you could have destroyed them. Buried them deep in the recesses of your mind, and the loft, probably, but still there.

I down the last of my lukewarm coffee and return to your letter.

I didn't want to start another page. Bah! Humbug! I'm afraid you'll just have to put up with more boring drivel while I fill up this yawning gap (I mean yawning). Dreadfully sorry and all that. All what? Oh that! Don't worry, I'll wipe it up in a minute. And mind the black pudding's paid for. Cost me my underwater trombone and my banana-benders, and stop turning into an armadillo when I'm talking to you. Mad? Who's mad? Not me. Never. It's just that when someone mentions Fizzix that I begin to... er...begin to... to... huge melons and frozen beans. Who needs Wedgie Benn when we've got semolina? Bongos are to tennis balls wot foam cushions are to Rockall. Cough and the world coughs with you – fart and you stand alone. Wobblebum flurgle hooblecrud spode Dunlop Bognor Regis, n'est pas? I'll take the three on the left, matey. Next to the one with the egg-whisk and the extendable probe. And who told Napoleon he could come back in here? You know the mess he made last time. He might've left his purple vest on, or did he put it in the bedpan again? Erkle numbford gronkle plingewort snoog, as Shakespeare put it, and who are we? Pass the sponge, Nurse.

Tapioca Pudding & Lotsa Love, see you soon – write sooner!

Marty xx

Bonkers. There's no other word for it. Joyously, wondrously bonkers.

Chapter 10

Hanging On the Telephone

I wish I could read my letters to you. As much as I'm enjoying this reminiscing, it's all rather one-sided. I know for a fact my replies would not have been nearly as entertaining as your mad missives. I can't believe they didn't bore you to tears. I know if I was responding to you now, my words would be very different.

As I fold up the letter and slide it back into the envelope, I realise I'm hungry and head to the kitchen for sustenance. As I pop bread into the toaster and retrieve butter and marmalade from the fridge, my thoughts drift to that time when you were away at university, and to what was happening in my own life. I'd met someone and it was serious.

His name was Steve and he was the same age as you. That was the only thing he had in common with you though. I'd joined a youth club with my friend, Vanessa - we'd been at primary school together, but then went to different secondary schools. Our mums had brought us back together when they decided we should take on a paper round. As much as neither of us wanted to deliver the papers one evening a week, we were soon grateful to be reunited, and became inseparable.

Anyway, that first night we went to the youth club, Steve walked in with his friend, Dave. Vanessa and I barely noticed

Steve, because Dave was so much better looking. Still shallow at sixteen. Once we were all introduced, though, we both realised that, actually, Steve was the nicer of the two. I didn't find out until much later that, that night, Steve told Dave he was going to marry me.

Even though my relationship with Steve soon became serious, I still liked having you in my life but, naturally I suppose, our contact rather dwindled. Letters still came, but with ever increasing windows of time between them.

Armed with two slices of thickly buttered toast and marmalade, I reposition myself on the sofa and take up another of your letters. Even though Steve popped into my head like the toast from the toaster, thoughts of him soon go cold. I don't have the regrets about him that I do about you.

My Dear Lou,

Howdy-do-dere, and how goes the world with you? Sorry I've not written sooner but spare time's been scarcer than spare cash round here.

I've been rehearsing for 'Comedians' most nights for the past few days 'cos it goes on next week. Oh dearie dearie me. No-one knows their lines, there's no set, no costumes (and no talent) and we're on in a week. Not terribly good is it? It's great fun tho'. I wonder if I'll think the same after the old rotten tomato treatment?

I'm sure you'll be relieved to hear I'm doing as much work this year as I did last year (i.e. something approximating to bugger all), but wot the hell, I didn't come here to work.

The new flat's pretty good, apart from the dingy décor, cockroaches, rats, rising damp, falling ceilings, dry rot, wet rot, gut rot, mildew, fungi and an assortment of several unspeakable contagious diseases. Wonderful, really. No, honest, it is, You'll have to drop in if you ever come up this way, but remember to bring rubber gloves.

No place like home. (Me? Exaggerate? Never.)

I pause my reading. I never did come 'up this way' did I? I never visited you during those university years. I wish I had. Maybe things would have been different then… I continue reading:

Wot else have I been up to? Did I tell you on the 'phone that I had… er… a little accident with Brian, that little car of great personality, charm, character, (rust), at 3 a.m. one morning? Poor old Brian, I didn't mean to write him off. I don't think the traffic bollard was too happy about it either. Ho hum. I was stone cold sober at the time too. Anyway, I've got to bug off now and do some set-building. Write soon and tell me all your news, and let me know if you'll ever be up this way.

See you soon,
Lotsa love,
Marty x

You kept hinting back then, didn't you? Asking me to visit, letting me know you still wanted to see me. And we'd obviously spoken on the phone – you referred to it in your letter. I can still picture the old red telephone in the hall of my childhood home. I can still remember the phone number. Just four digits. That's how long ago it was. I bet I sat on the hall floor talking to you, with my back against the radiator, and the coiled cable of the telephone pulled to its limit, family members having to step over my legs to get past.

You never talked about girls in your letters from university. There must have been girls in your life, but you never mentioned any. Was that a conscious decision on your part? I wonder. Did you want me to think you were always available?

Just in case I came to my senses? But I didn't, did I? Not back then.

With a sigh, I pick up another letter.

Dear Lou,

Howdy doody and how goes the world with you? Me? I'm fine apart from chronic inflammation of the grindles and the galloping nadgers, but I've been told they'll clear up soon enough as long as I keep up the series of injections.

How's the job-hunting going? Or *has it gone?* (I realise this letter is a later one, written after my early, unhappy exit from school.) *Whatever you do, steer clear of Medical Physics – it's enough to bore the socks off even Masters of the Tedium League like Sir Geoffrey Howe. Yes, I think I can safely say I'd rather listen to an entire one of his speeches on the price of rice pudding and Britain's embargo on small white plastic teaspoon imports from Taiwan than work in Medical Physics again for any period longer than about thirty seconds. The highlight of the summer was the stylish blowing-up of a fuse:*

So, what else has ol' Mart been up to? Well, I've been helping to set up the lighting for the freshers' bop, done spotlight for one of the bands and been to three parties. I now know this is the definition of stupid. Mind you, I did manage to stay awake for most of my first lecture. Only another few hundred to go.

How's the ol' driving going then? Great fun, driving, you'll love it. I really miss it myself. I'll bet you'll be a real road-demon — mild-mannered and innocence itself until you get behind the wheel.

I'm stuck for anything else to say, except, of course, nurdle, sprung funkle spoodle dim fuddy bongo elkim sniggo glurdlespurt bin voomsk and Norman Tebbit. Hope you're having a bloody good time of it all down there where the sun always shines and party political broadcasts never get shown.

Tatty bye,
Marty x

I'm still smiling to myself as I put the letter to one side and pick up the next item from the shoebox. It's a Christmas card this time, with a picture of a robin using a sledgehammer to crack a walnut. My smile falls away when I open the card and read what you wrote inside. Well, less what you wrote, more what you drew. The message reads: *Multitudinous congratulations on getting engaged by-the-by.* And underneath these pleasant enough words? This:

Yep, you drew a mug, complete with an arrow pointing to it next to my name. I was the walnut, you were the hammer-wielding robin. Although, of course, I'd forgotten about this card over the decades, the memory of the pain it caused comes flooding back. You had added an addendum in brackets: *(Only kidding – I wish you only the best.)*, but your truth and pain was in that little drawing. And it was the first time I ever realised you could be cruel.

Chapter 11

White Wedding

The mug has got to me. Stupid, I know, but there we are. It's ancient history so I don't know why it's affecting me so much. Maybe I do. Maybe if I'm really honest with myself, it's because you were right. I was foolish. Young, naïve and totally in denial about my truth. And probably yours too, with hindsight. Good old hindsight. She's a bitch. And I was a mug.

I flick through the rest of your cards and letters from that period of our lives. There actually aren't that many. I think we both pulled away a bit after I got engaged, didn't we? You were no doubt hurting with any possibility of us getting together now gone. And I was probably smarting a bit from the mug incident, and choosing to ignore any pain I had caused you. I was still too young and too stupid to have any real depth of emotional intelligence, wasn't I? Actually, that's probably just another excuse, another denial, to make myself feel better. I must always have known how you felt about me. I'm sorry, Marty. I was insensitive.

And so our lives and our paths drifted apart. We moved on, whatever invisible thread that had kept us connected thus far had broken. Did I forget about you? I suppose I must have done – most of the time at least. I think there was always a little part of you with me though, somewhere in the recesses of my mind, often buried under the messy heap of the rest of my life.

I don't want to dwell on my life with Steve. This story isn't about him. It's about us. You and me. Martin and Louise. Star-crossed lovers? The Romeo and Juliet of our time? I don't know. Will our story ever really be over? I can't pretend my life with Steve never happened. It happened for sixteen years; not all of them unhappy, but most of them dull and uneventful. And the times that weren't dull and uneventful? Quite a few of them involved you, didn't they?

I suppose I must at least acknowledge my relationship with Steve… edited highlights – and lowlights – will have to suffice. We got engaged when I was eighteen, ridiculously young when I think about it now. I simply can't imagine Libby engaged to be married – I'd be horrified, as my parents must have been. I, however, was blind to everything except the desire to escape from my family into the arms of someone I knew would never let me down, would always support me emotionally, and keep me safe. Married at twenty-one… walking down the aisle knowing it's a mistake, but doing it anyway. For better or for worse. You weren't in the congregation, were you?

No. I'd invited you to the wedding. Don't ask me why. Tactless of me, I'm sure. Thoughtless. You didn't reply to the invitation. That door stayed firmly closed. Why did I want you there? I don't think I've ever really let myself think about that too deeply. Was there some small part of me secretly hoping you'd object and stop me from making a huge mistake? Who knows. Would it be arrogant of me to say I'm sure I was in your thoughts that day? Knowing what I know now, I don't think it would be. I'm sure you would have been sad on the day I got married. The final nail in the coffin of hope and possibility. Time for you to accept that I, we, were gone, and to mourn our passing and get on with your life.

I've finished eating my toast now, mostly consumed without really registering the action, and I pause to pick a few wayward crumbs from my jumper, dusting my fingers off over the plate, and reaching it onto the coffee table. I'm warm and comfortable on the sofa and feel no inclination to move, just to sink further into the cushions and the memories. I acknowledge the fact I'm already feeling a sad sort of nostalgia, but I know today I need to indulge it, wallow in it, subsume myself in it. And then maybe reflect. Or cry. Probably both.

I'm trying to remember how, or why, you came back into my life. I pick up another bundle of keepsakes from the box and try to assign some chronology to things. It's quite hard as not all the envelopes have legible postmarks. Some I can work out from the addresses they were sent to, others were hand delivered and some I have carelessly left without envelopes. Years of history passing through my hands, a one-sided account of our story.

A bright pink card catches my eye: a Snoopy Valentine's card. I vaguely remember receiving this. It's one of the earliest cards I received from you, when we were still at school I think, and I was still flattered to have an older boy interested in me. I open it and read the message inside. The last thing you wrote was: *1 down, 9 to go*. I can feel a furrow between my eyebrows as I try to recall the meaning of the cryptic message. It dawns on me; I think I told you to ask me out again in ten years. I'm right, aren't I? I had totally forgotten about that. I think it was my way of keeping you interested without the complication of the one-sided attraction interfering with our friendship. I did want you in my life, Marty. I just didn't want you the same way you wanted me. Maybe it was selfish of me, but I wasn't ready for you then.

Chapter 12

The Drugs Don't Work

Ask me again in ten years. That would make me about twenty-four if I take it from my age when we met. I'd been married for three years by then. Were you married too by that time? I think you were. Did I know? I have no idea. My memories from that time are misty and vague. When I think about my years with Steve, there is so little that's remarkable.

What were you doing back then? I wonder. Plodding through life – eat, sleep, work, repeat – much like me? Or were you really living? I know I felt trapped and unhappy much of the time. Steve had wrapped me up in cotton wool and stood me on a pedestal, shielded from the world, cocooned and unable to grow, like a caterpillar unable to metamorphose. If I had been able to reach metamorphosis with Steve, I would have emerged as a drab, brown, little moth. But at least I would have had wings. But he would never have let me fly, clipping my wings and keeping me grounded by his side, never to achieve my colourful, soaring potential.

I don't think I have ever reached my true potential in this life, except maybe for brief periods of time, before slipping back into the safety of my cocoon, my comfort zone. I remember how unfulfilled I felt within the confines of my marriage, and how my butterfly soul longed to break free, but I was so young when I met Steve I didn't know how. And I couldn't hurt him anyway, however much I longed to be free to find out who I really was. My emotional growth stopped at sixteen, I think, institutionalised by my relationship with a man I now realise was controlling. At the time I just thought it was love. That bitch, hindsight, again.

I remember being depressed for much of my twenties. It was the start of the anti-depressants - Fluoxetine, Seroxat, Venlafaxine, Mirtazapine – and the counselling, both of which have recurred throughout my life. I desperately wanted to be free of Steve, but there seemed to be no way out. I remember when the change happened, began at least; when I pulled apart the layers of my silky cocoon, and peeped out at the world. It was when, after two years of counselling, I decided I had to make up for dropping out of school and get a degree.

For me to go to university meant Steve had to make huge sacrifices. I think he must have realised that, if he didn't bend a little, we would break and he would lose me. My counsellor had shown me what my life could be, and I knew I had to try or I would shrivel and die.

I was twenty-eight when I went to university. It was terrifying and exhilarating all at once. I know I was looking for an escape and, for a while, lectures and seminars and making new friends was enough. A tunnel had formed ahead of me for the first time and a small glimmer of light was visible in the distance. There was a shadowy shape silhouetted there. That shape was you.

University was life-changing. It can have borne no resemblance to your own experience, of course; I was a mature student and a married one at that. There was only the academic aspect for me, none of the parties and socialising you used to write about in your wonderfully zany letters. For me, probably the most enlightening thing was having access to email for the first time. It sounds crazy when I think about technology now; how Libby would laugh at me in bewilderment if she could see me back then, fumbling my way around a UNIX system. I had my first email address, and a new way of communicating was suddenly open to me, which no-one else need know about. I remember enjoying the feeling of control it gave me, a new feeling of power, being able to tentatively reach beyond my safe little shell.

I don't know why, but I wanted to reach out to you in those early days at uni. Was it because you'd shared your own experiences a decade or so earlier? My only reference to this academic world was through you, and maybe I wanted to return the favour? I don't know if that was the reason. Could it have been because I was so desperately unhappy at home and looking for an escape? I honestly don't know, or don't remember, the reason, but I absolutely do remember sending you a postcard around your birthday, addressed to your mum's house, and including my email address. I had no idea where you were living or if you'd ever receive the card.

I don't remember how long it was before I got your email, that fateful message that reconnected us, and would change the course of both our lives so devastatingly.

Of course I don't recall the exact words you wrote in reply, but I do remember the gist of that first email. You said your mum had forwarded the card and you memorised my email address before your wife tore up the card. I wonder what you'd told your wife about me to make her react like that? She hated me even then, didn't she? Before I'd even given her reason to.

Being on campus meant I had control over my time more than ever before. Steve had no way of knowing if I was genuinely there to study, or just to be away from our stunted life together. Unlike a job, the hours of which were a known quantity, he no longer had the power to control my time. Looking back now, I wonder how much of my power I gave up willingly, rather than had taken from me. It was just easier not to resist, not to push back.

We started to email regularly, didn't we? I got a computer at home, not only on which to write essays, but to connect to the university server and email you. I vividly remember getting up in the middle of the night sometimes to check for messages from you and to send mails back. It was reckless, I know, but also thrilling and life-affirming. I'd never been someone who took risks before. I must have been desperately unhappy. Or maybe I wanted to be caught? I don't know, but I got away with it and our correspondence remained a secret.

How long was it before you came to visit me on campus in Canterbury? You took a day off work and drove down to meet me for lunch in the Gulbenkian coffee shop. I remember not being able to eat the baguette I chose, I was just too nervous and excited.

One thing I don't understand about our reunion was my attraction to you. It was so profound and undeniable, and yet I'd never been attracted to you physically before. You hadn't changed, not really, so I must have done. Or was I simply so unhappy and desperate for a distraction from my life off campus that I fooled myself into those feelings? At the time, I simply don't know. I can only acknowledge that those feelings would prove to be all too painfully, wonderfully real.

Chapter 13

Mad Love

Shuffling through another pile of letters, I find a batch addressed to me at my college on campus, Rutherford College. I remember you being chuffed I was in the one named after a physicist. Having a pigeonhole there meant I could receive not just virtual letters, but actual ones too, and you were soon sending me cards, letters and little gifts. Amongst the envelopes are little gift bags and boxes; a matchbox with a tiny note inside – it had once contained your last Rolo; a fat envelope which still includes a piece of burnt pizza, the grease stains of which have seeped through the paper, and smudged your words. Just as well it went stale and hard, rather than rotted. I can't begin to tell you what a source of joy they were to me, a little oasis in the desert of my life with Steve. Even now, decades later, I feel a little smile and shiver of remembrance. I began writing to you at your work address, didn't I? Careful to mark the envelopes 'Private and Confidential' to keep my words and our feelings safe from the risk of discovery.

Just as your letters from your university days had delighted me, so too did these new missives, only more so. Much, much more so. For these letters had taken on a whole new dimension; my feelings had caught up with yours. It had taken more than those ten promised years, but I had fallen in love with you, and was about to enter the best and worst period of my life, to experience highs where I could touch the sun, and lows as bleak and black as a never-ending night sky without stars.

Looking back, I don't know how we managed to meet as often as we did. It must have been easier for me back then, for you had to take time off from your job as a Project Manager. But our attraction was an irresistible force neither of us could, or wanted to, deny. I could feel my wings pressing to be free, knowing that with you I could soar. Maybe one day I would fly too close to the sun, and pay a terrible price, but back then all I cared about was you, us, and our undeniable love.

I shuffle some of your letters into date order and begin to read. The first one's dated December 23rd 1996, some twenty-one years ago.

Dearest, dearest Lou,

Just a few short minutes to scribble you sweet nothings. That's all I can do. Grab any spare minute to jot down a word or two. Anna's just gone to feed the neighbour's cat. (I remember it hurt when you mentioned your wife – I didn't want her to be real to me, a painful reminder that you couldn't be mine, not really.) *Time enough for me to say thank you once more for a wonderful, if scary, few hours. Nothing has passed through my mind since I left you without working its way around thoughts and memories of you, of us. I've had my Christmas – Christmas has come early. I could hold you and hold you for an eternity, and still it wouldn't be long enough. Strange. My only regret now is that we had too much self-control! No guilt for being with you at all. How could something which feels so, so right, so natural, so beautiful, ever be wrong? I miss you so very much already. Good grief. Five and a half hours! What am I going to be like after a couple of weeks?! I can't bear to think about it. I ache for you so very much. I don't think I ever knew what 'yearning' meant before now. All I have is a vision of your lovely, smiling, giggling face to pull me through. Memories of your laughter, memories of your close, breathing warmth with emotions flooding over us and between us in ways and means and intensities which can never be known. For all this, I thank you, and pray we can be together again soon.*

The letter pauses there and I pause with it. I remember how it felt to be with you those first times. I can vividly recall how just the touch of our hands was filled with shock and awe. I'd never experienced such a physical thrill before. I had so little experience. I honestly had no idea that the touch of another human could literally take my breath away, cause it to get stuck in my throat as electricity coursed through my veins, lighting me up from the inside. And you always saw that light in me, didn't you? For you, I shone. Times of relative innocence, when we clung to each other, when our feelings intensified, but we didn't take the final step; before the point of no return. But we couldn't have turned back then, could we? Even if we had wanted to...

Anna's just gone next door for the next feed, so I've got a few more minutes. Since I left yesterday you've been constantly with me, in my heart and in my head. You've consumed me with feelings for which I have no name, with such overwhelming passion that there is no room in my head for anything else. No room in my aching heart for anyone else. Dear God! Less than a day!

I've been thinking, analysing, soul-searching all day long. All night long too. All I can find is you. I've come to the conclusion the only things that keep me here are the two cats and the mortgage. If it was just Anna, I could leave. I'd hate it, but I could do it. But it's not. If I leave, she'll lose the home she loves and the cats love. Is that daft? Yes. To leave her is one thing, but to give up her home is another. Bugger. What do we do, Lou? I love you, you know I do. I feel so trapped here, but so free and alive with you. I wish I could talk to you again. You have become my home. You are to me all that matters in my life. My moments with you are the memories to carry me forward through this time of desolation to the next ecstasy with you. I'm sorry I love you, Lou – I know it makes things so complicated. But love you I do. To your core. I'm smiling again because I hold your face in my head. I hold your warmth in my heart. With those small things, I can see daylight again. I have to hold onto them, close, tight, constant. You are with me now. You are with me always. You are my smile, my daylight, my dreams, my private universe. How I wish we could run for shelter and never return. Uh oh - time to go again. Feel my love through the ether, Lou. It's always there, reaching out to you.

I close my eyes and remember how it felt in those early days. I didn't miss the 'private universe' reference either – the song by Crowded House which we made ours. I reach for my mobile and tap it into Google, then close my eyes once more, listening to the song for the first time in many years. 'Promise of love is hard to ignore… Labor of love is ours to endure… I will run for shelter/Endless summer lift the curse/It feels like nothing matters/In our private universe.' The effect on me is profound and I can feel silent tears trickling down my cheeks until I taste them at the corners of my mouth. I don't bother to brush them away.

We both felt trapped in our lives but neither of us knew how to escape without causing great pain to the people we'd made commitments to. Easier to hurt ourselves and each other, and make do with snatched, secret moments of bliss, than hurt Steve and Anna. Would it have been more sensible, less painful, to have put a stop to things then? Before things went any further, and the emotional connection became a physical one? Could we have prevented boundless heartache that way? Maybe. But we didn't want to, did we? We wanted the pleasure, despite the pain. And the pain was excruciating, wasn't it? It tore at our very souls. And we transmitted it like a virus to the two other people who also loved us.

The song finishes and I wipe my sleeve roughly across my face, clearing my eyes so I can continue reading your letter.

Next instalment: 2nd January 1997

Well, it's been a week now since my last scribble. Have my feelings for you changed? Not a jot. Each waking moment passes with thoughts of you, and I live from one phone call to the next. Now you're away at your in-laws and it's going to be ages before I can speak to you again, and it's gnawing at my insides, clawing at my soul. I have a ravening hunger for you, for your touch. I need you here, now, part of me. To be with you is to set my heart soaring and experience passions without limit. I close my eyes now to relive your exquisite kisses in my mind, and wonder how long it will be before my stomach stops turning somersaults again. I want, no, need, to hold you close once more. To kiss and caress your perfect form. To feel your soft warm skin on mine. These are the thoughts that guide me though each day-like hour. It seems forever since I last beheld you, and an age before I shall again. Be assured that between those times my heart is truly yours, and ever shall be.

Ever shall be… I know you meant this at the time. I know it felt real, and I believed it with every fibre of my being. Can it ever remain true, without nurturing, without some small speck of returned affection? I honestly have no answer, Marty. I know you were agonising over your feelings for me, and I know I was doing the same. I pick up your letter again, and the darkness has crept in.

What's wrong with me, Lou? I should be happy here. I have a beautiful wife who loves me to death, a wonderful home, a secure well-paid job and two cats, which I adore. Why do I want to throw it all away to live with you in a shoebox? How can I hurt this woman I exchanged vows with six years ago? What kind of monster am I? Why can't I tell my emotions to take a running jump, to blot you from my mind and return to Anna the feelings she has for me? Because I'm a complete git, that's why. You should hate me.

I'd better go before I get too depressed. I just wish you were here to tell me everything will be alright, kiss me softly, and stroke my head as it lies across your chest.

I'll leave you with this:

I love you, Lou. I love you more than I could ever tell you, even if I had a very big dictionary. The scary thing is that I don't think I need to tell you, and I think you feel the same. You are my soulmate, my love, my life. With each breath, each step, each and every heartbeat of my aching heart I know that to live without you is to live a lie, to know that each day away from you is a terrible mistake. I just wish I knew how to break the lie and live the truth, to put the mistake right. Perhaps I do. I just don't have the courage to devastate an innocent life, and one I care deeply about in spite of all my feelings for you.

My love is forever yours, Lou. May we meet again soon and be free.

All my love,
Marty.

I'm crying again, with the pain of remembrance and the hollow echo of our long ago love. The agony and the ecstasy. Your words were my words; I too was living a lie but could not see a way out, couldn't break the heart of the man I'd exchanged vows with. But, equally, couldn't deny my love for you. That innocent birthday card I'd sent you with my email address on had started an unstoppable avalanche of feelings, which only gathered in size and momentum and power over time, and which threatened to destroy everything in its path.

Chapter 14

I Will Always Love You

I read the next few letters, and I can feel the agony of your dilemma. I remember the agony of my own. You told me over and over how much you loved me and wanted to be with me, and that anything else was wrong, was to live a lie. That our love was undeniable. That we must, we would, find a way to be together…

And I did my part. I found my way and the strength to leave Steve. Knowing I would have you was enough for me to make the break. It nearly destroyed me, but I knew I couldn't live my lie any more. Despite the pain, the relief was immense. I was still at university and life was difficult, but I could cope with anything knowing we were that much closer to being together. Properly together.

But you couldn't do it, could you? You kept on telling me how much you loved me and longed to be with me, but it wasn't enough, was it? For all your protestations of undying love for me, you still couldn't live your truth.

Thursday 20ᵗʰ Feb. '97

Dearest Lou,

Yes, I still love you. Volcanically, uncontainably, everlastingly. So there. It's about 6 p.m. now and I've run off to a conference room and locked the door so I can scribble a few lines in a bit of peace and quiet. Don't know why I didn't think of this before. Probably because my mind is already full of thoughts, memories and hopes of you. Not that I'm complaining. Any hint of you, anything at all is so welcome.

What a marathon phone call. I wish it didn't have to end, all the same. Your voice is a joy to hear. I just wish I could see you, too. What a pair we are, each looking for that piece from the other to give in to what we already know to be the truth:

I love you.

You love me.

Everything else is a distraction to be discarded. You doubt me because I'm with Anna. I doubt you because you're back-tracking on the openness of your love for me. The one is the cause of the other, a circle that has to break. Which will be broken. By me.

Bold words, Marty. I was back-tracking, I know. But do you not understand why? I was trying to protect myself from a devastating heartbreak when you failed to leave Anna, time and again. I'd proved my love for you by walking away from Steve, and yet you doubted me. I was the one who had the right to doubt, Marty.

It is so simple. I love you. I adore you. I ache to be with you every minute we are apart. We are carved from the same soul, and it can only be right to bring the two halves home. It can only be wrong to keep them apart.

You are so beautiful. In my mind now I have fixed an image of your face looking down at me in a half-light, hair falling around your face, that smiling perfect face and those smiling, so happy, eyes gazing into mine, through them, into the heart of all I am, searching for the love I freely offer back, without pause, without end, without hesitation. Smiling because the search is instantly rewarded with each glance. And I can feel your love for me. It's not delusion or imagination. It is real, honest, as intense as mine. I've said to you before that I feel what we have to be even, mutual, shared. Not one-sided, or distorted. And you agreed. You looked at me deeply, and agreed, leaning slightly towards me as you did so.

I did agree with you, Marty, and didn't I prove my love for you by leaving Steve? Weren't you the one who couldn't breathe life and truth into the words you wrote to me. Can't you understand why doubt started to creep into my mind, when you couldn't do the same? Why I started to wonder if I was just some lovesick fool, kidding myself we would be together. I started to believe you could never, would never, leave Anna. I'd hurt Steve, but at least I wasn't living a lie any more, whatever happened with you and me. I wanted to believe your words, Marty, I really did, but there was the issue of self-preservation…

You know it's true, Lou. Through all of this, through all of your self-doubts and guilt and torment, you know in your heart that you feel for me every bit as much as I feel for you. And you freely admit you don't doubt what I feel for you to be the truth. Please admit your own feelings. Set them free, don't smother them with thought.

When we were together, I did believe in your love for me, and in mine for you. It may be a cliché, Marty, but actions really do speak louder than words and, when your actions didn't add up to us being together, what was I supposed to think? I understood how hard it was for you to leave Anna – of course I did, because I'd had the same heartbreak with Steve. But how could I go on believing in the power of your love for me, when you continued to choose her over us? I understood. That didn't make it okay. I skim the rest of your letter, but I know what I will find there: more protestations of your love for me, that were getting harder to believe.

The next letter is dated February 26th. I'm not sure if I want to read. I know what it will say. Roughly, anyway. But I've started on this journey, so I might as well stop at every station.

Hallo you.

Thank you so much for ringing. I do so love to hear your voice, which lifts me above the grey fog descending over my life at the moment.

I'm glad you still get delighted by my excruciating ramblings and my lumberingly incoherent and inadequate expressions of the love I hold for you, the passion I find so impossible to contain. May it always be so. I keep finding old emails in which you expound your love for me, too, and I hold onto them ever so tightly to keep the dark terror of your withdrawal at bay, praying that all you said is just as true now as I knew it to be then. Deep within me I do feel it to be true. Deep within you I'm sure you do too. But you're right, of course, I have been pulling back lately to protect myself as I feel your fears and doubts plaguing you, and twisting what I know to be such an inviolate truth. A bloody scary truth at that. I could never have felt this way about you, Lou, if the very same were not inside of you, reflecting back into my eyes, into my soul.

You are forever part of me as I am forever with you. We could run away from it, of course we could. We could pretend it isn't there, put back on the blinkers and go back to something far less scary. But it would still be there, with us always. We would always know that we had the chance, a single chance, to live and love as never before. The chance of a lifetime with someone whose company the other would always cherish and never resent. A chance of happiness beyond anything else. Do you want to turn your back on that chance, Lou? I don't. I love you. I can still feel your love for me across all of your doubts and fears, across all the miles. Let it free, Lou, let it live. If you don't, something within us both will wither and die, and neither will ever be truly whole again.

Another lecture. Sorry. I don't mean to do this – I just tap into a vein and my heart takes over. I know how much you have to deal with and I know that heads get in the way. But my head has got me into huge messes before now, because I didn't follow my instincts, didn't have the courage to be honest about my feelings and their value. I don't intend to make that mistake here. All my feelings are bared to you. You terrify me, but delightfully, and I love you. I will ever love you to your very core.

I feel resentment now, as I must have done then, all those years ago. You accuse me, berate me, blame me. But what had I done wrong? Maybe it was just easier to blame me, than to admit that actually your feelings weren't strong enough, powerful enough, to surmount the obstacles in your way. I was there, in the middle, waiting for you to join me. But you didn't. Couldn't. How long was I supposed to wait? To hope. To believe. I wanted to believe you, desperately, but the more time that passed, the more painful it became. Your words started to seem empty, hollow, when not backed by action. It was breaking me, Marty. You were breaking me. And you used my pulling away to justify your lack of action.

Chapter 15

Time After Time

It's hard to piece it all together. Everything that happened. Everything that didn't happen. I pushed you away, or you pulled away... who knows? But the thread broke again and we disappeared from one another's lives.

You stayed with Anna. I tried to heal. I had no choice. I just had to get on with my life.

How did we find each other again, you and I? Do you remember? I've found copies of emails I sent to you dated July 1999 – you included them in one of your letters to remind me of my feelings, and my declarations of love for you. They were sent from my work email address at the insurance firm I temped at after graduation. They're the only examples of my side of the story that I have, I think. Proof, on paper, in black and white, of the brilliance and colour you brought to me, to my life.

22/07/99 08:22

Hello gorgeous, and wow.

I can't believe how the past two years just melted away last night. They might as well never have happened. If anything, my feelings for you were even more intense. I didn't think that was possible. All I wanted to do was fall asleep in your arms and sleep the first real sleep for a very long time. I still do. I slept for about two hours last night – you probably got about the same. I couldn't stop my stomach from turning somersaults and my heart was permanently in my throat. Any hope that I would see you again and realise I was over you has turned to dust. I can't be unhappy about it though because only with you do I feel really alive and complete. I love you, Marty. Hard luck.

I can't write much now, but I just wanted to say thank you for last night. Coming home was bliss. I only wish I could stay there forever, safe in your arms and so sure of our love.

Until later, take great care my love. My life.

Lx

The next one is from the following day, at lunchtime:

You have opened the shutters to my heart once more. My life is so dark and empty when you're not in it, Marty. You have brought such joy to me. It's so hard to believe that something that feels so right is wrong. Being with you always feels so natural, like it's meant to be. I am drawn to you irresistibly, no matter how much space or time comes between us. Te amo.

The next email you've included is from August 19th:

It was absolute heaven to be back in your arms again. It's been hard being away from home for so long. I love you with a passion unaltered by time and distance, and always will. I miss you so much now and yet I'm so happy to have found you again. Thank you my love, with all my heart.

You've also copied in a poem you wrote for me. There are quite a few amongst the shoebox contents. Some were sent as first drafts, messy and scribbled on whatever piece of paper you had to hand. Some were smudged by tear stains. Others had been copied out more legibly and many bore your trademark drawings.

Your face beyond description
Your smile beyond words
Your body beyond dreams
Your scent beyond perfume
Your taste beyond nectar
Your laughs beyond joy
Your eyes beyond bewitching
Your mind beyond dazzling
Your touch beyond physical
Your soul beyond compare
All these are yours. Yet you give them freely to me.
Thank you for sharing so much.
All I can offer you in return is my love.
And so I do. Beyond all measure.
Take care, enchantress. Goddess of all my dreams.

My reply is dated September 1st:

Morning, my love. Thank you for the beautiful words. Amazingly I feel all of those things when I'm with you. As you've already said, there are no words to adequately describe what we have. Just know that I love you more than I ever thought possible and that will never change. I can't wait to see you again, to hold you and be held. I have never known contentment like it. Utter bliss.

What was it that overtook us, Marty? How did we just pick up like that, after the heartbreak of the last time? The years just dropped away, the pain of loss a forgotten memory. What madness consumed us, reunited us, overtook us, a fever in our brains and our bodies? Like the unthinkable, almost unendurable, pain of childbirth, forgotten sufficiently to do it all over again. No words of recrimination or forgiveness were spoken, or indeed needed. Why was that, Marty? We were both so hurt, so broken when it didn't work out before. Why did we risk the hurt all over again? Nothing had changed. You were still with Anna. And I had worked hard to rebuild my shattered life. Why did we do this to ourselves, to each other, again? Risk everything. Again.

I put down the pages and lean back with a sigh, momentarily back in the room, back in the present. This journey of remembrance is a rocky road, and I feel the bumps now as a sort of echo from the past. The highs with you were the highest, Marty, you made my spirit soar. But the lows, the lows, they destroyed me, they shattered my soul into a million tiny shards.

Chapter 16

Run to the Hills

The pain is dull now, a muted memory, ink on a page bleached by the sun, a faint shadow of a scar where a livid graze once tore. All things gone but never quite forgotten. What would I tell my thirty-one-year-old self, after consulting with my old nemesis, hindsight? Run for the hills? Get out while you still can? While the power is still yours to take. Maybe. But would I have listened? I doubt it. When you were in my life, Marty, you were all-consuming, an irresistible force I could not withstand.

I look up from my seat on the sofa and let my gaze drift out of the window. The autumn sky is bright and blue; not the brilliant blue of summer, but the faded baby-blue of a crisp autumn day, deceptive, concealing its truth until you open the door and the chill air greets you. There are crossed trails from aeroplanes, sky kisses, and a glider in the distance. As I watch its graceful sweep across the horizon, I recall a much bumpier ride in a small plane that took us to Cornwall for a stolen weekend.

I'm sure if I looked hard enough I could find the exact date we went to Cornwall. I know it was when I was at university. We must have become such accomplished liars, you and I. Were you perhaps on a course, and I staying with a friend? How did the guilt not destroy us? Maybe because it never felt wrong, did it? You and I being together always felt like the most natural thing in the world. We didn't feel like bad people, doing a bad thing, when we were in each other's arms. I know we were both wracked with guilt at other times, but never when we were together. Never when we were in our private universe.

I remember that weekend so vividly, much of it anyway. We flew from Gatwick to Plymouth and hired a car, which you drove to a cottage you'd rented in the middle of nowhere. I can picture it now, with views over rolling green fields to the cliffs and the ringing of a buoy bell out at sea. It was February! Yes, I remember now, it was February, but the sun shone for us in a sky much bluer than today. We were blessed that weekend. In so many ways.

I'm ready to think about Cornwall properly now, and I get up and pad through to the hall where I retrieve the photograph from its hook on the wall: the one of me taken on those rolling green fields, a brilliant blue sky behind me. Settling back into my moulded corner of the sofa, I study the photograph. I look so young. And happy. I look like the happiest person on earth. And honestly, I think I was, Marty. Apart from you. For you were equally as happy. I truly believe that, Marty. In that moment, we were perfectly and completely happy.

And completely in denial, of course. For it couldn't last, could it? It was just two stolen days, snatched from our real lives, to give us a taste of what life could be like. It's like that awful quiz show, the darts one – you know the one I mean: 'Here's what you could have won.' Utter torment. Two days which gave us a tempting glimpse of what domestic bliss really looked like, before we were catapulted back to our stark realities, which could only have been made so much bleaker and blacker.

I'm not wearing a coat in the photo. I remember the jumper, though. I loved it all the more after that weekend with you. We couldn't believe how mild the weather was, could we? It was as though the universe approved of what we were doing. The sun shines on the righteous, right? Wrong. I looked it up. 'The sun likewise shines on the righteous and the unrighteous.' We were kidding ourselves that we weren't doing anything wrong. But that weekend, we had never felt more right.

It was the first time a front door was ours, the first time you lit a fire for us, the first time I burnt a pizza. The first time we shared a bath together, and a bed that was ours, and the fusing of our bodies was sublime. They were such precious hours, Marty, and confirmation we should be together; that to deny each other was to deny the very existence of love. I believed that weekend would be the turning point for us, that we must find a way to be together, properly and permanently.

Do you remember the walk down to the rocky beach? It was so steep and treacherous, following the paths made by creatures more intrepid than us, maybe sheep or goats who had none of my fears of falling. Our path was always so, but the arrival always worth it. I believed back then that, if I did fall, you would catch me. I can picture us on the shoreline. I can remember sitting on a sea-smoothed rock and letting my fingers sink and wriggle in a rock pool, feeling the cold water make them tingle. My senses were so heightened back then, every atom of my being singing the song of us, of our perfection, our eternal love. I could believe it then, that we would find our way to each other forever. I'm straining now to retrieve a memory from a gossamer thread, a wisp I can't quite grab, make more solid. It's something to do with a diamond, or a sparkle in the water. I'm sure we talked of marriage that day...

More clearly than that though, I can remember the pain of that weekend coming to an end. It had been so perfect, so utterly idyllic; if only we could have stayed there, pretended for a bit longer. But we had to go back, didn't we? As we did every time. Was this time different? I don't remember. Did we have renewed hope that we could find a way to be together? We must have. That time can't have been for nothing. It meant so much.

They served us sandwiches on the plane journey home. I can't remember what was in them, only that I felt really nauseous and couldn't eat mine. I'm not sure if I realised then my period was late, or if that came later, after I got home. The panic that I might be pregnant combined with the hope I dared to feel that a baby would surely bring us together... but it was just Mother Nature playing a cruel trick as, days later, my period arrived, perhaps delayed by the constant stress I was living under. I have wondered, over the years, what would have happened if I had been pregnant with your child then, Marty. Would that have been enough to make you leave your living lie with Anna? The life of an innocent, born into love. I have to believe it would have, because I still believe what we had then was real. But that's irrelevant anyway, isn't it? Because I wasn't pregnant then, and we were no closer to a solution.

Chapter 17

Secrets and Lies

The memories are kind of blurry after Cornwall. Do you remember what happened next? I know slipping back into our 'real' lives must have been nigh on unbearable, having had the spotlight shone on our true desire, a play within the play; that little snapshot of perfection. That spotlight must also have glaringly illuminated the chinks in our walls that were threatening to become gaping chasms at any moment. Surely Anna and Steve must have been able to see through them? Through us? To our truth. That we absolutely must be together.

Or were we such proficient actors, liars, that our secret remained undetected? I sometimes wondered if they knew but chose to ignore it, neither wanting to admit to such a painful truth. I still remember what agony it was to be so trapped by Steve's love and my vows to him; my inability to break those vows and his heart. Sometimes I told myself he'd be better off being free, free to find someone who loved him as much as he loved them. But for Steve it was always me. Only me. As you say too, repeatedly and often in your written and your spoken words. Only me.

I lay the framed photograph of myself down with a sigh. Ancient history now. That woman, that girl, is long gone.

Would anyone see a sparkle in my green eyes now? See dreams and possibilities, still, in the lines on my face? You would, wouldn't you? Even now, after everything, I still believe you'd see the young woman you fell in love with all those years ago.

I pick up another bundle of letters from the shoebox: they're from the summer of 2000. The start of a new millennium and certainly a new start for me. There's a gap in our written history. Something happened the previous summer, didn't it? We'd rekindled our affair; it barely took a cinder, did it, Marty? Because it was always there, our love, just beneath the surface, waiting to re-combust, wasn't it?

Before I dive headfirst into this next chapter, I heave myself up from the sofa, my bladder reacting to the copious cups of coffee I've been drinking. My body's seized up after sitting for so long, and I again become aware of the aging process. (I think Mother Nature may well be related to Hindsight; a first cousin, perhaps. And Wishful Thinking. Maybe related by marriage.) She's doing her worst with my body, now I'm fifty. I can feel the changes taking place, feel things starting to shut down, now that they're no longer needed, now that I have fulfilled my duty on this earth and produced a child to continue my lineage. Will a man ever want me again? The thought pops unbidden and unwelcome into my head. I shake it away. That's a thought for another day, when my head's not already full of you.

So certain was I that you and I could make it work this time. There was only one obstacle for us to overcome now: Anna. I really believed you could do it this time, after our reunion had been so incredible. And when you did, I would be waiting, free to welcome you into my open, loving arms, to share everything, and bring you home forever.

I knew it wasn't going to be easy for you to leave Anna, of course I did. And even though your previous attempts had failed, somehow I still had faith. You instilled that faith in me, Marty. You told me so many times how your love for me was 'infinite' and 'everlasting' and for us not to be together was simply wrong. And I believed you. I pushed my pain and fear deep down where the sun couldn't shine on it and make it grow, and I believed. Hope filled my soul; I only needed to be patient a little longer.

You came to see me at my sister's that summer. Do you remember? We sat in her back garden, on a blanket on the lawn, and we told her. Told her we were in love; blissfully, unrepentantly, feverishly in love. And she was happy for us, even though she didn't really approve. Because she could see the love between us, and even she couldn't deny it. Sharing our secret with Laura made things so much more real; admitting our feelings to someone in the family, 'outing' our relationship had to mean something. I close my eyes and I can recreate that picture of the three of us, even now, the sun blazing down on us, righteous or not. In that moment, I don't think I'd ever been happier.

Are you there now too, Marty? Back in that moment? Close your eyes and go back. Take my hand and go back...

Chapter 18

Un-Break My Heart

Laura hugged you when it was time to go. It felt like we had her blessing, didn't it? In spite of everything. We wanted some time alone before you had to begin the long drive home, and you suggested a drive into the countryside. We didn't go far; just to the edge of a quiet field off the side of a single-track lane. It was a cornfield, golden in the sun, on that brightest of days.

You were quiet when we stopped. Your mood had changed. I could sense a dark cloud hanging over you. I remember a feeling of pressure in my chest. I can feel it again now. That awful tightness, heart pounding in your chest, nausea gripping your throat – like the feeling when you have a near miss on the road.

'What? What is it? Marty, you're scaring me.' I'm sure I was squeezing your hand and trying to meet your eyes. But you couldn't make eye contact with me. And there were tears rolling down your cheeks. Did I tip your head up with my free hand? I wonder. Needing the reassurance I always found when I looked into your eyes. I wasn't prepared for what came next. Nothing could have prepared me.

'Anna's pregnant.'

Can you see my face, now, Marty? Can you see once more that, in that instant, when you uttered those two words, something broke in me? All these years later, I can still feel the world spinning out of control; the shattering of everything, every hope and dream and belief.

I grabbed the car door handle and wrenched my hand out of yours, just needing to get away from you, from your words, and the agony they'd inflicted. I can hear my sobs as I almost fell from the car and ran away down the lane. I just had to get away from you. I don't think I even registered what direction I was running in; if it was towards Laura's house or not. I just had to put distance between us. I simply couldn't believe what you'd told me; to do so was just too painful. It was a truth I didn't know how to acknowledge, accept or understand.

You ran after me, didn't you? It didn't take you long to catch up with me. I could barely stay upright through the sobs that wracked my body. You tried to still me, wrapping your arms around me, holding me tight even as I tried to claw free, shushing me all the while.

'Lou, stop, please, stop. Listen to me. Listen.'

I didn't want to stop though. Didn't want to listen to anything else you had to say. You'd said more than enough; everything, in those two words.

'Nothing has changed, Lou. We can still be together,' you tried to make me hear.

But everything had changed, Marty, couldn't you see that? Didn't you understand?

'It's you I love, Lou, only you.' Pleading with me.

But your words meant nothing now, Marty. You literally broke my heart. Those two words had pierced my chest as surely as if they were daggers, and nothing you could say could undo it.

And then the fight just went out of me and I went limp in your arms. I went from feeling everything to feeling completely numb in a split second. As I stopped fighting, you released your grip and I used that moment to step back and away from you, pushing you away, both my hands on your chest. You were crying, tears streaming down your face, a face filled with panic and fear at what you'd done. But I was overtaken, not by calmness exactly, but by something like it; a futility, a resignation. There was no more point in anything. In fighting, in running, in trying. Maybe even in living. Certainly not in listening to you, and the excuses that were spewing out of your mouth like vomit.

'Lou. I'm sorry, I'm so sorry, you have to forgive me! She tricked me. Anna tricked me! She stopped taking the pill without telling me!' Through the tears, and the snot now streaming from your nostrils. I think I hated you in that moment. I know I lost all respect for you. Something in me went hard and cold, plunged me into icy blackness. I didn't want you anywhere near me, and I turned away from you, walking now, and definitely in the direction of Laura's house.

Still you followed, pitifully asking for my forgiveness.

'Please, Lou, please! Forgive me. You're the only woman I've ever loved. Will ever love. Give me another chance. I'll make it up to you. Don't let Anna come between us,' you sobbed.

But you couldn't see, could you? Anna hadn't come between us, Marty. You had. Anna was just doing whatever she could to hang onto you and the marriage. Could I blame her for that? But you? You had let me believe that yours was a marriage in name only, and the physical side of the relationship was over. And now here you are telling me your wife's pregnant because she stopped taking the pill without telling you. No, Marty. She's pregnant because you had sex with her. While you were having sex with me; stupid, gullible, me.

You killed our love, Marty. Not Anna, not your unborn child, not me. You. Even if I had still wanted you, do you really believe you could have left a child, however conceived, when you couldn't leave the mother you claimed not to love?

Still you begged, pleaded for my forgiveness, my understanding; promised me the world could still be ours. But that world had spun into oblivion, Marty. The moment you uttered those two life-altering words, it had spun off its axis and been catapulted into the furthest reaches of the galaxy, taking my love for you with it. There was simply no coming back from that moment, not for me anyway.

I couldn't even feel your distress that day, Marty. Looking at your tear-stained, snot-covered, face and obvious terror, I felt nothing. Some critical component in me had simply shut down; maybe a subconscious act of self-preservation. A switch had been flicked into the off position in my brain. If I had to assign any feeling to that moment, it would be contempt, I think; not a feeling I realised I even had in my repertoire. You lost more than just my love that day, you lost my respect too.

I remember walking down the lane, calm, composed, icy cold to your overheated, panicking, pleading presence beside me.

'It's over, Marty. Hear me when I tell you. It's over. We're over. Done. Finished,' I tell you, adding emphasis to the words with a sweep of my hands.

I don't remember arriving back at Laura's. I don't remember at what point you gave up and left either. My memory cuts out somewhere back on that lane, the fields of golden corn on either side, the only witnesses to the scene that just unfolded, golden heads nodding sadly as I passed.

Chapter 19

Return to Sender

I return to the present with an exhalation of the breath I've been holding. I think that's the first time I've revisited that memory properly in all these years. Of course, it still has great poignancy, but it doesn't evoke the kind of pain it once would have. I suppose time, that great healer, has done its thing.

It was a strange time for a while, I remember, after 'the end of us'. There was no need to 'get over you', no weeks and months spent sobbing into my pillow, no mourning period for our lost union. I was as over you as if we'd never been. Whatever broke that day, in that lane beside the nodding heads of corn, had circumvented any such need, and I was grateful. I'm not sure I would have survived otherwise.

And so I just got on with my life without you, landing a new job and embracing all the new and exciting possibilities that came my way. It felt good to be free, not just from my marriage, but from the years of our affair.

I had cut all contact with you and asked that you respect my decision and leave me alone. But you couldn't do it, could you? You couldn't accept me telling you it was over, and for good. I must be in some sort of state of denial as far as you were concerned. Did you think you'd just wear me down eventually?

Don't you think that was kind of arrogant? You broke my heart, Marty. No, you didn't just break it, you shattered it into smithereens so spectacularly I could no longer feel.

I didn't answer your letters and cards, even though they kept on coming over the weeks and months. I gave you no encouragement, no reason to believe I would change my mind, but still you wouldn't give up, would you? But do you know what's worse than that, Marty? What's worse than your total lack of respect for my decision? I'll tell you, shall I? Because I don't know if I ever said this to you… You still chose to live a lie. Through all of this, you never once had the courage to be true to your so-called feelings, and leave Anna.

You would still rather live your safe little lie with a woman you claimed not to love, than be alone with your truth. You would never have left unless you had the guarantee of me waiting for you, would you? And maybe not even then. At least I had the courage to get out, Marty, to finally be honest about my marriage and face whatever awfulness ensued. How could I ever respect you now? You were a coward, Marty; spineless and weak, and undeserving of my love. Maybe if you'd had the courage to leave Anna and prove to me your words weren't just so much hot air, things could have been different. But you didn't, did you? And still you couldn't accept responsibility for what happened between us.

Did you think your persistence would gradually break down my defences? I have to tell you, it did the opposite. It shored them up, made them higher, stronger, more impenetrable. And then it started to make me angry. You know better than anyone how little anger I have in my DNA, but I started to get angry you didn't have the decency to leave me alone to get on with my life. I needed you to back off, but I had no idea how to get through to you, to make you hear me. And so the letters, the cards, and poems continued to arrive. I don't even remember what I did with them all. Certainly I don't have all of them here in this box. Did I put them back in the post marked 'Return to Sender'? I should have burned them.

I have found one poem you must have written during this time. It's scribbled on a tatty bit of paper that's obviously been screwed up at some point – whether by you or me, I don't know. I can imagine you screwing it up and tossing it in the bin, and then having second thoughts, retrieving it and sending it to me. A bit like our relationship, eh, Marty?

Dappled sunlight dances quiet,
Summer sun upon my face.
And yet my heart beats cold, so cold
Without you in my arms' embrace,
Without your smile's gentle grace,
Without your giggle's echo close,
Without the soul I love the most.
All that matters is not here.
All that's left is my own fear.
All the summers yet to come,
All the love that's left to run.
All the life within me still
Without you remains unfulfilled.

What was the point, Marty? What was the point of all those words of loss and grief and sorrow? To make me feel guilty? To make you feel better? What had I done wrong, Marty? What did I have to feel guilty about? I'd given you so many chances to be with me, but you failed to take them, didn't you? And then when I genuinely thought we had a chance of being together, you screwed it up in spectacular fashion. Only this time, I wouldn't let you retrieve us from the bin, smooth out the lines and try again, would I? Can you honestly blame me?

It didn't stop there though, did it? When letters through the post triggered no response, you upped the ante. I suppose I should be grateful that at least you didn't name me in any of the more public declarations of your feelings. I haven't thought about all the nicknames we had for each other for such a long time. They probably sound ridiculous now. One such pet name was 'GSP' which stood for 'Gorgeously Smashing Person', I think. It was so long ago. A lifetime. Anyway, 'GSP' was how you addressed me in some of the notes that started to appear in places other than through my, or my mum's, letterbox. I started to find A4 sheets of paper pinned to trees where I used to walk my dog. I couldn't miss them; they stood out bright and white against the bark, and you chose your target trees carefully. It was kind of unnerving to think of someone walking my route and trying to see through my eyes, even you, Marty, the man I'd been so in love with, for so long.

Did you think I'd be flattered by the attention? By the lengths you went to? Was I supposed to think it was romantic? Maybe once, I would have, Marty. But then it just felt creepy and kind of stalker-ish. I started to wonder if you were watching me, or following me. I knew realistically that you probably weren't – you lived too far away for one thing, and work and family would have left little time for being some sort of crazed peeping Tom. But it was unsettling all the same, and the anger that had been simmering inside me began to bubble. Even I had my limits, Marty. Even I could only be pushed so far. But you kept on pushing, didn't you?

You found another way of getting to me, even from a distance, and pieces started to appear in the local newspaper you knew I took. They'd be in the 'Announcements' section, addressed to 'GSP' or one of the other names only I would recognise. Mostly they were just small boxes containing declarations of undying love. The bubbling inside me became a rolling boil and I knew I needed to release it. I knew I had to find a way to stop you, to reclaim my power and force an end. I can actually remember making the call, Marty. I can picture the phone box I used to ensure you couldn't pick up my number, and the words I spoke.

'It's over, Martin. It's over for good. I don't love you anymore, and I never will again. You have to accept this and stop harassing me – stop all the letters, everything. If you don't, I will have no choice but to phone your mum and tell her to make you stop.'

I don't know if I actually said goodbye, or if I let you speak before I hung up the phone. I know I was shaking. However I felt about you back then, it wasn't an easy call to make. You forced me into it though. I couldn't make you hear me any other way. You couldn't hear my silence. You left me no choice, Marty, and I was pretty pissed off you forced me into behaviour completely alien to me. It was the only way I knew would make you stop. I knew the threat of telling your mum would be enough. You had protected her from the knowledge of us when we still had hope of being together; I knew you would not risk upsetting her now, when we were over.

And it did work, pretty much straight away. You couldn't resist one last piece in the paper, though, could you? Had to have the last word, the final say. I've found a copy of the piece you sent me. A bigger box this time. Much bigger.

GSP

You had no need to use so cold and sharp a blade in your last call, nor drive the savage wound so deep. You have your wish. I am easy to avoid, and will not seek you out. Yet I could not let things end in such darkness after so much light, so I write you this. I would far sooner say it to you alone and not the world, but you didn't allow that. Know you are constantly in my thoughts and in my heart. However much I wish you weren't, and fight it. You fill them both. Still. Always. I love you as much now as I have ever done, as much as I always will.

I remember all the times across the months when we lay skin-to-skin, times we fused in mind, body and soul. You are amazing, wonderful. I remember how each curve of your smiling face caressed my eyes, your laughter my ears.

I remember your silk-smooth back; your exquisite hands; your touch, your magical, electric touch. Your hair falling around your face, your perfect skin; your thighs; your lips. Your taste. Watching you beside me, smiling as you slept in the half-light before dawn. And all this mesmeric beauty

outshone by your astonishing mind, your sublime soul. I remember it all. These memories are the gentle warming winter sun upon my heart and time can fade none of them for me. I love you completely, and as I can love no-one else.

I remember your touch

I remember your words

I remember your eyes

I remember your fire

I know the difference. I try so hard, but cannot hide from it. If you say you can, then it was never there, and all my fundamental faiths in life and love – crystallised in you – crumble to dust and scatter in the winds of pale existence. I can never believe that. I came home, and know where it is. Who it is. If I search my soul, I find you living there. You can never make me believe you don't feel the same, behind it all.

Yet you are free of me just as long as your heart desires. You need never fear me rearing my ugly head.

I wish you only happiness, in this and every year. If you are happy, I would never risk upsetting it. You must know that. I just wish, this once, I understood. Never doubt how deeply I love you – it lies far beyond all measure, all imagination, and is immune to time.

And should you ever, ever get in touch it could cause me only joy. In weeks, years, or decades, unto the day before the end of never.

I'll always pray one day that we'll both find home again. I accept that day may never come. But so I pray. I remember and I smile. Until then, wherever you are, be happy.

Good luck, you daft and lovely Smasher.

Take great care of yourself.

All my love everlasting.

Rampler

Xxx

(See sonnet 116)

Chapter 20

Bitter Pill

Heavy stuff, Marty. I don't feel angry anymore though. If I stop to try and work out how I feel after all this time about what happened all those years ago… A little wistful, perhaps. Certainly I wonder what life might have been like if we had made a go of things; if you'd managed to leave Anna, before. Before you got *her* pregnant. But could you, would you, ever have left? You weren't able to before the baby, before Esme, so how can I believe you'd have had the strength to leave once you'd held her in your arms? And, anyway, would I have let you?

I never wanted to be a homewrecker, Marty. Yes, I wanted you more than I've ever wanted anything or anyone in my whole life, and the thought of breaking up a marriage was bad enough. But breaking up a family? I'm not sure I could have lived with the guilt of that. It's all irrelevant, anyway, isn't it?

I should probably let go of your hand now, get off the ride down memory lane and do something constructive with my day off. Honestly, though, I know full well there's no point; I know the way I'm feeling I'll achieve nothing. Today, I just need to immerse myself in the memories and see where they take me.

I pick out another handful of pages from the shoebox and a

few small photographs shake themselves out, demanding to be seen. I gather them up, shuffle them into a neat little pile, and look through them. They're photos of Esme, your daughter, some of just her and some of you holding her. She's not very old in them. I guess they range in age from maybe a few weeks to about nine months. She looks like a smiley baby. And you look like a proud and happy father. It was hard for me to see those pictures of you, Marty. Then and now. You'll never know how hard.

I wonder now how you crept back into my life? When you decided it was safe to? How long you thought I would stay angry and demand your absence? It wasn't long, was it? Just a few short months, where I was simply getting on with my life without you in it. I guess you always knew me well, knew any anger I felt would burn out quickly without the oxygen of contact from you. I locate the letter that came with the photos of Esme, and settle back into the cushions to read once more:

Dearest Lou,

Still my one true love. Always.

Find a few pictures of Esme enclosed, which I scanned at work.

Go on, open them. Have a look. Should help you push me further away.

Beautiful, isn't she? I hope you meet her one day. I still hope you'll be her step-mum one day. So there.

Please read this. It is the last such letter you'll get from me. I wrote most of this in the small hours of this morning between tears. Then transferred it here to get rid of the unsightly blobs, and tone it down. If you've got PMT, maybe wait a week, but please. Please. Read, don't skim. Alone. Quietly, alone, carefully, to the end, several times. It's our lives. It's not about jealousy. It's about loss. And truth. Feel the words. Feel what's behind them. Don't get angry. Just feel. Understand me. Understand you. If you can't feel it now, don't throw it away. Read it again in a month or two. A year or two. Ten. Keep it, read it, feel it. Take your time. You have all the time in the world, now.

Anna knows. She knows I still love you, have done for every moment since Christmas '96. Apparently she knew a while ago. I've just confirmed her fears. Says I've been calling your name in my sleep for years. Never said a word about it. Imagine that. It'd been brewing for a while. Month by month since you stopped things. I've been trying so hard to let you go, as we both 'did the right thing'. Pointless. It got worse, not better, as the months went by. I tried to ring you a few times before, you remember? But you couldn't talk. Wouldn't talk. Didn't offer your mobile. I should've pushed, but no. Still 'doing the right thing'. Anna's not daft, she knows things have been wrong and getting worse. Just not why. She ran away to mother to let me think. She didn't expect me to still be there when she came back. I shouldn't have been. I shouldn't have been there six months ago. Then this Sunday I could hold back no more and the truth came out. She knows.

She still wants me. She must really love me. I said we should talk. Not looking forward to it. She'll be hard to resist, knowing the pain she's in, the way she'll use Esme to encourage me to stay. I've told her you don't want me now, and she says I'll get over you. I won't. I can't. I've tried so hard for so long. Every time I look at Anna, every time I look at Esme, I'll know I should be in your arms instead.

I wish I could talk to you alone, hold your hand, seek warm reassurances from your loving eyes. I wish I could hold you. I wish *you'd run away to Cornwall or Stornoway with me. I wish I hadn't been such a complete arse and cocked things up so comprehensively.*

How do I go on being a father living such a lie before those innocent young eyes anymore? To teach Esme that it is better to live a lie than to fight for what you know to be true and right. I don't love her mother. I love you. Look at the photos, Lou. Look at them. Can you begin to understand the pain of lying to her every day, day in, day out, pretending to love her mother when I love only you?

It's not being kind to Esme, not in the long run. I believed I stayed for her, but it slowly dawned she'd not thank me for living a miserable life, for lying to her. She'd blame herself for ruining my life. Leaving Esme for you is the best thing I can do for her. She'd want me to be happy. I can never have true peace in my soul as long as that half crystallised in you is not beside me. I'm so sure you still feel the same deep down. If I left her for you… That is worthy and right. But to leave her for nothing? How do I leave Esme for you when you deny me?

I'd miss Esme. Dear God, I'd miss her as much as I've missed you. But I know she'd be in good hands and give Anna something to focus on without me. I'd still see her. And I'd be living in truth again after so long. I could look my daughter in the eye as she grows up. So clear are things now. But too late, you say. Too late.

It's not too late, Lou. Not yet. We can still have children of our own just as beautiful as Esme if you let me give them to you. And born into love, not a sham. Such love. I can be with you in a 'phone call.

If you want me, call me. Anywhere. If I don't fly to you there and then, I deserve all the wrath you can muster. But you stand to gain the world.

I still have faith in your love, wherever you buried it. I know

I saw it briefly through your magical eyes, just inches away on your sofa. Before you felt it rising too, and pushed it far back down. I know it frightens you to risk reawakening those incredible forces which caused you so much pain. I know you're hiding from me now, and for good reason. Afraid of me stirring truths you've worked so hard at concealing from yourself, which I know you needed to do to survive. But the truth will not be hidden forever. It will haunt you always. Take it from one who knows. Don't give into fear. There is so much yet to gain.

I pray one day you'll set your love for me free again, that time and truth defeat the fortress round your heart, too. It's not the love that causes the pain. We do, by denying it. If we listened to love, we would both be so much happier already. Be true to your heart and the rest will follow.

You can still have fun with me, you know. And we can live the peace of Cornwall every day, have everything we dreamed of for so long. We can live it now. If only you let us. We are so close to everlasting happiness. You must know that, in your heart. Please, don't wait too long. Don't give up one pretence of happiness only to replace it with another. I know you're having fun for the first time in so long, seeing someone who can spend money on you, take you places, make you laugh. It must seem such a relief after all you've been through, and I can see how you believe yourself to be content. My timing is so awful. But I can't believe you'll ever be serenely happy with anyone, not as you can be with me. Never home. Short-term fun, not long-term fulfilment. Does he love you? Can he ever love you as I do, as I always will? Love you for all you are, for all you will ever be. I find this so hard to understand, after we fought so hard and for so long to be together, and it cost us both so much. You'll never share anyone else's soul. You know as

well as I do where home is, you know where it is.

You have no reason to believe me, I know. I am so sorry for so much. The problem was never doubting my love for you, only the right thing to do. I thought I was 'doing the right thing', but I was looking at the wrong choice. It wasn't Esme or you. The choice was truth or lie. Choose truth, and I have both you and Esme. Choose lie, and I have neither. By choosing Esme, I chose the lie, without understanding what it meant. Now the right thing to do is so clear. Allow me to make the choice again, please. Please, Lou. I just didn't understand the question. Now I do. A bitter, bitter lesson. I choose truth. All I can do is wait and hope. Only you can choose now. Whatever you do, follow your heart and not your head. Don't make my mistake. Don't allow six short months to take away two lifetimes of such happiness and completeness. My timing is so crap, but I am sorrier than you can ever know. All this mess is my fault, I know, but the choice now is yours. I fall at your feet. Please, choose me. The other half of your soul. Choose truth.

In the meantime, I pray for your every happiness, and genuinely will you all the luck and love in the world. If you are truly happy, then I am happy for you. If not, if things don't work out and your defences do crumble, call me. Any time. Any year. Never hesitate for a moment. Follow your heart, listen to your soul. Actually, never hesitate to call me anyway, about anything, any time. Gossip, news, just hello. Any contact is always such joy. Please talk to me. If you want to, call. Never be afraid.

I won't write like this again — just cards. Any more would push you away, and I could not bear to lose my dearest friend as well as my one true love. But these words are from the heart, and they stand for my lifetime. Don't be angry with me. Keep them. Read them and reread them. You lose nothing by doing so. I had to try,

had to fight for what I believe to be true and right. To try and be heard from so far away. You are possessed of such indescribable, breath-taking beauty in every way. Sublime within and without. And so you will remain, however the passing years may write themselves upon you. Beauty and light beyond all description. Goddess. Dearest goddess of all my dreams. I love you until death do us part, and probably beyond. You live in my heart forever, and I adore you for all time.

But now, I set you free. I will always hope and pray for your return. I am so afraid. I live for you.

Time to stop rambling.

May you one day see a froglet, a sparrow, a sunset, and the same cascade begin for you as it did for me. And bring you to realise who to share your life with as no other, who to grow old beside.

A single call, Lou. All we need. No waits, no promises, no doubts. A single call. Take such good care, my one love. My heart and soul reach out to you always. Feel them. As I am sure I still feel yours.

Sonnet 116 still stands.

Marty xxx

I love you, I love you, I love you.

I look up Sonnet 116, even though I pretty much know it by heart:

Let me not to the marriage of true minds
Admit impediments. Love is not love
Which alters when it alteration finds,
Or bends with the remover to remove:
O, no! it is an ever-fixed mark,

That looks on tempests and is never shaken;
It is the star to every wandering bark,
Whose worth's unknown, although his height be taken.
Love's not Time's fool, though rosy lips and cheeks
Within his bending sickle's compass come;
Love alters not with his brief hours and weeks,
But bears it out even to the edge of doom.
If this be error and upon me proved,
I never writ, nor no man ever loved.

Wow. That was heavy going, Marty. And so full of contradictions and confusion. If that's a representation of what was going on in your head at the time, you must have been in a pretty dark place. Did I feel sympathy for you? Back then, when I first read it? Honestly, I don't know the answer to that. I think my reactions to the letter may well have been as schizophrenic as your words: anger, sadness, disbelief. I wonder if I had to reply to the letter now, what I'd say to you? Not for the first time, I wonder if my letters still exist, and wish I could read them. It's difficult to know how I would've responded, now, with the passing of so much time. I'm a different person now, aren't I?

Chapter 21

RSVP

Dear Marty,

Thank you for your letter and photos of Esme. (Would I have said thank you? I wonder. Probably, in spite of everything that had happened between us, I think I still would have thanked you – that's just the way I am.) *She's beautiful - you must be very proud.* (I think I would have sounded formal. To start with, at least.)

There's so much to respond to in your letter, and so much confusion; the ravings of a madman almost. Do you realise how much you contradict yourself, Marty? How with one breath you tell me you only want my happiness, while in the next you're questioning my new relationship and telling me I'll never be truly happy with anyone but you. Don't you think that's arrogant? After everything you put me through, to suggest you're still the only man who can ever make me truly happy? It's almost like you're cursing me, planting a seed of doubt you hope will germinate and grow into a realisation that you're right. It doesn't matter how many times you say you only want me to be happy, Marty, I don't believe you. Are you really so convinced I'm just suppressing my true feelings and one day my defences will crumble and I'll come running back to you?

So, Anna knows, and has for some time. I feel sorry for her. She deserves better. We all deserve to be with someone who loves us as much as we love them. Did you ever stop to think that staying with her was selfish, Marty? Before Esme, before all that. Didn't you think it would be better to leave so she could find someone to love her the way you said you loved me? To stop living a lie; live your truth and let Anna find hers? Do you know what I think? I think you're spineless. I think you make excuses and blame everyone but yourself for the way your life's turned out. It's all my fault we're not together – I wouldn't let us try again, I wouldn't let you. Do you know how pathetic that makes you sound?

Is it really my fault you're lying to Esme every day, as you put it? No, Marty, it's not my fault! Man up and own your decisions, your mistakes, your responsibilities. Do you not see how you made me lose respect for you? You ask how do you leave Esme when I deny you? You leave because that's the honest decision for you, or you stay and you own it! You don't throw all the blame at my feet, Marty. Let's be honest here: you'd rather live a lie with Anna and Esme, than be alone. Everything else is just so much crap. I owned my mistake and I ended my marriage because that was the right thing to do, and it's better to be alone than living a lie. You had the same choice, Marty, so don't blame me for your decision to stay.

Your letter goes round in circles. One minute, it's all so clear – you shouldn't stay for Esme, she wouldn't want you to be unhappy because of her, and the next you might as well stay if you can't have me. Leave and stop living a lie, stay because I've said it's too late for us. On and on and round and round. You didn't understand the question before. It wasn't Esme or me, it was truth or lie, you wrote. For God's sake, grow a pair! The one thing you fail to realise, Marty, time and time again, is that your choice to continue living a lie is why I no longer love you. You lost my respect, and with it my love. You never managed to leave, to prove to me you could actually do it, so why would I ever give you that kind of power over me again?

You say I'll never be truly happy with anyone but you. I guess I'll take my chances...

Does that bear any resemblance to my original reply, I wonder? If indeed I did reply. I think I must have done. I would've been angry at the injustice of your words as I saw them; pissed off that you insisted on blaming me for your life choices. And using the promise of having a child, children, together... that was low. Honestly, Marty, what did you really expect me to say? That I'd welcome you back with open arms, and give you another go at breaking my heart? It was about self-preservation, Marty. It was about survival. I'd patched my heart up too many times and the seams were forever weakened where I'd stitched it back together.

Chapter 22

Give Me a Sign

I take up another letter, this one neatly typewritten, and start reading. The opening paragraphs are further outpourings of your love for me: 'inexpressible joy', 'wonderment', incandescent beauty', 'astonishing power'. You expressed your love so much and so often and in such exalted terms, Marty, but it was never enough, was it? Never enough to bring you to me for good. I wonder if I stopped believing it? If it became overkill? Anyone reading your letters now would, frankly, need a sick bag. God knows why, but I'd agreed to see you. I don't understand what was going through my head back then. I know I was seeing someone new. I read on.

So why did I come? Why get up at such an unearthly hour and spend six hours in a car just to see you for two when you're seeing someone else? So little time to see you, and you were so tired. I craved to stay, to carry on, but you were clearly agitated by the passing time and the threat of discovery. Edging away from windows and doors. So very tired. Me too. All I wanted was to curl up beside you, rest your head against my chest. To drift off in your arms for my very first real rest in an eternity, experience that peace so long denied me which only you can provide. So very long.

I just had to come. We never really got into the 'why'. I was just so happy to be home again, however briefly. I was just intoxicated again by you, and needed to soak you up as much as possible. To replenish such a depleted soul. As we talked, and sat, and just 'were', I couldn't bring it up directly. There was no time, and you were so tired. But so many questions are unanswered, and I'm trying so hard to understand. I'm not making much sense. No change there, then.

But I'm so much less afraid since seeing you again. Because I've looked deep into your eyes and seen your love reflecting back into my own, despite all you try to do to deny it, and force it down. Wishful thinking? I really don't think so.

Friday. What a horrific day. Why did I ring you? I'll tell you why. I wasn't going to tell you, but I suppose Sunday doesn't make much sense unless I do, and I hate holding things back from you.

I was going to ask you three things: 1) Do you love me? 2) Do you want to hold me in your arms forever? And 3) Will you marry me? If the answer was yes to all three, I was going to come down then and there to begin with you again, to start from scratch. To leave Anna and Esme, the house, the cats, everything. Just the clothes I stood in. Begin again with just truth and love. So sure was I that you would say yes, that you still felt the same as I. Then you dropped your bombshell before I could ask, and the steel claw tore and twisted inside. Never have I been so suddenly and completely alone as I was in that moment. To be so sure of a new beginning, that this time it would work, that now you'd had time to get over Steve, you've a place of your own where we could just BE. And I had the strength at last to leave and come to you. To spend the weekend imagining our new life together, caressing souls once more in peace and harmony. To come home at last, for good.

And then the bomb fell and swept it all away. You've met some-one else. Too late. Too fucking bastard late. God, my timing is so crap. My love for you is so strong. And now I am adrift far from shore, not really knowing what I can believe any more.

I so wanted a sign from you on Sunday that you wanted me to stay. Once I'd seen you, and known my love to be as unfaltering as ever, my passion just as explosive. Just a sign that you still wanted me. I came so close to telling you about Friday then, and what I'd planned to say, but I couldn't bear disrupting your new life if you had found happiness without me. You didn't know what to say, you said. All I wanted to hear was 'I love you'. But you just wanted me to go.

Sunday 13th. Unlucky for some.

And then, most cutting of all, you turned away from me as I bent to kiss you goodbye. If anything, that hurt more than the bombshell. It wasn't as if I was going to launch my tongue down your throat. A soft, loving kiss. But you turned your head aside. And now I don't know what to believe any more. My love for you is so infinite, but now I don't know where yours is. Dark doubts overcome me. One minute I'm so sure I saw it in your eyes, the next I wonder if it was ever there at all. Was it ever there as strong as mine? If it was, where is it now? Sometimes I am so sure. Others, all is lost and I doubt everything. How could you be doing what you are doing with him if you still loved me? Arrghh! I hate hate HATE this.

All I am sure about is that my heart and soul belong to you and you alone. For all time, and in all ways. And I love you beyond words. There are two words I never really understood before I fell in love with you, but now I am part of them. They are part of me. One is 'eternity', the other is 'infinite'. My love for you is truly infinite, boundless in every respect and each dimension. Immeasurable in power, intensity and depth. There is no limit on my love for you, and it will last well beyond my simple lifetime. Which brings me on to eternity. That is how long I will love you for. I now believe in the immortal soul, and you are bound to mine forever. I scrawled some nonsense once about my love for you being like thunder at night, echoing to the farthest reaches of uncharted space and time, surrounding dying embers of stars as yet unborn. Quite good that bit. And still true. We had thunder on Sunday night as I cried. I've already said that if there's a heaven, I will find you in it. If you are not there, then it is not heaven. I will always hope we will find it together on earth one day. Somehow.

Take such good care, you most wonderful and amazing of women. My hope will never die, but for now I'm going to hide away in a corner and gibber quietly to myself. I won't bother you again for a while, as I recover and build defences again, but I'll never really believe it's the end. Because there is no end to my love for you. It has barely begun, surrounds you always, and you can draw on it whenever you wish.

All my deepest and everlasting love,
Infinitely and eternally yours.
Marty
xxxxx

Another powerful and confusing letter, Marty. For all the contradictions, though, the one thing that never wavered in your letters were your declarations of love for me. With everything that happened between us, that remained constant, didn't it? However much your love for me was tested, you always came back to it as an undeniable truth. It was so strong.

Why couldn't I grab hold of it and just hang on for dear life? I know I'd met Jon and thought I was in love with him but, if I'm honest, what Jon and I had didn't have even a fraction of the sheer brilliance of our love, Marty. No man could ever really make me feel the way you had. I could only kid myself for so long, though. It didn't take me many months to realise that I was fooling myself about my feelings for Jon. It was just a brief infatuation that burned out quickly. That never really happened with you, Marty. No matter what happened, I couldn't quite extinguish the true spark between us.

I must have confused the hell out of you. I'm sorry for that. I didn't mean to. As much as I tried to resist the pull of you, those invisible threads – that spiritual connection – could never really be broken, could it? As much as I tried to deny our love – to you and to myself – you saw it still, didn't you? Sometimes, the shutters over my eyes let you see in for the briefest glimpse of the love I still had for you. But then, just as quickly, the shutters went down again and I retreated back into the safety of denial. If I didn't love you, you couldn't hurt me. And it worked. Most of the time.

Were you really going to ask me to marry you? We'll never know now, will we? If only we'd been braver. You know my excuses, but what were yours? Really, Marty, what were your excuses? Why didn't you make the leap of faith and show me you really were committed to being with me? Did you never think you needed to show me, to prove to me, that you were genuine by being on your own? That you had to end the relationship you were in to prove you could begin anew. It felt like you were always hedging your bets. Does that make sense? It felt like I was always the one taking all the risks. You still had the safety of your marriage, the warmth of hearth and home with Anna and your daughter, if you couldn't have me. I think I lost respect for you because of that.

If only you had had the strength to pack a bag and just come to me, Marty, before it was too late, before all my defences went up… What might life have been like for us? We could have had the dream, lived the fantasy. Maybe we could've had it all, Marty. Instead of which, I settled for nearly fifteen years with Alan, a man I never loved. I told him I loved him. I wanted to love him. But I never really did. Because I never *could* fall in love again. For I never stopped loving you. He was good to me though, and he was, and is, a wonderful father to Libby.

I feel like I've wasted my life, Marty. I honestly feel the only worthwhile thing I've ever done is have my daughter. I pray she doesn't make the same mistakes as her mother. I want her to have the happiness I was denied. Maybe that means I have to tell her about you, tell her not to be afraid to love, not to be afraid to take a leap of faith and live her truth.

I wonder what I would have said, what would have happened if you had asked me to marry you that day? Thinking about it now, even after conferring with my old nemesis, hindsight, I honestly don't know the answer. Would your proposal have been enough to break down my defences, a battering ram to the portcullis? Maybe. I don't know. I'd done such a good job of burying my true feelings, hadn't I? But maybe that's what you needed to do… storm the fortress and rescue the fair maiden from the demons who kept her prisoner within. You needed to bound across the moat, Marty. You needed to be the knight in shining armour. You needed to rescue me. At the end of the day, though, you weren't prepared to take the risk any more than me, were you? You wanted guarantees. But love doesn't come with guarantees, does it? There's no getting your money back when it all goes wrong.

You said I turned my head away when you went to kiss me goodbye. I know that must've hurt you, and I'm sorry. Do I know now why I did it? Was I afraid you would try and take more than I was willing to give? Or that you would taste on my lips the love I still felt for you? Could I have carried on the deceit if our lips had met? I don't know. I'm sure I didn't do it as a way of hurting you, but of protecting me.

Chapter 23

Words

Dearest, dearest Lou,

Just a simple letter to say goodbye, and pass on my warmest wishes for your future, wherever it may lead. How hard that is. You are without doubt so far and away the dearest, most beautiful, wonderful soul ever to have touched my life, and your happiness is more important to me than anything. If making you happy means keeping away from you, then I have to comply. I could not bear to stand between you and happiness. I only ever want to carry you there. I just wish I could understand, this once.

Another 'goodbye' letter, eh, Marty? How many of those did you send me over the years? Always promising it will be the last one, always saying you'll keep away from me, let me get on with my life. You never did, though, did you? Not for long, anyway. And somehow I always let you back in; sometimes a little, sometimes the whole damn way. It was like a scab you couldn't resist picking at, never quite letting it fully heal. Every time, just when I thought you'd finally let go and moved on, you'd re-open the wound, pick, pick, picking at it until it bled. And then the healing would have to start all over again, the resulting scar a little bigger, a little deeper each time it healed over. Kind of masochistic, don't you think? It was hard on me too, Marty. I had my own scars.

Thank you for saying goodbye on Friday. Sorry I broke down. I had resolved not to. I wish I could have seen your face and held you in my arms once more. I do so in my mind and in my heart each day. I said I'd keep you updated of the situation with Esme and Anna. I suppose what it comes down to is that if I can't devote myself to you and your happiness for the rest of my life, I have to devote it to Esme. However much I resent her for keeping us apart. Whatever life I live with her mother, I will do what I can to make her feel happy and loved. She is a wonderful child, and I'm a damned good father, even if I say so myself.

So, we spoke on the phone? To say goodbye. I don't remember, I'm afraid. So long ago, Marty, so much buried pain and regret. I think I'd hardened my heart to you, hadn't I? Ever since you told me about Anna's pregnancy. I am sorry you still weren't happy, hadn't moved on from me, from us. I think I hoped fatherhood would be enough to salve the wound of you and me. I'm sure she helped, of course, but it's a different sort of love, isn't it? The love of a parent for a child. I know my love for Libby is the most powerful thing in the world; it burns with an intensity the like of which I could never comprehend before I held her in my arms. And it never waivers or diminishes, does it? If anything, it grows as they do. I would give my life for my daughter.

You wrote of resenting Esme for keeping us apart. That surprises me, knowing you as I do, and knowing the depth of your love for your child. It's really not her fault though, is it? Esme is innocent. An innocent. The same as Libby. She didn't ask to be born and, as far as I'm concerned, has no blame attached to her. Anyway, it's pointless attaching blame to anyone now. It happened. Your marriage to Anna wasn't as dead as you led me to believe, and whatever feelings you had for her resulted in a child. At the time – when you told me about the pregnancy – it felt like a betrayal, which is ridiculous, isn't it? Anna had every right to a physical relationship with you, her husband. She was the betrayed. By you. And by me. It never felt like that though, did it? We always felt right, and true. It still shocks me you were sleeping with both of us. It's something I've never been able to get my head around. It just seemed so out of character for you. For the you I thought I knew, at least. I think it made me wonder if you could do that, what other deceptions were you capable of? It made me doubt everything, Marty. But, most of all, it made me doubt your love for me.

I really don't know if Anna and I can get back together after the things I said. Things that can never be unsaid, and which in any case are as truthful now as when they tumbled out. We're going to go away together for the week of our tenth anniversary as you suggested. We'll see. Neutral ground. Interestingly, neither of us told our mums about the split. Mainly my sister telling me not to on my part, I must say. That will probably help hold things together. Anna's brother hates me. Hardly surprising.

You know how hard it was to live a lie with Steve. It will be doubly difficult for me to live a lie now, and multiplied several times by the innocent eyes of Esme. But I'll see what I can do if

Anna allows. For me, there could never be anyone who could replace you. I could never be happy with anyone else. Even to try and recreate something so spiritually intense and unique with another would never work, and would plague me each day by betraying a love so pure and total. It could only ever feel a pale substitute. I might as well try to build the Taj Mahal with pink Lego. Superficially similar, but so far removed from the real thing. There can only ever be one, and I would always know the difference. I have one true love, and to leave Esme for anything else would be wrong. So if Anna wants me to stay with her again for Esme, there seems little sense in not doing so for now. My duty. Never my love. I'll raise my mask again and hide behind.

The Taj Mahal made out of pink Lego… now there's an image to conjure with. Is that all *we* were? I wonder. Just a pale imitation of the real thing? If we were everything I believed we were, would you still have been sleeping with Anna? Or is that just something men do? Any port in a storm and all that. For all your proclamations about how I was the only woman you could ever love, blah, blah, blah… was it all just so much hot air? Or am I confusing love and sex? You made me believe they were one and the same though, Marty; that when we made love it was something precious, something almost spiritual. So, what was it with Anna? Was it just sex? Just physical? Meeting a need? Did you think about me when you were with her? In her? I never asked you about it, did I? I don't think I could've handled it then. Whatever you'd said.

I can be happier devoting myself to Esme than being apart from you both. And it's what my sister says I should do, and all my friends. They all say I should loathe, detest and despise you for what you've done to me. For ruining my life, Esme's, Anna's, for being so fickle in your emotions and continually breaking my heart. That I've had a lucky escape and I'm well shot of you.

They cannot know, cannot understand. You have shown me what true love can be. Its power, its sensual and spiritual wonder, its eloquent magnificence; its amazing ability not only to bring a soul to understand eternity, but be part of it and share it with another. You did that. No one else could, or ever will. I can share so much with you, you alone. As Blake said:

To see the world in a grain of sand,
And heaven in a wild flower;
Hold infinity in the palm of your hand,
And eternity in an hour.

With you, I experienced all this. Experienced the wonder of the entire universe. Only you. Only with you can I share these things. I simply love you, can do nothing but love you, and will adore you for all time.

I remember those paragraphs, Marty. I think, of everything you ever wrote to me, this made me the angriest. I still don't know why you felt the need to tell me. You should hate me, but you don't? Am I supposed to be grateful, or something? That, in spite of the fact I ruined your life, you still love and want me. Well, hoo-bloody-ray, lucky me. God! I'm getting angry now, Marty, and it's ancient bloody history. How dare you?! What the hell did you tell your sister and your friends? Nasty old Lou, one minute she wants me, next she doesn't. Does she love me, does she not? Boo hoo, poor old Marty. You must really have painted a picture of me as the villain of the piece. I don't

118

suppose you bothered to mention the fact you let me down time after time, promising to be with me, but never making it happen. Telling me I was your one and only true love and then getting your wife pregnant. I bet you loved playing the victim? Letting me take the blame. The responsibility. I hated you in that moment.

Re-reading this letter now, nearly two decades after it was written, is strange, Marty. I can still feel echoes of the emotions it must have aroused in me back then, but with a – I don't know... a sort of clarity; with the benefit of age and experience, perhaps. I can read it as more of an observer, with more detachment, I guess. It was all so raw back then. I'm struck, as so often with your letters, by the contradictions. Honestly, Marty, if I was a psychiatrist, I would have had serious concerns about your sanity.

I accept you believe now that our love cannot be rediscovered, that it is past. Please accept from me my undying belief that it awaits us still. Accept I might, just might, be right. However remote or unlikely, at least admit to yourself that if your present path does not lead where you think it will, then it can still lead back to me. I will welcome you at any time with open arms and open heart. I can never change how I feel about you, try as I might. And I can never believe your love for me has died, never believe I'm just flogging a dead giraffe. I know you say our chances are remote, but I cannot allow my hope to flutter and die completely in the bitter storm of these past weeks. To lose that hope would destroy me utterly. I have my dreams and my prayers. You are in them both.

The giraffe's dead, Marty. You killed it.

I will never call you again, never contact you again if that is your wish. Except for Christmas and birthday cards so you know I remain alive, and how to find me should I move. I'll only send them to your mum's. I would never risk upsetting any new-found happiness you might have. Please let me know if your mum moves. If you ever want to contact me for anything, never hesitate. Know I will always welcome any word, any sight. Any contact with you is a joy to be treasured. But it must come from you. I will not come to you, will not seek you out. Except, of course, through my heart and soul, reaching out across the night, across the years and miles. You have my word.

Never contact me again? I have your word? You must have been joking! When were you EVER true to your word? If you'd really wanted me to be happy, don't you think you would have left me alone? Let me move on with my life, let the scab fully heal. Don't you think you were being selfish, Marty? I think your letters were all about you, really, about meeting your needs. They had nothing to do with what was best for me at all. They were just your way of trying to ensure I couldn't quite close the door on you, to try and stop me from ever being happy again. Not without you. Selfish.

You can help me, though. It is far easier for me to leave you if I know you are not hiding from me. The very worst thing for me is not knowing where you are, how you are, even if you still draw breath to delight the world with your life. Please, help me by never hiding. It would drive me insane. Insaner. Not knowing, wondering, worrying, imagining. If you can trust me with the knowledge of (roughly) where you are, how you are, keep me up to date

and write, however rarely, then I can get by so much more easily.
Even if you tell me you're divorced, remarrying, pregnant, become
a Mormon, run off with the Brazilian football team, anything.
Anything at all. I will remember you fondly, smile that you are
happy. Happy that you can tell me. That gentle warming winter
sun upon my heart will continue to shine. I will always be your
friend, and wish you well. Never judge or condemn.

There's a little glimpse of the old Marty there. The funny, crazy boy who used to write to me from university. Whatever happened to him? He used to make me smile. Not cry. But then, wasn't that the same boy who called me a mug for getting engaged? Maybe I should've heeded that warning? And why should I make it easier for you? Did I owe you that? Did I owe you anything?

I've set up an email account for you. Well, for me actually. So I
can write to you but not risk upsetting your life. I needed to talk
to you, express my feelings when I couldn't see you, talk to you,
write to you. So I set up a Hotmail account to send them to. The
first few are probably a bit strange, but might help you understand
my frame of mind through this. Or lack of it. Trying so hard to
understand you. And for once, partly failing. I'll send the odd
thing over the weeks, months and years when my feelings get too
much and my soul is screaming. Only you and I know it's there.
But you need never see them if you don't want to. At least it will
stop me trying to send you post and relieve any temptation I may
have to call you.

The Hotmail account. I'd forgotten about that. I wonder…

I just tried to log in to it. How stupid, to think it would still be in use after all these years. I never did look at the emails you sent to it. An act of self-preservation, perhaps? Am I curious? What else could you possibly have said in them that you didn't put in your letters over the years? It's just another example of what you needed though, Marty, don't you see that? It wasn't about me, or even us, it was about you needing somewhere to spew your thoughts and feelings when I denied you access. How long did you continue to send emails to it? I wonder. When did you no longer need it?

I'll let you have my new address too, should Anna and I not make a go of things. Probably in your birthday card. If I can write to you, and think one day you might read. If all the time I can know where you are, that you are well, that you are out there somewhere and happy. If I know the path between us remains open should things ever change. If I know these things, then that will get me by. And you will be free of me for as long as your heart desires.

You'll also know where I will be once a year. Every sixteenth of December, eleven to twelve a.m. in The Chapel of the Holy Innocents at the Cathedral. Weekends moved to the following Monday (so this year I'll be there at 11 a.m. Monday 18th). Only illness or death will prevent my attendance. Well, possibly car breakdowns. If you want to do some Christmas shopping, I'd love to catch up with you. This or any year. Talk in sanctuary about how each other's lives are going. Maybe grab a pizza. I would never plead to share your life with me, don't fear. Or try to kiss you. Anything ahead for us must only come from you. You know my feelings, know they will never change and there could never be anyone but you. I accept in all probability you will never allow us to be together now, but I will always welcome a smile, a conversation, to replenish my soul. An innocent hug if you allow. And always, always, hope for more.

All my deepest and everlasting love is yours, yours alone, and surrounds you always.

Wherever you are.

Whoever you are with.

Marty xxxxx

P.S. Sonnet 61

Is it thy will, thy image should keep open
My heavy eyelids to the weary night?
Dost thou desire my slumbers should be broken,
While shadows like to thee do mock my sight?
Is it thy spirit that thou send'st from thee
So far from home into my deeds to pry,
To find out shames and idle hours in me,
The scope and tenor of thy jealousy?
O, no! thy love, though much, is not so great:
It is my love that keeps mine eye awake:
Mine own true love that doth my rest defeat,
To play the watchman ever for thy sake:
For thee watch I, whilst thou dost wake elsewhere,
From me far off, with others all too near.

Chapter 24

When You Come

I must have replied to your letter when I received it. I think I would've been too angry not to. It's the injustice of it, Marty. I feel a shadow of it now, as I must have felt the full glare of it then. It wasn't fair to lay the blame all at my feet, and I wouldn't have taken your words lying down; no way. I'd've been on my feet, fists raised, ready to defend myself. Metaphorically speaking, anyway.

I know my reply must have made some sense to you, because I've found your next letter.

I read my letter again yesterday. So clear is your side now. I'm so sorry. I was simply trying to express my own thoughts, feelings and confusions. I really cock things up sometimes. Throwing away the middle page helps it read better. Please never think I blame you. You have only ever shown me the joy that life can bring. You are the most amazing woman on this earth. Your sublime and captivating beauty, pouring from your soul and radiating from your skin, your incomparable eyes, this will keep me spellbound for an eternity. I love you utterly and it is with you always. Cornish fires burn eternal.

So much time has passed since this all happened, Marty. I still find it impossible to make sense of. I suppose I haven't let myself stop and really think about it before now. Maybe I'm having a mid-life crisis? Long overdue, probably. To be honest, my whole life feels like one long crisis. Would it have been different, better, if I'd spent it with you? I never told you this, but I did go to the cathedral on December 18th that first year you said you'd be there.

I don't know why I went. Some masochistic trait I've always had where you're concerned? I'd told you we couldn't be together. Ever. But still the thought of you persisted. Still I couldn't quite excise you. I took the day off work, telling people I was going Christmas shopping, which was actually true, but not the whole truth. So help me, God.

So, December 18th 2000, so long ago, but the memories of that day are so vivid. It had turned really cold, hadn't it? When I got in to the car that morning, the ice had made beautiful patterns on the windscreen. I sat looking at them for a few seconds before I could bring myself to spray them away with a can of chemicals. The weather was a blessing because it meant I could wear a woolly hat and a big scarf up around my chin without looking conspicuous. Not a disguise, exactly, but I was definitely trying to conceal my identity. For I had no intention of actually meeting up with you that day.

I did wonder if you would actually turn up at all. They had forecast snow showers for later that day – the first of the winter – and I thought maybe you wouldn't risk not being able to get home again. Back to Esme, and to Anna. I had to go, though. I had to know if you'd meant what you said in your letter: that you'd be there come hell or high water.

The car took ages to warm up and I sat in it blowing on my hands. Is it just me who doesn't wear gloves to drive in cold weather? I wonder about that every winter. Stupid, I know. I remember hearing something about not wearing gloves to drive, unless they're proper driving gloves, because they could slip on the steering wheel. Or something like that. It's funny the things that stay with you. Hear a snippet once and it's with you forever. A bit like you, Marty.

Can you guess what CD I listened to on the drive to Canterbury? Yep, Crowded House. Who else? I haven't listened to this album for such a long time. Always thought it would be too painful. It was. It is. But that day was different. It was about subsuming myself in you, in us. Wallowing, much as I am on the day after my fiftieth birthday. If I could advise my thirty-three-year-old self, would I tell her not to go? Not to torture herself? Probably. I'm damn sure she wouldn't have listened though. Then, or now.

I used the park and ride, knowing the city centre would be absolutely heaving with Christmas shoppers, and there would be zero chance of finding a parking space anywhere. Even at the Park and Ride, I was lucky to find a space, and the bus I boarded was full, the windows running with condensation. Squeezing myself next to a frazzled-looking woman, I smiled briefly at her, before retreating into my head once more. I didn't want to engage with anyone today. I just wanted to be in my private universe. I was glad to escape the stuffy confines of the bus, away from the inevitable coughs and sneezes on board. Coughs and sneezes spread diseases. Another of those things you hear once and never forget. Like you, Marty.

Pulling my bobble hat on and bunching my scarf up,

I headed towards the cathedral. The streets were already heaving with shoppers, some looking stressed out, others obviously relishing the festive season. There was a Christmas market in the High Street, the sweet and fragrant scents of mulled wine and hot chocolate mingling in the air. Everywhere was so crowded. I abandoned all thoughts of doing any shopping myself. It was nigh on impossible to get near any of the stalls and I began to feel claustrophobic, even though I was outside.

Ducking off the High Street and down a less-busy side street, I headed in the general direction of the cathedral, head down, not meeting anyone's eyes. And just hoping I wasn't on a collision course with you. I was very early, so I just hoped I had beaten you here. You were probably still on your way, still in the car. If you were coming at all. Were you listening to Crowded House too? I wonder how you were feeling? If part of you believed I would be there, waiting for you in the Chapel of the Holy Innocents. Or if I would walk in and find you sitting there. And you would take me in your arms... and... and what? You'd glue me back together?

The streets got quieter as I got further away from the main shops and the market; still bustling, but at least you could walk in a straight line, without dodging and bumping into people. It was too early to gain access to the cathedral, so I found a café close by, peering through the steamed-up windows trying to see if there was a table free. Chancing it, I went in and was relieved to find a two-seater table just back from the window. I couldn't see out so I figured you couldn't see in either. I ordered an Americano and allowed myself to relax, removing my hat, coat and scarf and letting my mind drift.

I don't know if it was a good cup of coffee. I just sat there, cupping it in both hands and staring at nothing. Why the hell was I there if I didn't want you anymore? I didn't know then and I don't know now. Was I looking for some sort of confirmation? Well, no better place than a cathedral for that, I think wryly. Maybe that was it, though. I just needed proof that you were genuine. That what we'd shared was as real as it had felt at the time. As real as I still believed it to be, somewhere deep down inside me, even if I didn't care, didn't dare, to acknowledge it.

I remember wishing I could see out of the café's window, so I could spot you when you arrived. *If* you arrived. I hadn't really thought through my plan for this particular hour of my life. It really was too cold to lurk outside, so I decided to finish up my coffee and head inside the cathedral to find a suitable place to wait, somewhere I could see visitors arrive but they couldn't see me.

Stepping through the doors into the magnificent cathedral filled me with awe, as it always did, and a feeling of peace. Something happens on the threshold and all the stresses and strains of modern life somehow can't gain entry, repelled by some invisible force-field. They're left like dripping umbrellas to be collected on the way out. Taking a deep breath in and slowly releasing it, I allowed myself to be lulled, closing my eyes for a couple of seconds before heading into the nave to begin my search for a suitable place to wait. I had to work on the assumption that you would head straight for the chapel. The Chapel of the Holy Innocents, where we had spent so much time together, alone and quietly breathing, content just to be in each other's presence. Cut off from the outside world, from our real lives. The irony is still not lost on me. We were not innocents.

I think it was about ten-thirty when I sat down. I'd found a seat almost completely hidden by a pillar, up towards the choir, from where I could see each new arrival at the main door, but they couldn't see me. My heart was pounding with anxiety and anticipation. I'm not sure what scared me the most: seeing you or not seeing you.

I see you. I'd just checked my watch and it was ten fifty-six and, when I looked back up, there you were. You came, Marty. You came. I held my breath at the sight of you; messy dark-blonde hair above that so familiar face. That face I'd held in my hands so many times, gazing in to the blue eyes that contained my whole world for a while. You're wearing a dark woollen coat and scarf over jeans. No hat. You never really did hats, did you, Marty? Nothing could contain that wild mop of yours.

You stopped for a second on the threshold, much as I had done, no doubt transported to another plane as I was, passing through some ancient time warp. I risk a breath, my heart pounding in my chest, and watch as you start to walk, willing you to turn to your left and head straight for the chapel. But you don't. You keep on coming towards the nave, towards me. Panic fills me and I lean further behind the pillar, silently praying you don't look over in my direction. I'm not sure how long I wait before I risk a peep around the pillar; it feels like an age, but is probably only seconds. I spot you, from the back this time. You're leaning over and lighting a candle, one of many now flickering in the dimly-lit space. Standing upright again, you pause, and I can almost hear your silent prayer.

I realise I've been holding my breath again, and that my

hands are clenched, nails digging into my palms. Every atom of my being is tensed, waiting, anticipating, ready for fight or flight if necessary. Only when I see you turn towards the chapel do I feel myself relax, the sense of panic subsiding a bit. I had thought you might somehow sense my presence. Stupid, I know, but the way you always spoke of your love for me being spiritual, ethereal, I wondered… Anyway, you didn't, but I can't help wondering what would have happened if you had found me. Maybe I wish you had…

I follow you with my eyes as far as possible, losing sight of you as you turn into the chapel. It's a tiny chamber, with only a couple of pews, and I imagine you sitting down on one of them. And waiting. Alone with just your thoughts and memories for company, wondering if I'll show up. I did show up, Marty. I just didn't have the courage to see you, to speak to you. I don't really know what I was afraid of. Loving you, or not loving you? It was never that simple, never that black or white.

I knew now that you were there, that you would stay for the full hour, hoping with every passing minute that I would show up. I wanted to get closer to you, to see your face, so I got up from my hiding place and walked up the opposite side of the nave, knowing I needed to approach the chapel from the same direction you had; that way I could see into the chapel from behind where you'd be sitting.

Stepping as quietly as I could, I slowed and stopped just before the chapel door, peeping though the window-space in the ancient walls. You were sitting exactly where I knew you would be: the same pew that we used to share. But now you're all alone, hunched over with your elbows resting on your thighs and your head buried in your hands. I can't hear any noise, but I know you are crying. Putting my hand to my mouth to suppress a sob, I turn and walk quickly towards the exit.

Chapter 25

Diamonds and Pearls

The jigsaw puzzle of us is still confusing; I'm still trying to piece it all together. I suppose it's a good reflection of the state of our minds back then. I take up another of your letters; it's undated, but refers to the Hotmail account, and to a gift you sent. I'm guessing it was October then, my birthday. October, 2000.

Lou,

I don't know what you have or haven't read. I don't know if you even read my last sprawling ghastly letter, let alone if you've ever looked at your Hotmail account I mentioned in it (to send things to, for you to read if you want, but avoid if you didn't). Perhaps you will one day. Many are quite dark, but they're getting better. The darkest I don't send.

I do understand what you're trying to do. I always understand you, given time. I just need to look inside. I still understand you better than you understand yourself half the time. Maybe I'd be doing the same in your shoes. Then again, maybe I wouldn't. What I do know is that I love you as much now as I have ever done, as much as I always will. As much as I always, always, always, will. I wish I could begin to tell you how much. Its unimaginable strength. Its relentless insistence. I can never hide from it for long. A simple fact, not words on a page. There are no words. No words at all. Understand that. Neither of us can touch the sky, but we both know where to find it. And it is as real as the ground on which we stand.

Wherever you are, whoever you are with, know you live forever in my thoughts and in my heart. You fill them both. I sent a small present. I won't send more. I hope you like it. If filled with my love, it would contain enough energy and light to power a thousand suns for a thousand years. Yet this is as a single grain of sand, the smallest speck taken from the Saharan dunes of my love for you, which rolls until the very sunset of my soul. A love filling any space between us, in miles or in years. It exists beyond all physical bounds, and surrounds you for eternity. Yet a desert it remains without you to share it, to provide the cool, pure crystal spring of life in which to bathe and be enveloped by a serene peace and beauty like no other. You make the desert bloom.

I have one heart. It is yours.

I have one soul. It is yours.

I have one true love. It is ours.

All my deepest love rests with you alone, and so it will for evermore.

Take such care, you most amazing, most beautiful of all minds and souls.

All my love. Forever.

Marty xxx (Sonnet 109)

So much for no more letters, just a card on my birthday and at Christmas. So much for leaving me be, letting the scab heal. Still you insisted on pouring your heart out on paper; still you insisted on telling me I was wrong. What if I was, Marty? Was that for you to decide? Wasn't that my choice, my decision?

I'm wondering about the gift you mention. There's only one thing it could have been, and it's sitting on my dressing table right now, this very minute. I wore it last night to my birthday dinner and haven't got round to putting it back in my jewellery box yet. I probably shouldn't have kept it. I honestly don't know why I did. It's a delicate pendant of emeralds and diamonds. It's the only valuable thing you ever gave me. In a monetary sense anyway. You should know, though, that it's no more precious to me than that small, plastic giraffe. I wear the necklace twice a year: on my birthday and on Christmas Day. Don't ask me if that was a conscious decision. It just sort of happened, and then it became a tradition. I wear it tucked into whatever outfit I have on though. I know if people saw it they would ask me where it came from, who gave it to me.

Libby saw it once. She was about sixteen, I think, and raiding my jewellery box for something 'vintage' as she put it. I remember laughing.

'Oi! Cheeky! I'm not that old!' I'd retorted, giving her a light shove. I remember. We were sitting side by side on my bed. My jewellery box was open in Libby's lap, and she was holding items up, one by one, and examining them.

'Sorry, Mum! You know what I mean though. Something a bit classier than all my tat from Claire's Accessories.'

'I do have your Great Granny's double strand of pearls, if they're any good,' I told her, the little faux pas already forgiven.

'Hmm, not really feeling pearls.'

'No, you're not really a twinset and pearls kind of a girl, are you? I never was, either.'

134

'Yep, I definitely take after you, that's for sure,' Libby said.

'You are so much more than me, Libby. You are most definitely the best bits of both me and your dad. Never forget how amazing you are. How special. And loved. You are so loved, Libby.' I'm getting maudlin and over-sentimental.

Libby pokes her tongue out and pretends to stick her fingers down her throat, rolling her eyes at me. I can't help laughing.

'Yep, you're no better at taking compliments than your mother.'

Libby returns to rummaging through the jewellery box, lifting out the top tray and placing it on the bed beside her. I catch my breath, realising one little box in the bottom compartment contains your necklace. Maybe she won't open it. If she does, maybe she won't ask. I hold my breath, as she removes and rejects one thing after another. Until, finally, there's just one small green box remaining.

My hand goes to my throat as she takes out the box and opens it to reveal the emeralds and diamonds glittering upon their white satin cushion.

'Wowsers, Mum! This is gorgeous. Why've I never seen it before? Don't you ever wear it? God, I'd wear it all the time,' Libby gushes.

'Oh, that old thing. It's nothing, just something I was given one birthday,' I try to downplay it with a dismissive flick of my hand.

'It's certainly not nothing, Mum. It must have cost a bomb! Did Dad give it to you?'

I wish she would just let it go, close the box and put it away. 'No, no, it was from someone I knew before Dad. Anyway, I've got another old jewellery box around here somewhere – let me

135

see if I can find it. Might have more luck with it.' I start to get off the bed, eager to distract Libby and change the subject.

But she won't let go. 'Well, whoever it was must have thought a lot of you, to get you something so valuable. What was his name? It wasn't your first husband, was it? Steve? You never really talk about him.'

I'm happy for her to think it was Steve. 'Well, it's ancient history, another lifetime. No point going back over old ground. We got married too young, that's all.' How can I tell her about you? How can I tell her I was having an affair with a married man? How can I tell her the truth? I couldn't bear Libby to think badly of me.

'I guess so,' she says, shrugging and accepting my response.

I close my eyes for a moment, letting my breathing return to normal.

And that was that. Libby closed the box, declaring the pendant 'too precious' to borrow and putting it back in its hiding place in the bottom of the drawer.

She was right, of course, it was precious. In spite of everything that had happened between you and I, Marty, much of our time together had been precious. But, while the necklace is real and exists in my world, our love feels like something other-worldly, something that existed in a fantasy bubble on a far-off plane. Something ethereal that couldn't cross over into the real world. And it appeared you were never going to let me forget it.

Chapter 26

Photographs

I pick out another of your letters, again undated, and without even a 'Dear Lou' at the start. I think maybe you really did start out writing these letters to yourself, didn't you, Marty? I wonder if there were others that you didn't then send to me? Others that were maybe sent as emails to the account I never looked at, afraid of the pain and the darkness I would find there.

Why do I write this? Will I ever send it to you? I doubt it. I think this is more for me to try to understand myself than you. If I ever do send it, then maybe it'll give you an insight into my mind. Trying to get an insight into yours by self-discussion. Not a lecture, please don't take it as such. Just a sprawl of mind and heart in bewildered freefall, trying to make sense of the incomprehensible and impossible. The gibberings of a lunatic under the influence of the approaching full moon. The ravings of a madman, yes, but a madman so in love. A love as true and deep as ever existed in this world. It is wonderful. And it is yours.

Thank you for Saturday. I cannot begin to express my feelings for you, and how they swelled as Esme got to know you in those short hours. Your beauty continues to radiate unbounded from the centre of everything you are, and bursts through the surface to bathe me in such incomparable light after what seems like an eternity of darkness. The sun shone in my heart again after an Antarctic winter of desolation. For this and so much more besides, I thank you.

The photos have come through now. They are indescribably beautiful. They are my life encapsulated. As I gaze upon them reliving the memory, the mountainous waves of emotion surge over me once more and dissolve my face into tortured expression and the same endless tears washed across me through Saturday night. Unknowable combinations of light and dark, joy and pain, beauty and tragic waste. The two women in my life whom I adore – each day I lie to one and ache for the other. I have neither, and neither has me. I have only one escape, but cannot take it because… why? I cannot understand, why? Why do you not take this happiness we have both already touched?

I know you must be emotionally exhausted and so confused after the past eighteen months, but can you really not feel the forces raging across the ether between us still? Seething and boiling under the mask you present to the world, and even to me? Tapping at your heart with the truth you seek so hard to deny and escape from? Perhaps you really don't. But if that is so, then there really is no such thing as true love, and all I hold dear about what happened between us is about as meaningful as an episode of 'Emmerdale'. I do believe I touched eternity with you, Lou. Saw things, touched things, became things, which changed me forever, opened up my soul to awareness of truth and beauty beyond any attempt at description. And shared them. With you. Only with you.

How can I be so sure? How can I know what you appear not to? All I can do is tell you of a night in Cornwall. I'm sure I've told *you before, but it bears repetition. A night in Cornwall when all my dreams came true.*

A night when you were beside me, the woman whom I adored to the very core of her mesmeric soul with every ounce of my own. When you were with me, made love with me, slept silently beside me, skin next to mine, breathing. Breathing. In that room, in the half-light before dawn as I watched you sleep beside me, in awe of your beauty bathing the night. As you smiled gently in serene peace to match my own. Everything that mattered was with me in that room. My entire life was in that room, and nothing else. You were then and are now, everything. And I know it just as surely this very moment as I weep. Weep recalling the same certainty I felt weeping at your beauty then, salt trickles across my cheek in the still of that February night.

Silent tears of utter joy at the certainty we had become one, and somehow forever. In ways which cannot be undone however we may attempt to do so. My soul had grown beyond itself, and fused with yours. That is what I knew then. It is what I have known ever since that night. It is what I know now. Whatever cliché you may use to cloud your mind and heart, whatever water has passed under the bridge or boats have been burned in the drive to move on and turn over a new leaf. Whoever else you may have lent your heart, it does not matter. I simply know that if I search my soul I find you living there. How can I do that if you don't find mine within yours? That, in essence, is what I don't understand. And will never be able to understand for as long as I live.

I can understand you deciding not to be with me for the sake of holding a family together, however misplaced. I can understand you doing what you can to get on with your life without me as a result, and accept your choice. What I can never understand is your denial of a love so true as ours. You may choose to live apart from it, but please don't deny it. For that is to deny everything which means anything to me. It means there is no love, there is no God, no eternity, no soul. It means there is no me.

There are a thousand reasons to be apart, but I can offer a thousand counters to any reasoned argument you may present. There is only one reason to be together. That is love. There is no answer against love. It is a thing of the heart, the soul. The mind has no dominion over it, for all its futile attempts. Logic and reason don't count here. I still have faith in love. I still have faith in you.

Love is everything. If I have learned anything throughout this, it is that simple fact. Love is everything. And you have all mine. I would be lying if I told you otherwise. You have all of mine, Lou. All. Forever.

What was it I wrote in my Valentine's card?

Forever is not simply a measure of time.

It is timelessness. It is a place, a truth. It is home. It is peace. It is beauty.

It is you.

I remember. I remember that day, Marty. God only knows why I agreed to meet you, and your young daughter. Temporary insanity? That's all I can put it down to. Or some deeply-held masochistic desire to see this little person who'd stolen you away from me, through no fault of her own. To see you as the loving father I always knew you would be.

I rummage through the shoebox for the photographs I know will be in there somewhere, having become separated from the letter. And there I am, holding your daughter, holding Esme. And we're smiling. Both of us. And I know you were too,

Marty, smiling as you took the photographs. It must have been a bittersweet moment for you. I know it was for me. I look so young. And Esme is just perfect. She took to me straight away, didn't she? That must have hurt too.

I'm trying to cast my mind back to that time in my life, to understand why I agreed to the meeting. It's hard to piece it all together now – like you said, a lot of water under a lot of burned bridges. But I always let you back in, didn't I? I could never resist your pull for long. I only let you back in so far this time, though. Did you ever really understand it was an act of self-preservation, of survival? It didn't matter how much you declared your undying love for me, I couldn't let myself take the risk. I couldn't believe that, if I asked you to come to me, you'd actually be able to leave this time. Leave not only Anna, but Esme too. Besides, how could I have lived with myself knowing I'd broken up a family? That was something else you never really understood. You wanted me to be the reason you left them. Why couldn't you see I wasn't able to bear that burden, shoulder that blame? You should have left for you, Marty. If that's what you wanted. You needed to accept the responsibility, not put it all on me. And then, when you were free, maybe, we could have been together. It's all such pointless speculation now, though, isn't it?

You wrote of Cornwall again in this letter. Do you think I could've forgotten all that we shared that weekend? Or all that it meant? I never could. I never will. You weren't alone in your feelings then, Marty. But there was still hope in my heart back then. I still had faith in our love, and in you. After you told me about Anna's pregnancy, I lost that faith. I simply couldn't sustain it after that bombshell. I could no longer make a leap of faith and believe you would be there to catch me. Was I wrong? I don't know. I know you think I was, but I couldn't help it. I couldn't risk it…

Chapter 27

You've Got to Hide Your Love Away

Dearest Lou,

I found out yesterday (18th December) that you'd moved – by chance from the chap you used to live next to, as I was about to post your Christmas prezzie through the door. After you hid from me. He said I should speak to the landlord to get your forwarding address, but no joy. He didn't have it. Either that or you got a friend from work to call me back and fib about not knowing where you'd gone to put me off, and it wasn't the landlord at all. Still, I had to try.

You know I'd never use your new address. Never turn up uninvited, or lurk. I said I'd only post to your mum's after you moved, and so I will. But it hurts so much that you don't trust me, or are afraid of me. It just helps me to know that you're OK, and I can place you. A way to contact you in an out-and-out emergency that doesn't rely on those dreaded mobiles, blasted SMS' or potentially weeks of delay at your mum's. Something I'll never use if you don't want me too, but would comfort me so much to know is there.

Be happy in your new home. Be happy always. Please, let me know you're OK from time to time. May you feel my deepest love surround you, wherever you are. I hope that one Christmas, or any time, you'll catch up with me face to face. To warm me with your incomparable smile again. Is that so very much to ask?

Just a small present and (very small) card to your old address for Christmas. And a card to your mum's. Hope you get them eventually, and like them. I hope you get this. I wish I could have given them to you in person, just seen you again for even a few minutes. It's so dark this time of year, and I miss that amazing light that shines from you alone. I miss it so very much. It's been so long.

So many things I wanted to give you this Christmas. So many things throughout all your life. So much to share, yet can be shared with no other soul on this earth. I love you so much, Lou. Beyond anything I could ever describe, yet every bit as much as I know you can still remember. In all this world, through all time, know that to be constant. Take such care, sweet goddess.

In the meantime I'll go back and stick my head in a bucket of soggy cold rice pudding to try and cure my insanity. Chances, slim.

All my love. Forever.

Marty xxx

I can't help but smile at the final paragraph. A tiny glimpse of the old you, Marty. A little flicker of the crazy boy I used to know. Rice pudding and insanity. As for the rest of the letter? You're right, I was hiding from you, Marty. I had to. You'll never know how much I've regretted that over the years, how much I wish I'd made different decisions. For us all.

Chapter 28

Laura

Dearest, dearest Lou,

Thank you. Simply, thank you. For your smile. For your laughter. For the wrinkling of your exquisite nose as your giggles dance across your beautiful, beautiful face and upon my ears. Upon my heart. For your eyes, your incomparable infinite eyes, flooding my soul with the unique and intense blaze of light, colour and warmth. And love. Still, love.

Thank you for your touch, that touch like no other upon this earth, that touch that passes through my skin to caress the innermost depths of my eternal soul. Thank you for holding me. Within your arms, breathing, breathing. Gentle, soft, warm, close. And your hair cascaded around your smiling face, its delicate scent filling my lungs as I close my eyes and remember. Remember it all. Feel it all. Peace, beauty and truth like no other. Such infinite peace. For this, all this and so much more, for sharing eternity again if only for a few short minutes, I thank you.

I love you, Lou. I can do nothing but love you, love you with a raging irresistible power of such intensity as I cannot begin to express, yet know I need not try. Feel it with you. Don't think. Feel. Clear your mind and feel. Don't you miss the depth? The beauty and power, the totality of a love filling each dimension to infinite extent? I don't doubt you feel love for Jon. I don't doubt part of you still feels love for Steve. But I also know that no man can ever begin to love you as I do, as I always shall. As you cannot begin to love anyone as you loved me. As you still love me, somewhere. Deep. Hidden. Yet pressing for release against that fortress around your heart.

Perhaps Jon was a bridge to carry you across the chasm between Steve and your true future. But the bridge itself has only a short span. An exciting journey, but not a destination. Perhaps your holiday with him will show you that, if you don't already know. Know that time to be better shared with me. Moments. Scenes. Time.

I'd met up with you again, obviously. What the hell was I doing? I was obviously still seeing Jon at the time. I do see the pattern though. Every time my life was going wrong, I reached for you. You were still the one person I wanted when things got bad in my life. You mentioned me going on holiday. I only ever went on one holiday with Jon, and to be honest the relationship was on the rocks before we touched down on the island of Mallorca. I really thought he was the one, but I know we split up soon after we got home. It pisses me off to think that I might never manage to hold down a relationship with a man, Marty, do you know that? For all the hurt you caused me, I still couldn't find a man who made me feel like you did; I still couldn't find the other half of me. Is that really because you were my soulmate? Is there really only one? That doesn't seem fair.

The ringing of the landline breaks through my reverie. Talk about saved by the bell, eh, Marty? I debate briefly whether or not to answer it; I'm really feeling quite anti-people today. I can't ignore the insistent ringing, however, and putting the letters to one side, I heave myself off the sofa, making those ridiculous groaning noises as I do, and wondering idly why it is I can no longer sit down or get up without making them. Another little foible of my advancing years. Joy. As I plod to the hall to answer the phone, I make a little promise to myself to consciously try not to do so any more. Fifty is really NOT that old.

Picking up the handset, I say a silent prayer that it's not my mother. Or my sister.

'Hello,' I answer, crossing my fingers.

'Oh, you are there.' It's Laura. 'I was about to give up.'

Damn, I think. 'Sorry,' I say. 'Took me a minute to heave my ancient self off the sofa.'

'What? Oh, never mind. I was just ringing to say I hope you enjoyed your birthday meal last night. I hope Dad didn't ruin it for you, like he does most things.'

So like Laura. Say something nice… and then ruin it.

'It was lovely, thank you. And thank you for organising it – I really appreciated it, and it was lovely to all be together, even Dad. Libby's pretty good at managing him these days.'

'Well, yes, of course… typical of Charlie not to show his face though. Not that I believed for a minute he would show up.' Laura, keen to keep off the positives.

'I know, he's not the most reliable of brothers, is he? He does have his problems though.' I still want to believe the best of Charlie, to make excuses for him, even though he lets me down time after time. My choice of words is, however, like a red rag to a bull.

'Problems?! Any problems he has, he brought on himself,' Laura huffs.

I'm really not up for a debate on the whys and wherefores of our younger half-brother right now. Easier to let it go, I think with a sigh.

'Well, it was a lovely evening anyway. Always lovely to see you, Nigel and Richard. Richard's really shot up again, hasn't he?' I say, trying to steer the conversation away from Dad and Charlie. It works.

'Yes, he's going to be at least six feet, I think. Such a good boy.' For all her faults, Laura cannot be accused of not being a proud mother.

'And handsome, too. Like his dad.'

'Well, I think he's already much better looking than Nigel. And sparkier too, if you ask me.'

I didn't, I think, feeling a pang of sympathy for Laura's henpecked husband. 'Well, I think you did awfully well picking Nigel, he's definitely one of the good ones. Gives the rest of us hope,' I say, trying to keep things light-hearted.

Laura harrumphs, unable to conceal her dissatisfaction with her spouse. 'He's about as exciting as a wet weekend in Clacton these days,' she says nastily.

'Have you ever had a wet weekend in Clacton?' I ask. 'You shouldn't knock it 'til you've tried it. Might be loads of fun.'

'Don't talk nonsense. It would just be wet. And miserable. Limp. It would be limp. Like Nigel.'

There's no point arguing with Laura when she's in this sort of mood. I'm still trying to think of a suitably un-inflammatory reply, when she carries on.

'Honestly, Lou, I'm seriously thinking about leaving him.

Or having an affair. Or both.'

'Blimey, Laura, steady on! I'm probably the last person who should be dishing out relationship advice, but don't do something you might live to regret.' Or worse still, not live to regret, I think to myself. 'Look at what happened to me all those years ago.' I'm not sure if I want to say your name, aloud, to my sister. Taking a deep breath, I commit. 'With Marty. Look how that ended. He broke my heart.'

'Marty! There's a blast from the past! Whatever happened to Marty? Did he stay with his wife after getting her pregnant? I suppose he did. I haven't thought about that day in my garden for years.' Laura's voice softens. 'He really did love you, Lou. You could see it in his eyes. He adored you.' She sounds wistful.

'For all the good it did me,' I retort, not ready for anyone else to get sentimental about what might have been.

'No, really. He was obviously head over heels in love with you. If only that cow of a wife of his hadn't deceived him and stopped taking the pill.'

'You can't possibly blame Anna?' I can't believe what I'm hearing.

'Why not? She trapped him,' Laura says matter-of-factly.

'She hardly trapped him – they were married.'

'All the more reason she should've been honest. Deciding to have a child should be a joint decision. She lied.'

'So did he, Laura, so did he,' I sigh. 'She knew about us. Anna. Anna knew. That's why she did it. To try and hang onto him.' I don't know why I'm telling Laura this.

'Holy crap.' Laura rarely swears.

'Indeed. Apparently he used to call out my name in his sleep.' What am I doing? Why am I still talking about this to her?

'Double holy crap.'

'Yep. She must really have loved him.'

'Well, I think she should have had more self-respect. I'm damn sure I wouldn't want to stay with a man who called out another woman's name in his sleep. I bet he thought about you when they were having sex!'

'Jesus, Laura! Don't!'

'What? He probably did. Imagine that – him thinking about you while impregnating his wife,' she cackles. She's enjoying this far too much. I need to nip it in the bud.

'Well, anyway, it's ancient history, isn't it?' I say, relieved that at least she doesn't know about all the times you and I re-kindled our affair over the years.   'I suppose so. Shame, really, you made a good couple. Looked right together somehow.'

'Well, whatever we were, let it be a dire warning to you, Laura – affairs never end well. And Nigel really is a good man. Don't hurt him.'

'I know, I know. Take no notice. I'm just one big perimen-opausal mess at the moment. Fine one minute, then the next I could quite happily take an axe to someone.'

'Good lord! Maybe it would be safer to have an affair then?' I joke. 'I feel your pain though, sis. I'm not exactly symptom-free either.'

'It's a bloody nightmare!'

'Yep, literally in my case. Non-bloody-stop!' It feels strangely comforting to have something in common with my sister. Even if it is just hormones. 'I'd like to start dating again, but the prospect of sharing my bodily goings-on with a new man is just hideous,' I sigh.

'Ooh, yes, hadn't thought of that. What man is going to

want to have an affair with a woman my age? Maybe I'd better stick with Nigel. Good old reliable, solid, Nigel.'

'Thanks! I'm not much younger than you! Are you saying I'm past it?' I'm only half joking. Laura's simply voicing things I've thought myself.

'Don't be daft!' Laura says. 'Plenty of life in the old dog yet.' She laughs.

I'm going off her again. 'Woof.' I reply.

Laura's still laughing. It's actually really good to hear her laugh. She doesn't do it enough. We've rather lost our way as sisters over the years. Maybe that's my fault? I don't know. It would be nice to get back to being friends again. Maybe, just maybe, I could trust her again.

'We should go shopping sometime, maybe get some lunch. Like we used to,' I suggest, keen to offer an olive branch while things are cordial.

'I'd like that,' Laura answers, with no hesitation. 'Right, I must go and hunt for something for dinner. You are lucky, Lou, only having yourself to think about. Speak soon.'

'Yes, speak to you soon. Take care. Bye.'

I don't feel lucky to be on my own, I think sadly as I hang up the receiver. I just feel lonely. And I miss you, Marty. I still miss you.

Chapter 29

Lonely Boy

Oh hell. There's nothing quite like other people's problems to take your mind off your own, is there? I'm already carrying the burden of the knowledge of Laura's dissatisfaction with her marriage. I've told her I'm the last person to offer marriage guidance, having cocked it up twice, but she persists in confiding in me and asking for my counsel. I suppose I'm qualified to tell her what *not* to do. And I've told her *not* to cheat on Nigel. But, isn't that rather hypocritical of me? I wonder. And would I have listened to anyone telling me not to have an affair with you, Marty? Probably not. The heart wants what it wants, after all. We all have to make our own mistakes, don't we? No good trying to learn from others'.

Do I really think Laura would have an affair? As much as she moans about Nigel, I think deep down she does love him. Maybe, like all women of a certain age, myself included, she's just feeling a sense of life passing by too quickly, of time running out, of being 'past it' and no longer being desirable as a woman. God knows, as a single woman, I'm terrified of growing old with no one beside me. Anyway, Laura's problems aside, I wasn't prepared for what happened next.

It was a few days after my birthday and I'd not long been

home from work, battered by another day spent dealing with complaints about the hospital – the tea was too hot, the ward was too cold, the doctor was too foreign, the nurses too brusque – when the landline rang. Groaning inwardly, I picked up the receiver.

'Hello,' I said, trying to sound brighter and breezier than I felt.

'Hi, Lou, hi. It's... er... it's Nigel.'

I can't remember a time when Nigel has ever rung me. Except perhaps when Richard was born. 'Oh, hello, Nigel. Is everything okay? It's not Laura, is it?' My first assumption is that something must be wrong with Laura for Nigel to phone me himself.

'Oh, no, no, Laura's fine. Sorry, didn't mean to scare you.'

'That's okay. It's nice to hear from you. Whatever the reason,' I add, with a laugh.

'Okay, good, I... um... I was wondering, if I... could I... possibly pop round? Come and see you, that is, when it's convenient?' Nigel says. Eventually.

'Yes, of course, any time really. After work,' I tell him, hoping he can't hear the curiosity in my voice.

'How about tonight?' Nigel asks, his composure regained.

'Um... yes, why not,' I say, cursing myself for being so bloody accommodating when all I really want to do is have a long hot soak in the bath with a long cold drink of gin.

'Thanks, Lou, what time suits you?'

A quarter past never o'clock. 'About half seven?' I say. 'If that works for you?'

'Yes, yes, that's perfect. I'll see you then. Thanks, Lou. Bye. Bye.'

'Bye, Nigel. See you later.' I hang up the phone, wondering what on earth he can want to talk to me about.

I'm still wondering as I make myself a quick bite to eat and get changed out of my work clothes. I've come to the conclusion it must be something to do with their wedding anniversary, which isn't that far off. Maybe he's planning a trip or a special present and wants some advice.

The doorbell rings at exactly seven thirty, and I smile to myself at Nigel's punctuality. Not a minute before, so as not to inconvenience, not a minute after, so as not to disrespect. *You really are the most solidly reliable man I've ever met, Nigel*, I think as I pad through to the front door.

'Hello, come on in. Can I take your coat? Don't worry about your shoes.'

Nigel steps in to the light, and I'm struck by how dishevelled he looks. By Nigel-standards, anyway. His hair, which is usually so well-groomed, is looking decidedly ruffled, along with the rest of him, frankly. Yes, ruffled is the best word to describe my normally composed brother-in-law.

'Thanks, Lou,' he says, handing me his coat, which I hang on a hook under the stairs, and giving his shoes a rub on the doormat.

'Can I get you a drink? Cup of tea? Or maybe a whisky?' I ask. To be honest, he looks like he could do with one.

'Er... actually, a whisky would be great. Thanks, Lou. No ice.'

'Go through to the lounge, I won't be a sec.'

I grab the whisky and two glasses from the dining room and take them into the lounge, where Nigel has taken a seat in one of the armchairs, and is perched nervously on the edge of the cushion. His right leg is jiggling up and down and he's chewing on his thumbnail in a very un-Nigel-like manner. Perhaps he needs this whisky more than I realised, I think, furrowing my brow as concern kicks in. I pour out a stiff finger for each of us. I don't really like whisky, but I know Nigel won't like drinking alone, and I plan to just nurse my glass.

'Cheers!' I say, passing a glass to Nigel and clinking it with my own.

'Yes, cheers, Lou. And… er… thanks for seeing me.' I've never seen Nigel so discomposed. It's unnerving.

'Of course. Any time. What's on your mind?'

'Well, I… um… I don't really know where to begin,' Nigel says, looking noticeably uncomfortable.

I wait, giving him a chance to find his words, but I can't bear his discomfort and jump into the silence.

'Is it about Laura?' I prompt.

'Well, yes, sort of, I suppose. It's more about me, really. This isn't easy for me.'

'No rush. Take your time.' I don't want to push him.

Nigel slugs back the amber liquid in his glass, wincing slightly as the whisky burns its way down his throat.

'I'm having an affair,' the words shoot out of his mouth and hit my ears like bullets. I wasn't expecting that. I immediately try and shake the shock from my face, but I'm sure Nigel saw it.

'Shit,' I say, deciding honestly is the best policy. 'Wasn't expecting that.'

'Oh God, Lou, you must hate me. You can't hate me anymore than I hate myself.' Nigel looks defeated.

'Jeez, Nigel, I don't hate you. I could never hate you. You're pretty much the most decent man I've ever met.' I want to reassure him, comfort him, even though he's just told me he's cheating on my sister.

'But… after what I just told you…?' Nigel looks confused. He'd obviously expected me to berate him. But pot, kettle, and all that.

I shrug. 'All you've told me is that you're human. Like the rest of us. We're none of us perfect, especially in my family. I have no right to judge you, Nigel.'

Nigel visibly relaxes, sitting back into the chair, leaning his head back and exhaling the longest of breaths. 'It's such a relief to tell someone. You can't imagine the stress I've been under.'

Oh, trust me, I can, I think to myself. I get up and walk over to refill his glass. 'You can get a cab home. I think you need this.'

'Thanks, Lou. I don't know how it started, not really. Or why I let it. I was just so… I don't know… so bloody lonely, I think. Laura's been so cold towards me, for such a long time…' Nigel looks at me, nervous about speaking ill of my sister.

'It's okay, I'm sure there's nothing you can say about that sister of mine I haven't thought myself,' I reassure him with a wry smile.

'No, she's not an easy woman to live with. You know me, Lou, I've always tried to be a good husband and father, a good provider… All I ever wanted in return was to feel loved and appreciated. And wanted.' Nigel looks a little embarrassed.

'I get it,' I say, urging him to continue.

'She emasculates me. Nothing I ever do is good enough. All I wanted was some small sign that she still loved me, still wanted me. But all she ever did was knock me down. Sorry, I'm not blaming Laura, it's not her fault…'

Well, it kind of is, I think. 'No, no, I know. I understand. We all need affection. You're only human, and you can only take so much, before something has to give.'

'I just needed to feel wanted again. I needed to feel like a man again,' Nigel says sadly.

'I get it, really I do. Do you love this woman?'

Nigel hesitates. I suspect it's not because he doesn't know the answer, but because he's afraid to admit it out loud to his sister-in-law. He takes a deep breath before looking me straight in the eyes. 'Yes, I do. I love her.' He breaks down then, tears streaming down his face, partly from relief, I think, at having shared the burden.

I get up and retrieve the box of tissues from the side table, pulling a few out and passing them to him. Nigel wipes his face and blows his nose, calmer again now he's confessed all. Well, nearly all. I suspect there's more to come.

'God, it's such a relief to have told someone. I'm sorry it had to be you. There simply isn't anyone else I could tell.'

'You don't need to apologise. I'm glad you felt able to tell me. I'm glad I could be here for you. You must've been under a huge strain. Can I ask how long it's been going on? You can tell me to mind my own business.'

Nigel looks sheepish. 'Almost six years. Six years this Christmas, actually.'

'Shit,' I exclaim, unable to hide my shock.

'Shit, indeed.'

'Is it anyone I know?' I ask, pulling a face that says I hope it isn't.

'Yes. It's Karen.'

'Karen? Your secretary Karen?'

157

'Yes. I know. It's a cliché.'

I shrug. 'Clichés exist for a reason. You work closely with someone, day in, day out, build a relationship of trust and mutual liking – it's kind of natural, really. You didn't go looking for an affair. And these things happen. There's another cliché for you! She's worked for you for donkeys' years, hasn't she?'

'Yes, twenty-three years. When it happened, she said she's been in love with me for most of them.'

I bring a picture of Karen to mind. Imagine a spinster librarian from the sixties and you're not far off. Neat and tidy are words that spring to mind, with her trim figure and hair always fixed back in a French pleat. I always thought how lucky Nigel was to have her as his secretary; she was so obviously devoted to him, and did so much more for him than her secretarial duties dictated. Much more, clearly, as I now realise.

'I did wonder why she never married. Makes sense now if she's been in love with you all this time.'

'She's a wonderful woman, Lou. And she's never pressured me to leave Laura or tried to cause trouble for me. She's only ever shown me love and kindness. But lately, with the atmosphere turning even frostier at home, I've started to think I'd rather spend the rest of my life somewhere else.'

'With *someone* else,' I add.

'Yes. With Karen. She deserves so much better, so much more, than I've given her.'

We sit in silence for a while. I know what I want to say to Nigel, but I'm conflicted by feelings of loyalty to my sister, however difficult she may be. After a while, Nigel breaks the silence.

'What do I do, Lou? Tell me what I should do.'

'Oof! No pressure there!' I'm also remembering my recent conversation with Laura about how unhappy she is in her marriage. But still, it's not really my place to tell Nigel what to do, is it? I suppose all I can do is offer an opinion, without making any recommendations. Right, Lou, be Switzerland. And pray there isn't an avalanche of backlash coming your way any day soon.

'Okay...' I begin. 'This is what I think. And please bear in mind it's only my opinion. Ultimately, it's up to you and Laura – well, and Karen, I suppose – to come to a decision.'

Nigel nods. 'Yes, of course. Understood.'

'Okay, well, before you do anything, you need to wait until Richard finishes his 'A' Levels. It just wouldn't be fair to turn his world upside down now. You've waited this long, so another few months won't make any difference. I think you need to stop seeing Karen, apart from at work obviously, until then. You can't run the risk of being found out before you're ready. I'm sure she'll understand. Be honest with her though, Nigel, always be honest. If she is the one, then she deserves that. And if she is the one, she'll wait a bit longer for you. As long as she knows the hope is real.'

He nods again. 'I know she'll understand.'

'Good. But equally, if you're not serious about a future with Karen, you must tell her. Don't keep her hopes up if it's never going to be anything more than an affair. That would be cruel.'

'I do want to be with her. It's all I want.'

'After Richard finishes school, then I'm afraid you're going to have to face the wrath of Laura. I don't envy you that, I really don't. You know she's going to lash out big time – you'll just have to weather Storm Laura and know that the storm will pass and she'll calm down. Do you tell her about the affair? I honestly don't know if you should or not. I think maybe the sting of that would be worse than believing you've just fallen out of love with her. She will hate feeling like you've made a fool of her. Does that sound deceitful? It's a hell of a white lie, I know. But if it protects Laura, maybe it's the way to go. You'd have to wait a little while before going public with Karen, of course.' I stop talking for a while. It's kind of bizarre to be discussing the potential end of my sister's marriage so matter-of-factly with her husband.

'I don't want her to hate me.' Nigel looks distressed by the thought.

'Well, I'm afraid she's going to. For a while, at least. But I think you might be surprised when the initial shock wears off. She deserves to find someone who wants to be with her the way you do with Karen.' Jeez, I sound so calm. And kind of wise. So much easier to give advice than to take it.

I can't help thinking again about my recent conversation with Laura and her thoughts on Anna lying about coming off the pill. She'd said she wouldn't want a man who didn't want her. I'm really hoping she meant it, and that after the initial shock of Nigel leaving, she'll be relieved.

'Thank you, Lou, really, thank you. Everything you've said makes so much sense. I'm not going to lie – the prospect of telling Laura scares me to death, but the alternative is unthinkable. I simply can't imagine my life without Karen. I don't want to. Do you think Richard will be all right?' The worried look returns.

'Yes, I do. He's got a good head on his shoulders – like his father. Most of the time!' I can't help laughing. 'Just make sure you and Laura are on the same page when you talk to him. I know amicable might be a bit too much to ask at the beginning, but hopefully, for Richard's sake, you can present a united front. He just needs to know you both love him and none of it's his fault.'

'Yes, yes, of course. I'm sure we can manage that,' Nigel says, nodding vehemently.

'For all her faults, no-one could ever accuse Laura of not wanting what's best for her son.' I smile at Nigel. 'It'll be okay. I'm sure of it. Another whisky?'

'Why not? One more for the road. I have a feeling it's going to be a long and difficult one.'

'Maybe. Focus on the destination.'

We share another whisky – at least Nigel does, I'm still nursing my first – neither of us feeling the need to break the comfortable silence that has settled between us. Eventually, Nigel looks at his watch.

'I'd better be on my way. Do you know the number for a taxi firm?'

'No need. I can drop you back. I haven't actually drunk that much.'

'Oh, if you're sure. Thanks, Lou. For everything. Especially for not judging me. It means a lot.'

'You're welcome. Any time. But remember, that was all just my opinion. You have to do what you think is right. And I'll be here for Laura, and Richard, whatever happens.'

Chapter 30

Written in the Stars

I drop Nigel at the end of his road, just in case. Neither of us wants to risk Laura seeing my car and having to explain why we were together. I have form, after all, and my sister's not the most trusting of women, with an inclination to think the worst of people. Although, of course, in this case she'd be right. Just not about the woman.

Nigel is planning to say he had drinks with a client and got a taxi home. He's going to collect his car from my house sometime in the morning. I'll be at work, so there's no reason for Laura to be anywhere near my house while Nigel's car's parked there.

Driving back home, my mind is still buzzing with Nigel's confession. I'm pleased he felt able to confide in me; I still think he's a decent man, and the secret was tearing him up. I know how that can feel. But, on the flip side, Laura's my sister and I feel horribly disloyal right now. I know she's not an easy woman, and that she no doubt has made Nigel feel less of a man over the years, but... blood, thicker than water and all that. Another cliché based in fact. I'm trying to imagine how I would feel in Laura's shoes. It's an uncomfortable dilemma. Would I want to know the truth, and sooner rather than later? If she ever found out what passed between me and Nigel tonight, it would destroy my relationship with her. As it is, I'm faced with lying to her. For the rest of our lives.

I pull up outside my house again, the space I'd vacated in front of Nigel's car still free thankfully. It's a relief to close my front door on the world once more. I need a drink now. Just not whisky, I think, heading into the dining room and grabbing the bottle of Bloom's. Pouring myself a generous measure over ice, and adding Fever-Tree and a wedge of lime, I head for my favourite armchair, sinking into the cushions and curling my legs under me. I take a big glug of the gin and tonic and sit like that. For about thirty seconds. Then I realise I'm too bloody old and inflexible to sit comfortably like that anymore. With a sigh, I manoeuvre my legs out from under me, pulling a footstool over to rest them on instead. My mind can't keep up with the aging of my body. Shame there's not a tartan rug handy, I think grumpily.

I'm feeling my age, Marty. I'm starting to feel old. I hate it. It terrifies me. Fifty years old, and still alone. We were meant to grow old together, Marty. Weren't we? Wasn't that what was written in our stars? How did we screw it up so spectacularly? Hearing Nigel speak about his affair with Karen brings it all back; how his face lit up when he talked about her, and how certain he was of his feelings. Will he be able to do what you couldn't? Will he be able to leave his wife and child to be with the woman he loves? I really hope so. Does that make me a bad person? Maybe. All I've ever wanted is for people to be happy, though. And Laura and Nigel are both unhappy, so why stay together? Nigel has a chance of real happiness, and surely Laura deserves the same opportunity?

The Nigel and Karen thing has put you firmly back at the front of my mind, and I remember the letter I was halfway through reading the other night when Laura phoned. Retrieving it from the top of the shoe box, I find where I left off:

I still believe and will always believe, that to truly move on we have to do so together. That any future spent apart is the wrong one for us both. I know this with such clarity and certainty. The future awaits us. Not going back. Moving forward. Living the lives we both deserve. The future is beautiful, is ours. But only together. I know this so surely. One day, and soon, may you. If you truly want to live life for yourself, just raise the portcullis against which your bursting heart is pressed. Let your love flow again. Set your soul free again. You fought so hard, and for so long – and I do understand why. But you don't need to fight any more. Your best and happiest future lives with me, and it always will. And if these are the paths we had to follow to understand this, then it is not time wasted. The only betrayal of love is its denial, and its denial will betray you.

You sounded so sure, so certain, Marty. How could I doubt such passionate declarations? Why did I continue to resist the pull of you, insisting that I no longer loved you? Were you right? Was I in complete denial about my feelings for you? I know the shutters had come down that awful day you told me Anna was pregnant; some act of self-preservation that was the only way I could survive at the time. I also know I lifted the shutters enough to let you in part of the way, because we'd been together on and off since. But I could never let that guard down completely, could I? I think I was so scared you'd let me down again, and I couldn't risk it, however much I wanted to be with you. I wouldn't have survived another rejection. I did what I had to do to protect myself. Was it really what I wanted? Be honest with yourself, Lou.

I'm not sure honesty is always the best policy. I had perfected the art of resisting you, even if I was lying to us both. With that old bitch hindsight by my side, though, I know that deep down, suffocated by the protective armour I'd put on, the truth was all I wanted was to be with you. I wanted to run to you, Marty. I wanted to run to you, throw myself into your arms and stay there forever. I wanted to tell you I loved you, only you, it was only ever you. Infinitely. Eternally. You. But I didn't. I couldn't. And I hate myself for it. I hate myself for not taking that leap of faith.

All these years later, the memories still have the power to make me cry, and tears stream down my face now. I wipe them away with my fingers before they can reach my mouth and I taste their saltiness on my tongue. Bitter, sorrowful tears of a love lost, a life wasted. I don't want to taste them. I take another mouthful of my drink instead. Giving my face another wipe I return to your letter. I don't know why I'm torturing myself like this, Marty. Or maybe I do…

I'm under no illusions. I know your flaws, foibles, inadequacies. You're a neurotic, psychotic old ratbag with dire PMT, mood swings, shambolic health and bouts of manic depression. But you also possess the other half of my soul, and I love you so completely, so utterly, that no time, no barrier, no wall, no distance, no words, nothing, can ever, ever overcome it. A love so infinite as to weather all. And it is yours. All you have to do is take it.

Perhaps the breaking up of a family stops you. Do you focus on that to shore up your defences when they begin to sag, when the pressure inside your fortress begins to crack the walls? Perhaps you feel you can't take the responsibility, you don't want my daughter turning into a neurotic like you. Well, don't. Are you listening?

My child. My responsibility. You won't be breaking a family, I will. Breaking it for reasons of truth and love. Because I don't want to lie anymore, because I don't want to resent an innocent for denying me, and you, happiness any more.

Our best future is the one we share. I know it. I think you do, too. Bring us home, Lou. One day. Soon. Forever. Bring us home.

Listen to your heart. Be happy. Be yourself. Live life for yourself. All this means one thing, when you're ready.

Be with me.

I love you. Completely. Forever.

Marty xxx

I'm not convinced you could have left if I'd called. Could you? What would really have happened if I'd picked up the phone and said, 'Come to me, Marty. Come to me. I'm ready. I'm yours'. So many questions, Marty, and not a single bloody answer. You denied me the chance to answer, didn't you? I'm not ready to think about that though. Not yet. Maybe not ever.

Chapter 31

Making Plans for Nigel

I feel tired and drained the next morning, groaning when the alarm goes off and hitting the snooze button, desperate for more sleep, even if it is just ten minutes. Ten minutes later, I press it again, telling myself it's okay, I can use dry shampoo on my hair. I press it a third time. I can get away without having a shower this morning. I really don't want to face the day, the world. I've slept fitfully, my head spinning with Nigel's revelation, my own guilt about deceiving my sister, and thoughts of you, Marty. You always seem to be in my head at the moment, never far from the front, queuing, waiting impatiently for me to deal with whoever's in front of you.

Well, you're going to have a long wait today, I think, as I contemplate another day spent dealing with people's complaints; complaints that are often about friends and colleagues – people I care about. I finally drag myself out of bed, wondering if today will be the day I finally crack and walk out of the job I hate. I haven't really acknowledged how much I dread going in to work each day. Maybe it is time to look for something else? Any idealistic notions I had when I took the job have long since vanished.

I somehow make it to work on time, despite pressing snooze

a fourth time. Grabbing a coffee, I'm at my desk and checking my emails by nine, and it's head down until the post arrives at about ten fifteen. I open the first letter and begin to read, quickly realising I'm going to need more coffee to get through this morning. Picking up my mobile, I head for the canteen, where I'm trying to choose between a blueberry muffin or lemon drizzle cake (having by-passed the fruit bowl), when my mobile beeps. Text message. Taking a quick peek at the screen I see it's from Laura. Selecting both cakes, and an Americano, I head back to my office.

With my mouth full of muffin, I open my texts, wondering what Laura wants. Maybe she does want to take up my suggestion of shopping and lunch. Great! Building bridges with my sister is definitely overdue. A bit like quitting this job. I read the text. It's not about shopping. Or lunch.

Good morning, Louise. I popped by your house this morning to leave a pot of primulas on your doorstep. Can you please tell me why my husband's car was parked outside your house when I arrived? Laura.

Oh crap. The formality of the text message aside – that was just Laura's style – oh crap. Okay, think, Lou. She doesn't know you've read her text yet. Has she contacted Nigel? Phone Nigel. I quickly scroll through my contacts and hit dial.

'Answer the phone, Nigel. Please answer the phone,' I mutter to myself.

Thankfully, he does. 'Lou, hello, what a nice surprise,' he says.

'Er… yep. Nope. Not a nice surprise. Actually the opposite,

I'm afraid. Laura went to my house this morning.'

I can almost hear the penny drop and see the colour drain from Nigel's face before he answers. 'Oh crap.'

'Oh crap, indeed. I take it from your reaction she hasn't contacted you?'

'No, no, I haven't heard from her. Oh God, Lou, what do we do?'

'Honestly? Right now I have no idea. Thoughts?'

'God. None. Shit.'

I can tell from Nigel's uncharacteristically monosyllabic responses that he's gone into panic mode. Great. I suppose it's Lou to the rescue.

'Okay, just don't answer the phone to her if she rings you. Let me have a think and I'll call you back,' I instruct.

'Right. Okay. Thanks. Bye.'

Putting down my mobile, I lean my elbows on the desk and put my face in my hands, applying fingertip pressure where a throbbing has started behind my eyes. What the hell do we do? I wouldn't put it past my sister to turn up at the hospital if she doesn't get a reply quite quickly. How the hell did I get myself into this? And, more to the point, how do I get myself, and Nigel, out of it? I make up my mind, and redial Nigel's number.

'Hi, Lou.'

'Nigel, hi. I can't see a way out of this. Well, I can, but I'm not sure it's the way to go...' I begin, not even sure I should suggest it.

'What is it? Lou, I'm desperate.'

'Well, with your anniversary coming up, you could say you were plotting a surprise and needed me to help out... I don't know, maybe planning a city break or something and wanting

169

me to keep an eye on Richard.'

'Brilliant! Yes, that could work!' Nigel is starting to sound relieved.

'I'm really not sure it's the right thing to do though. Think about it… it would be kind of cruel, don't you think? Making Laura believe everything's okay between you, and then… you know. Like building her up before knocking her down. If you see what I mean?' I'm not sure I'm explaining myself particularly well.

'I do see that, but what's the alternative?'

'Tell her the truth. At least the abridged version. Just bring forward what you were going to do anyway.'

'God. But what about Richard, and his exams?'

'You need to hope Laura's instinct to protect her son is stronger than her desire to unleash her wrath on you.'

'Oh my God, Lou. What a mess. I'm so sorry to have dragged you into it.'

'Can't be helped. I would just rather we stopped digging now. I don't want to compound the lies we've already conspired in. Right, I'm going to reply to Laura. I'm going to tell her that she needs to speak to you. And hope she forgives me for my part in this.'

'I'm so, so, sorry, honestly.'

'I know. Let me know what happens. And I'm here for both of you.'

We say our goodbyes and I text Laura: *You need to speak to Nigel, Laura. But you know where I am if you need me. Lou x.* I don't envy Nigel, but my heart aches for my sister.

I can't stomach the thought of the coffee and cake now. It's going to be all I can do to get through the remainder of the day with any kind of focus.

I don't hear back from Laura, and the day limps by like a homeless man with two gangrenous feet. I don't think I managed to achieve very much at all, apart from a couple of very sub-standard replies to complaints about the state of the ladies' loos in A & E, which, frankly, I agreed with anyway. Five o'clock finally arrives, and I'm grateful to head home, albeit anxious about what will happen once Nigel gets home from work.

I got a text from him just as I was leaving work to say Richard had gone round to a friend's to revise after school, and he was heading home to speak to Laura. I texted back 'Good luck' and said a silent prayer for him. I can't help comparing Nigel's situation with yours, Marty. I absolutely believe he will follow through and tell Laura it's over. But then I believed you would too, in the beginning anyway.

I can't settle to anything at home. Finding the pot of brightly-coloured primulas Laura left on my doorstep triggered another great wave of guilt. It's sod's law this is happening just when Laura and I have started to patch things up. Maybe that's why though? The universe doing its thing – reuniting me with my sister so I can support her through this crisis? Things do happen for a reason, don't they? Well, usually, eh, Marty? I still haven't worked out the reason for us. Maybe we're the exception that proves the rule. Maybe the universe is closely related to Hindsight and Mother Nature? The three bitches.

I sit on the sofa, staring at nothing. All I can do is wait for the fallout. Which I'm sure will come. I don't know if that will be Nigel arriving on my doorstep with a suitcase, or a distraught sister who may or may not hurl a pot full of primulas at my head.

I wait. And I wait some more, stopping only to close the curtains and turn on a lamp. Finally, at about seven o'clock my mobile rings. My heart is in my throat as I check the display. It's Nigel.

'Nigel, hi. Is everything alright? Laura, is she…does she…?'

'It's okay, Lou. We're okay. Laura knows. She's calm. She says she'll speak to you tomorrow.'

'Thank God. She's really alright? Does she hate me?'

'She's really okay, I promise. And no, she doesn't hate you. I told her that, when I came to you for advice, you told me I should be honest with her. That you were giving me a chance to do the right thing before you said anything.'

'Oh! Thank you! Thank God. I've been sick with worry.'

'I know, and I'm really sorry, Lou, but I think it's going to be okay. We're going to talk things through properly now, before Richard gets home, and decide how to handle the situation.'

'Oh, good! Thank you for letting me know. And Nigel, please will you give Laura my love?'

'Yes, of course. And thanks, Lou, for everything.'

We say our goodbyes and I realise I'm shaking. The relief is palpable.

Chapter 32

Tell Laura I Love Her

I crash out early after my brief conversation with Nigel and sleep soundly, getting up to the first sounding of the alarm the next morning, showering and washing my hair, and feeling decidedly more human. I know the road ahead won't be an easy one for Laura and Nigel, but the hardest part is over, I'm sure.

Laura texted me first thing asking if I was free for lunch, and she's coming to the hospital at twelve-thirty. I'm not going to lie, I am a bit nervous about seeing her, conscious of the part I've played in what's happened. I just hope she knows I only ever had her best interests at heart. You can never really tell which way Laura will go, so I'm not completely easy as I wait for lunchtime to arrive. Today's batch of complaints is all about the food in the restaurant. Again, I sympathise. Yes, the I-think-it-was-supposed-to-be-moussaka was disgusting.

I meet Laura in reception right on time and give her hug, even though we don't normally hug each other. We're not from a family of huggers, but it feels like the right thing to do. I asks if she wants to risk the canteen food, telling her I think it's probably safe – they've just had their 'off' day. Them and the moussaka. We queue up for jacket potatoes and tuna – surely they can't get them wrong – and head for a quiet corner table.

I study Laura's face. Apart from dark shadows under her eyes, which tell of a sleepless night, she looks okay. Considering. She's calm, anyway, which is a relief. Wearing my tuna jacket would not be a good look.

'I'm sorry, Laura,' I say, reaching over and squeezing her hand where it rests on the handle of her knife. A sudden thought hits me and I risk a smile. 'You're not thinking about stabbing me, are you?'

She can't resist a slight smile, albeit tinged with sadness. 'No, not this time, Lou,' she assures me.

'Phew! Seriously, though, I'm so very sorry.' I'm treading carefully as I'm not entirely sure what Nigel has or hasn't told her.

'Thank you. It was a shock. Stupid me, didn't see it coming at all.'

'You're not stupid.'

Laura pulls a face. 'I don't know. I feel stupid. I should've seen the signs. Realised he didn't love me anymore.'

'I don't think it's that black and white. Don't beat yourself up.'

'It doesn't matter anyway. And honestly, I think I'm relieved. We probably should've split up years ago.'

Sod off, hindsight, you bitch. 'Don't say that – you've given Richard a stable, happy home all these years. That's worth a lot. They weren't wasted years.'

'Weren't they? I don't know. I could've been happy. Happier.'

'No point thinking like that though – you can't change it. Just got to deal with the now.' I'm still tiptoeing, unsure if Richard has told her about Karen or not. Although I can't imagine she'd be this calm if he had. 'What exactly did Nigel say?'

'Oh, just that he'll always love me, I'm the mother of his child after all, but that he's not *in love* with me and he thinks we'd be happier apart. That we both deserve to be happy and he knows he doesn't make me happy...' Laura's pain starts to leak out of her in silent tears that roll down her face unchecked. My heart is breaking for her, as I rummage in my bag for a tissue.

'Oh, Laura, I'm so, so sorry.'

She shakes her head, taking the tissue and wiping the tears away, getting the famous Laura control back once more. 'It's okay, really it is. I honestly am relieved. I'm just sad, I think. It feels like I've failed.'

'Oh my God, no, you haven't, Laura. You haven't failed. Shit happens, relationships end, it's no-one's fault. And our parents didn't exactly set a good example – show us how it should be done. Although, it could be argued they did a pretty good job of showing us how *not* to do it.'

'You're not wrong there,' Laura agrees. 'I hoped I would do better, though, be better.'

'And you are! You only have to look at Richard to know that. Please don't blame yourself.'

Neither of us has touched our food, which actually looks less appealing by the minute. 'So, what happens next?' I ask.

'Nothing. For now, at least. We've agreed to carry on as normal – well, as normal as possible – until Richard finishes his exams. Then we'll tell him together. Explain we've just grown apart and we don't make each other happy anymore. You know, present a united front.'

'See, you're already doing a thousand percent better than our parents!' I say, smiling at Laura. Another sudden thought hits me. 'Hey, we'll be able to go out on the pull together!' I'm laughing.

'Oh good god. Perish the thought. I am definitely NOT ready to think about the dating scene yet.' Laura fake shudders, but she's smiling.

'That's okay, you can just be my wingman,' I joke.

We sit quietly for a few minutes. It's Laura who breaks the silence.

'I'm sorry I haven't been a better sister.'

'Don't be daft!'

'No, really, I've been a cow, I know I have.'

I don't know what to say to her. She's actually not wrong.

'We're family – it would be weird if we got along all the time.'

'I'm going to try and be better. I make no promises on the dating thing though.'

'How about we both try and be better. I haven't exactly gone out of my way to be there for you either,' I admit.

'That's because I was a cow,' Laura says quite matter-of-factly.

We smile at each other. 'I'm glad you're okay,' I tell my big sister.

'Moo,' she says, laughing.

I'm still chuckling to myself as I head back to my office after seeing Laura off. Neither of us touched our lunch, but I'm so filled with relief I don't feel hungry. I daresay I'll be starving in an hour, but I'll worry about it then. I want to speak to Nigel before I do anything else. I call him from my desk.

'Hi, Lou. How are you? Have you seen Laura?' he says when he picks up.

'Yes, she just left.'

'How was she?'

'She seemed fine – genuinely. I think although she's terribly sad, the overwhelming feeling is relief. I know that's what I'm feeling!' I tell him.

'Me too. Honestly, and I know this is a cliché, I feel as though a great weight's been lifted.'

'Well, you know I love a cliché,' I say, laughing. 'Seriously, though, Nigel, I'm really happy for you. I know none of this can have been easy for you, but everyone deserves to be happy, and you have a chance at real happiness. Not everyone is strong enough to do what you've done. And, now I've spoken to Laura, I know she'll be okay too.'

'Thank goodness. I'll always love her, Lou, but it just wasn't enough anymore. Karen just makes me feel whole somehow. Does that sound pathetic?'

'God, no, quite the opposite. I get it. I think we're all looking for that someone who does that for us. Our 'other half'. You've been lucky enough to find yours, and now Laura has the chance to find hers.'

'Thanks, Lou. What about you? Have you not found your soulmate, your other half? It always surprises me that you're on your own.'

'Oh, I found mine a very long time ago. But we blew it, sadly. And no-one has ever been able to take his place. Not really. Hard as I tried to kid myself they could.'

'I'm sorry. That's rough. Laura's never talked about your relationships to me. I got the impression it was a closed subject.'

'Blimey. That does surprise me. I thought she'd have been only too eager to slag me off as the brazen hussy she probably thought I was,' I say, trying to sound more light-hearted than

I felt.

'What? No. I know your relationship with Laura has been strained at times, but she's actually incredibly loyal where her family's concerned. I know she bitches about your dad and Charlie, but she would still defend them to outsiders.'

'I think maybe I've misjudged that sister of mine over the years.'

'Well, she makes it bloody hard for people at times. I love her, Lou, but I don't always like her very much. I think maybe I have to shoulder some of the blame too, though. I don't think I've made her any happier than she's made me in recent years.'

'Resisting the urge to churn out a whole load of clichés here, but it takes two. Relationships are hard. I know they say you have to work at it, but you have to want to do the work. If something is fundamentally wrong, all the work in the world won't make it right.'

Nigel sighs. 'I guess so. It's not what I wanted for myself, or for Laura and Richard though.'

'No, I know. Been there, done that, got the t-shirt. Two t-shirts! But regret is such a useless emotion. Think of the positives – you've raised an amazing son together for starters. Nothing can change that.'

'I know you're right. I think it's just too raw at the moment. I hate the fact I'm breaking up our family.'

'Don't think of it like that. Richard would want you to be happy, will want you to be happy when you tell him. Karen has waited a long time for you, for happiness, and you both deserve it. I'm assuming you haven't told Laura anything about Karen?'

'No, nothing. I think you're right that we should protect Laura from that. I've spoken to Karen about it and she totally understands and agrees we should wait. She said she's waited this long, so what are another few months? I'm a lucky man.'

'Yes, you are, and I'm so pleased for you. Right, I'd better do some work. I've got a letter in front of me about the size of the spaces in the car park which demands my attention.'

Nigel laughs. 'Just tell them to get a smaller car!' he says, and thanks me again before we say our goodbyes.

Chapter 33

Get Ready

I think I'm ready. I don't quite know why I think it. Maybe it has something to do with the Nigel and Laura situation and being brave. Or turning fifty and feeling my own mortality. Or maybe it's just time. Probably long overdue.

Bottling it up, packing it away and burying it in the deepest, darkest recesses of my mind seemed like a good idea. Imagine my mind as one of those massive container ships in the middle of a vast ocean, loaded while I slept with thousands upon thousands of different coloured metal boxes, so that I have no idea which one contains this memory of you. It's taken nearly two decades for the cargo to be unloaded and now there's just one container remaining, waiting to be opened.

I'm going to open it, but I'm afraid. I'm so afraid that what I find inside will destroy me, destroy what little equanimity I have left. I think I'm going to need gin, the proverbial Dutch courage to open the door to the container, and I've poured myself a generous measure which I take with me to the lounge.

I'm ready. I close my eyes. And I let you in.

It's the fifth of April, 2001, and I'm in my car. I'm driving. Driving to meet you. 'Pineapple Head' by Crowded House is playing on the CD. I turn it up loud and I sing along, happy and hopeful and feeling more alive than in such a long, long time. I've asked you to come. It's time. Time to tell you I'm ready. I'm ready to take the leap of faith, to ask you to be with me. To trust that this time you will be able to leap with me. Time for us to be brave together.

The weather is awful, April showers at their worst, and my windscreen wipers are set on fast. I reluctantly keep my speed down, even though I'm impatient to arrive, to be with you. I'm trying to picture your face when I tell you and it makes me smile and sing even louder. I feel intoxicated at the thought of seeing you. I know, without a shadow of a doubt I'm doing the right thing and it feels amazing.

I've asked you to come to Canterbury and to meet me in The Chapel of the Holy Innocents at eleven o'clock. It seemed a fitting place to proclaim my love for you. I remember wondering idly if they would let us get married there one day. Wouldn't that have been amazing? Any tears shed that day would be happy ones, and would wash away all the heartbreak that had gone before.

I park in the multi-storey carpark, too impatient even for the park and ride bus journey. I was still too early, of course, but I had to be there waiting for you when you arrived. I didn't want you to get there before me. I'm still grinning like a loon as I go through the entrance, leaving my troubled past at the door with my dripping umbrella. I'm about to head to the chapel when, as an afterthought I head for the table of votive candles, as you had on that December day, and I light a candle to symbolise our love and how brightly it still burned in me, despite my best efforts to stifle it.

Then I take my seat on our pew in the chapel, and I wait. I

remember checking my watch every two minutes, impatient for you to arrive, and jumping up to peer out of the doorway just as often. I couldn't wait to make you the happiest man in the world. I knew just one look at my face would tell you everything you needed to know.

Five past eleven arrives and I write your lateness off to traffic and to car parking. Ten past, the same. I check my phone to make sure I haven't missed a call or text saying you'll be late. Quarter past. Twenty past. I'm starting to think you're not coming. But I can't believe you'd miss an opportunity to spend time with me. At half past I try phoning you, but get no answer. I text a brief *Let me know if you're coming* message and continue to wait. I start to wonder if this is payback for December the eighteenth, and the hour you sat in this very spot waiting, hoping I'd turn up. And being disappointed. Perhaps I was wrong about your feelings for me, after all.

I tried phoning you again, more than once, but each time your phone was unavailable. I waited until twelve-thirty, and then I had to accept you weren't coming. I remember heading for the exit, retrieving my umbrella and venturing back out in to the city, still keeping a lookout for you, half-hoping I'd see you hurrying along like Alice's White Rabbit, looking flustered at your lateness. *I'm late! I'm late! For a very important date!*

All I could think was that I'd left it too late, and that this time you'd had a change of heart. This time, you'd buried your feelings. I wondered if it served me right. This wasn't a fairy tale and I wasn't getting my happily ever after.

I didn't know what to do after I left the cathedral. Even though it was obvious you weren't coming, I couldn't bring myself to leave the city. If there was even the slightest chance

you might still turn up, having just been caught up in traffic, I had to be nearby. I wasn't quite ready to give up on you. Looking around the square outside the cathedral gates, I saw the same café I'd been in that December day and headed over to it. Shrugging out of my wet coat, I ordered a hot chocolate and found a table. I checked my phone again, but there were no messages or missed calls.

I felt totally adrift, not knowing what to do. I tried to find a rational explanation. If you'd had car trouble, you would have phoned, or texted to let me know. Maybe you were ill. Or Anna, or Esme, was ill? Maybe something had come up at work and you couldn't take the time off? Or maybe you just didn't feel the same any more. Maybe I really had left it too late. But how could I believe that to be true after everything you'd said in your letters? Infinite and eternal, that's what you always said. How could that have changed?

I don't know what made me tune in to a conversation between the lady serving behind the counter and a customer who'd just come in. He's saying something about being delayed because the M2/A2 junction was closed following an accident. Relief floods though me as I realise you've obviously been caught up in the same traffic as him. It's not too late.

The man keeps talking.

'Looked like a bad one – a dark blue Audi was on its down the embankment. Probably driving too fast for the conditions. I'd aquaplaned once myself and slowed right down. Didn't look as though any other vehicles were involved. Na the man says, shaking his head.

My heart literally missed a beat when he said it was a blue Audi. You drove a dark blue Audi. I try to shake it

Lots of people drive dark blue Audis. But the moment of panic becomes a ball of fear in my chest. I don't know what to do. I think I'm going to be sick.

I need fresh air, so I bundle my coat back on and head for the door, muttering a thank you in the general direction of the counter as I go. I can't breathe. I just need to get outside. Don't overreact, I'm telling myself. The chances of it being you are remote. Are they though? I counter, in a debate with myself. Right car, right road, right time. No, no, it's not you. It can't be you. No way.

The feeling of nausea hasn't subsided and has been joined by a lump somewhere in my chest which is making it hard to breathe. I don't know what to do. I don't know how to make sure you're okay. I decide to head for my car, and hurry off in the direction of the car park. Once safely inside my car, I start the engine and change the radio station to a local one, wondering what time the news and travel will be on. I check the time: one twenty-five, so there probably won't be any news until two o'clock, assuming it's on the hour.

I can't wait that long. I'll go mad. Who can I phone for help? It was before the days of smart phones or iPhones, and my ancient Nokia was less than useless. I decide I can't just sit there, powerless and terrified. I head out of the car park and head for the A2/M2 roundabout, not sure what I'm expecting to find, but knowing I have to do something and that's all I can think of. The traffic is still slow and has built up on the opposite side of the road due to people rubber-necking. People are ghoulish. I was about to join their ranks, and I peered across the carriage way, just in time to see a tow-truck pulling a dark blue Audi estate up the bank.

The feeling of panic increased. A dark blue Audi estate. Like yours. But loads of people drive dark blue Audi estates. It's impossible to make out a number plate or see anything else. As the traffic noses forward, I wonder what to do next. I try to apply rational thought to the situation. Okay… which hospital would they take an injured driver to? Realising it could be one of three, I'm no closer to knowing what to do. Deciding the only sensible option is to go home, I take the next exit. I turn up the radio as it nears two o'clock, praying I'll get more information about the accident and the driver. I think I forget to breathe as the news starts. All they say is that an accident is still causing tailbacks on both carriageways, nothing about the driver or any passengers. I suppose it's too soon for any real information. I release the breath I've been holding, still feeling nauseous. And scared. So scared.

Once home, I know there's no point trying to do anything except wait for answers. I put the television on the local channel, make a cup of tea and wait. I've tried your phone again, but it's still unavailable. It's just because you're in a meeting at work. You're just at home looking after a sick child. You're not lying injured in a hospital bed. You're just not. I'd know if something bad had happened to you. Wouldn't I? I'd feel it somehow, through those invisible threads that bind us. I'd feel a tug on them, I'd feel something.

I sit. I wait. I try to think rationally. The chances of it being your car are slim, aren't they? But you didn't show up to meet me… What could possibly stop you from coming to me? If all your protestations of love were to be believed, what could possibly stop you from coming to me, Marty? What did you say in one of your letters? *'Only illness or death will prevent my attendance. Well, possibly car breakdowns.'*

Finally, when I think I'm going completely mad, the early evening news comes on. I have to remind myself to keep breathing, and the feelings of nausea meet my trapped breaths in an uncomfortable ball in my chest.

'A man was taken to hospital following a serious accident on the A2 near Canterbury today. His car is believed to have skidded off the road due to bad weather conditions. No other vehicles were involved. The police have not yet released the man's name. In other news...'

Other news? No! There is no other news. I need to know. I need to know more. Who was it? What was his name? Fuck! I leap up from the sofa, and grab the Yellow Pages, flicking through the pages until I find hospitals. I will ring every hospital in the area if I have to. I dial the first number, for the nearest hospital, but I have a feeling they don't have an Accident and Emergency Department. I have to start somewhere though.

I get through to the main switchboard and explain myself. I was right, no A & E, the driver wouldn't have been taken there. The operator tells me to try Ashford or Margate. I phone the William Harvey Hospital in Ashford and explain myself again. This time, the operator puts me through to A & E.

'Accident and Emergency, how can I help you?'

'Oh, hello, um, I'm trying to find out if someone was brought in earlier today. There was a car crash. This morning...' I fade away, not knowing what else to say.

'Are you a relative?'

'What? No, but...'

'I'm very sorry then, but I can't tell you anything.' She does sound apologetic. Is that because she knows something, or because she can just hear the worry in my voice?

'Please… can you at least tell me if the driver was brought there?'

There's a pause. She's obviously weighing something up in her mind. 'All I can tell you is that a man was admitted around lunchtime today after being involved in a road traffic accident. That's really all I can tell you. I'm sorry.'

'Okay, I understand. Thank you for your help.' I'm shaking all over as I hang up the phone. I still don't know if it's you. I still don't know what to do. I can't bear feeling so powerless. Making up my mind, I grab my coat, bag and keys and jump in the car. I have to go to the hospital. Maybe they won't tell me anything, but I can't sit at home doing nothing.

Chapter 34

Right Here Waiting

It's starting to get dark when I pull into the hospital car park. I'm even more stressed now after road closures and diversions on the way there. Then I managed to drop the ticket as I took it from the machine at the barrier, struggling to open my door and retrieve it. I could feel the frustration of the driver behind as I fumbled about. I mouthed a sorry and raised an apologetic hand in the universal 'thanks for your understanding' gesture. I'm completely flustered as I hunt for a space in the packed car park.

I park, badly, and take a minute to calm my breathing and regain my composure, before heading for the doors marked 'Accident & Emergency'. The ambulance bays are full and there are a lot of people milling about, some having a sneaky cigarette before going back in to cope with whatever their own emergency was. I wish for a moment I smoked. I needed something to take the edge off.

I join the short queue at the reception desk, silently willing the people in front of me to hurry up. I'm struggling to stand still and am muttering under my breath like a mad woman, 'Hurry up, hurry up'. I must look like I've got the DTs. When I finally reach the front of the queue, I can see the receptionist thinking 'Oh good, another mad drunk, another strung-out junkie'. She smiles a tired smile and asks how she can help. I recognise her voice as the lady I spoke to on the phone. I repeat my earlier request, and receive the same answer.

'Please.' I'm not above begging. I just need to know if it's you.

'I'm sorry, if you're not family…'

I should've lied. I should've said I was your sister, or your wife. I should have been your wife, Marty. Please, God, let it not be him. Let me say yes to him, let me make it right.

I can see the receptionist isn't going to budge, so I turn reluctantly back to the crowded waiting room. There's one seat left by the vending machine, so I perch on it and sit there wondering what to do, my hands fidgeting. I must have looked like I needed a fix. I did. I needed a fix of you, Marty. I needed my phone to ring and for you to be on the other end, telling me you're sorry, you got called to a meeting at work you couldn't get out of. Or sorry, the battery died on your mobile. Or sorry, Anna's ill and you've been taking care of Esme. Anything. I could even have coped with you saying, sorry I just didn't want to see you, Lou. Anything just to hear your voice and to know you're okay, and not lying in a hospital bed with a broken leg and a bang to the head. You could be just the other side of the double doors past reception. So close. You could be so close.

I don't know how much time passes. Patients ebb and flow around me, copious cups of coffee get poured by the machine next to me, people cough and fidget and complain, asking the poor receptionist, 'How much longer?' How much longer do I wait? It might not even be you. I could be waiting for news on the wrong person. Except they would be the right person.

Anyone that wasn't you would be the right person, Marty. My heart would go out to them, of course, but all that would really matter is that you were okay.

The double doors open again. Everyone in the waiting room looks up when the doors open, hoping this time they'll hear their name being called, and their wait will be over. But nobody's going to call my name. I have no idea how to stop waiting though. This time when the doors open, a police officer comes out. I look over at him, taking in his tired face and serious expression. It's a face that's seen a lot. Too much. It's a world-weary face. It's a face that knows things. Too many things. I wonder…

I leap from my chair as he passes, stopping him just before the exit, calling out:

'Excuse me. Sorry. Sorry to bother you…'

He stops and turns back to look at me. 'Yes, can I help you?' He sounds weary.

'Sorry,' I say again, 'It's just…' I'm struggling for the right words, 'a friend of mine, I think he might have been in an accident. A car accident, I mean. Today, this morning. On the A2. Nobody will tell me anything. Only we were meant to meet and he didn't show up…'

'Are you a relative?' That question again, but still I'm unable to lie. Unable to claim you as mine.

'No, but…'

The police officer puts his hand up and stops me, 'I'm sorry, then, madam, I'm afraid I can't tell you anything.' He shrugs his face into an apology and walks away. 'I hope you have good news. Goodnight.'

'Th…thank you. Goodnight.' I'm left standing on my own

by the exit and I lean up against the wall. I'm honestly not sure I can support myself much longer. The not knowing is killing me. I don't know how long I continue to stand like that, overtaken by weariness and indecision. I should go home, I suppose. But if you're here, then that's where I need to be. If it is you. Of course this nightmare could be over nothing, and some other poor man is lying in a bed through the other side of the double doors.

I'm still standing like that when I become aware of someone approaching. Some lucky patient seen and discharged, heading for home no doubt, I think with a sigh. They don't walk out past me though and I become aware of them standing still a few feet away from me. Just standing there. I look up, wondering why they've stopped. It's a woman. She's obviously been crying. I don't know her, but she has a shocked look of recognition on her face.

'He's dead. Martin's dead. And you killed him!' She spits the words at me before sobs erupt from her and she runs out into the night.

Chapter 35

Secret to the End

I'm frozen to the spot, trying desperately to stay on my feet. Without the wall to hold me up, I think I would have sunk to the floor. 'He's dead. Martin's dead. And you killed him.' The words replay in my head on a hideous loop, growing louder and harsher and more real. I don't want to hear them, but they won't be silenced.

No… you can't be dead, Marty. It's just not possible. It's all just a horrible nightmare. Pinch myself and I'll wake up. You can't be gone. I would've known. I would've felt it. You wouldn't leave me. You wouldn't… We're not done yet…

I blink and try to focus. I feel calm. Or maybe stunned. Or maybe I feel nothing. I don't know what I feel. Anna. That was Anna. All I can think is that she shouldn't be alone, out in the night, somewhere, broken and grieving. I head out of the hospital and look around outside. I spot a figure hunched over the railing on the other side of the road and, taking a deep breath, I walk over.

I reach out and put my hand on her arm. 'Anna. I'm sorry. I'm so sorry.'

She looks up and into my face and I see a flash of hatred in her eyes before she breaks down and sobs wrack her body once more. I don't hesitate, taking her in my arms and holding her tight as her slight frame continues to shake. Silent tears stream down my face unchecked. I have no right to fall apart. This woman, this wife, Anna, the rights are all hers. If I have any strength left, I must give it to her. I have taken so much from her over the years. It is all I can give her.

We stand like that for some time, until the sobbing gradually subsides and Anna's body begins to still. As she calms, she pulls away from me, trying hard to regain her composure, obviously conflicted at taking comfort from me. The other woman. The woman whose name her husband called out in his sleep. The woman who threatened to destroy the family she had worked so hard to make and keep together. The woman she has hated for years. She wipes her face with both hands.

'He was coming to you, wasn't he?' It's a rhetorical question. She already knows the answer. 'The police gave me his phone. I saw the missed calls and the text message.'

'Yes. I'm sorry.' I know how inadequate my words are. There is nothing I can say that is going to make this any better, for either of us. 'I loved him,' I say quietly.

The briefest look of anger flares on her face before she gets herself under control again. 'He wasn't yours to love though. Was he?'

'No. I know. I'm sorry. I don't know what else I can say.'

'Nothing. There's absolutely nothing else you can say, because he's dead. He's lost to us both now.'

Tears are streaming down our faces, uniting us in our loss of you, however much we might not care to admit it. We'd both loved you and we shared the pain of losing you.

'You shouldn't be on your own,' I tell her.

'I won't be. My parents are coming to get me.'

'Good. Can I wait with you?' God, this is so weird, but I can't leave her, whatever she thinks of me.

She doesn't reply straight away. Maybe I've overstepped the mark? Why on earth would she want me anywhere near her? Then she just says 'Yes', and we stand there, side by side, not speaking any more, but not alone. It's only about ten minutes or so before a car pulls up alongside us. A middle-aged woman gets out and rushes to Anna, wrapping her into a tight embrace.

'Mum, oh Mum, he's gone,' Anna squeezes the words out just before the floodgates open and she starts to sob uncontrollably, her mother barely able to hold her up as her legs buckle underneath her.

'Oh, my darling girl. I know. I know, I'm so sorry, but I'm here now. And Dad's here and we'll take care of you.' Anna's mother strokes her head and speaks softly to her.

A man, Anna's father, gets out of the car and together they get Anna into the back. Anna's mother gets in beside her and they drive off into the night.

I'd stepped back into the shadows when the car had pulled up. I'm left standing there, alone, my hand over my mouth suppressing the sobs that have been trying to escape ever since Anna broke down when her mum arrived. I don't think Anna's parents even registered my presence, and I was grateful for not having to explain who I was.

I need to get home while I'm still capable of driving, and I half run to the car, closing and locking the door once I'm inside. I start the engine and somehow, on some sort of auto-pilot, I make it home. I don't make it further than the hall.

I'm revisiting this memory for the first time, and I feel the pain almost as acutely now as I did then. Closing my eyes, I'm right back there. There's a youngish woman there in the hall. She's collapsed on the floor, as if she couldn't hold herself up anymore. And the noises coming from her… they're almost inhuman, animal noises, heart-wrenching, devastating, howls of pain. Now she's crying out, 'No, no, no, no', over and over again, as if saying it will make it so. He's not dead. He can't be dead. It's just not possible. 'No, no, no, no.'

And no-one comes to her. No-one sees her pain, or hears her cries. No-one knows how her heart is broken. No-one can know because he wasn't hers to lose. He wasn't hers to grieve over. All this young woman's crying must be done in private. The only thing she can do for him now is protect his memory.

Chapter 36

Remembrance Day

How do I feel after allowing those memories back in, Marty? After re-living the horror of that day, that night, all these years later. I think I just feel desperately sad, really. Sad for a life cut short, for daughters growing up without a father, a mother forced to outlive her child. I think to lose a child must be the worst pain in the world. I know if anything happened to Libby, I would not want to carry on. Can you actually die from a broken heart, Marty? I know there were times when I wished I was dead too. Times when I didn't know how to carry on, if I could carry on. But I had to.

I remember living through a whole gamut of emotions back then; the stages of grieving I suppose. The initial numbness I felt, the denial you were really dead, didn't last long and then I was hit by an avalanche of pain and guilt as I tried to accept the truth. Anna had said I killed you. Her words would never leave me. In a way she was right, of course. You were on that road in the rain because you were coming to me. Because I'd asked you to come to me. I will carry that guilt with me to my grave. Then there were times I got angry, when I railed at you for not driving more carefully, and for not checking your tyres, after the inquest reported that the tread on two of them was below the legal requirement. I was so angry at you for leaving me, Marty. For denying us the chance of happiness. For a long time, I didn't think I could survive losing you. I'm honestly not sure how I got through the months of depression, or when it started to lift, just a little, and life gradually got a little more bearable, day by day.

Eventually life got to be more than just going through the motions, more than just surviving. I met and married my second husband, not because I was head over heels in love with him, but because I didn't want to be alone anymore and because I knew he loved me and would look after me. There was no point in holding out for a love like ours, Marty. That's a once in a lifetime kind of love. I knew I had to settle for something less. I thought I could make it work. He was a good husband and father. But he wasn't you. No-one was ever going to take your place. I think I just existed in some sort of half-life. Libby became my reason for living. My life was over, but I could still do my best to make sure she lived hers to the full.

Do you know what one of the hardest parts of losing you was, Marty? Not being able to talk to anyone about you, confide in anyone about my love for you and the desperate sense of loss I felt. Laura believed our affair ended the day you told me about Anna being pregnant. How could I tell her now that we'd carried it on? After everything I said. Everything we went through. She wouldn't have understood. I thought about Anna sometimes. I envied her. Does that sound crazy? It's true, I did. I envied that she could grieve openly, that people would understand why she was sad, and would support her through it.

But do you know what the absolute rock bottom was for me? What very nearly sent me past the point of no return in my grief and pain? I got a text message from your phone. I can't begin to describe how that felt, Marty. It felt like a cruel joke when I saw your name on the screen. For just a split second, my heart lifted, some part of me thought there had been a terrible mistake. And then just as swiftly, my heart plummeted. Of course, Anna had your mobile. It was the briefest of text messages:

Don't come to the funeral.

That was rough, Marty. Those five words nearly destroyed me. Would I have done the same thing in Anna's position? I suppose I might've done. I did understand, of course I did. She didn't want the added pain of your mistress being there at your funeral; a living, breathing, flesh and blood reminder of a painful truth. Anna knew deep down, even if she didn't care to admit it, that she'd lost you long before the accident. But she had to carry on the illusion until the bitter end, didn't she? From loving wife to grieving widow, with nothing but a happy marriage and planned baby in between. I did understand. She was protecting not only herself and her daughter, but your memory too.

But it was rough. I was struggling so badly with the loss of you, Marty; and the knowledge I would never see you again. Never. Ever. Forever. I couldn't make my brain accept it. There had always been you. Even when we weren't together, even when I thought I hated you, you were still out there, somewhere, loving me. The possibility of you, of us, was always there, a lighthouse guiding me past the rocks. I didn't know how to accept your light had gone out forever. I was cast adrift on a dark and stormy sea, with no hope of rescue, no hope of reaching safety.

I didn't even know when your funeral was. So many times I picked up the phone to ring round the funeral directors near your home to try and find out. Would they have told me? Would they have asked who I was? Just like at the hospital. Was I family? I don't know. It felt dangerous to know. I'm not sure I could have resisted the urge to turn up at the church, even if it was only to slip in late at the back, and to sneak out early, running away before I was found out. I needed to say good-bye to you. I needed the closure a funeral helps bring about. I couldn't have that, though, could I? I had to find another way.

I had to do all my grieving in private, and I had to find a way of saying goodbye privately too. I decided to retrace the steps of us, Marty, from our very first meeting at the pyjama party to our last.

I bought a bunch of roses before I set off in the car. First stop: Phil's house. I don't know if his family still live there. I drive past it sometimes and it's changed over the years, the front has been cleared of trees, revealing the house in all its splendour. I wonder if the cellar is still used for parties? I pull into the layby in front. The radio's on in the car, Heart 80s as usual, and they're playing Spandau Ballet's 'True'. I can feel tears threatening. I can't give in to them now, not at the start of this journey, or I will never make it through. Thank God they're not playing 'Tainted Love' - the first song we heard together, all those years ago, in our pyjamas.

As the song comes to an end, I undo my seatbelt and remove a single rose from the bunch lying next to me on the passenger seat. Checking the road is quiet, free of other cars or any pedestrians, I quickly jump out and lay the rose on the front wall. I'm back in the car a second later, my heart pounding. I try and analyse why I feel so anxious. I'm not doing anything wrong, am I? Not really. People leave floral tributes at significant places all the time. And this place couldn't be any more significant: the place I first met you, Marty, never dreaming then what that meeting would lead to.

The next place I want to revisit is my old grammar school and I drive the couple of miles before pulling up just up the road from the main gates. I undo my seatbelt, but I don't get out straight away, leaning back in my seat and closing my eyes. And there you are... standing opposite the gate, hands in your blazer pockets, your crazy hair sticking up, and that dopey smile on your face, expectant and excited as you wait for me to come out of school and find you there. Waiting for me. You spent so long waiting for me, Marty, didn't you? We spent so long waiting for each other.

I sit awhile longer, waiting for that fourteen-year-old school-girl to walk out. I can picture her face, my face, blushing a little at finding you there waiting. A little embarrassed, but secretly pleased. Crossing the road to meet you, handing over her heavy bag. As the young couple walk away, down the road, I open my eyes and return to the present. Taking another rose from the pile, I slip out and place it where you had stood all those years ago. I keep my eyes to the ground, hoping no-one sees me, hoping no-one wonders what I'm doing, or asks me. I don't know what I would say.

It's a few more miles' drive now. I've had to turn the radio off. Too many emotions threatened when they played The Communards' 'Never Can Say Goodbye'. Never was a song more apt, eh, Marty? No matter what happened between us, how many times we hurt one another, we kept coming back for more, didn't we? Only now I have to say goodbye to you, don't I? That's what this pilgrimage is all about. To try and achieve some sort of closure. Even though I know there can never be such a thing, not really. We'll never be over, Marty. Not in my heart or in my mind. You'll just be popped in a shoebox full of letters and love, and placed in the back of a wardrobe or under a bed. Out of sight. And maybe sometimes out of mind. Enough to cope with life, enough to move forward, anyway.

I arrive at the beach about twenty minutes later. I've been here many times since you and I were last here, but those times did not carry the same significance. Those times, there had still been the possibility of us; there had still been hope, however remote it may have seemed. But now death had shattered any chance of a future together. Would we ever have got our acts together, Marty? Would we both have said yes at the same time? You were coming to me on that fateful day. Was it to say yes, you'd be with me? As you had so many times over the years in your letters. Just call and you'd come. That's what you'd said. No matter how much time passed, you said you'd come to me; you'd leave everything and you'd be mine. I'll never know now, will I? But I choose to believe you were coming to say yes. It gives me no comfort though.

I pluck a third rose from the seat and walk slowly down to the beach, relieved to find it deserted. A weak April sun is pushing through the clouds, and the tide is about halfway out, leaving an expanse of compacted sand in its wake. This was where we came just before you went off to university, where we said the first of many goodbyes. Where the end of innocence happened. Just friends then. You meant so much to me, but I was still so young; too young to realise you were my soul mate. I think you always knew, didn't you? You were just waiting for my feelings to catch up with yours. And when they finally did...

I shake the thought away and continue up the beach, walking in a diagonal so I gradually reach the sea. Standing just out of reach of the waves, I close my eyes once more, until you're there beside me, laughing, carefree, and full of hope and possibility. Before my emotions become a tsunami to overwhelm me, I open my eyes and spin the rose into the foamy water, watching as it bobs about on the waves. I turn and walk away before there is a chance of the single flower being washed up on the shore again. I don't look back, getting into my car and driving quickly away.

It's fitting the next stop on my pilgrimage is Canterbury, following in the footsteps of so many Christians who travelled to visit the shrine of Thomas Becket. While mine may not be a religious journey, it is most definitely a spiritual one. My faith in your love was tested many times, Marty, but ultimately it survived. My first stop when I arrive in the city is my old university. Parking in the visitors' car park, I head straight for the coffee shop where we met. This is where I started to really fall in love with you. This is where my feelings finally broke through. I remember how surprised I felt. It was like someone switching a light on, illuminating what had been there all along. I just hadn't been ready to see it before.

I order a coffee and take a seat in the window, gazing out over the campus I haven't visited for quite some time. I can just about see my old college, Rutherford, and I remember the thrill of receiving your letters and parcels there. If only we'd got our act together back then, Marty. You would still be alive… It's pointless thinking like that though. I drink down my coffee quickly, and start to rise out of my seat, pulling a now slightly battered rose from my bag and placing it on the chair in one swift motion as I hurry out of the coffee shop. I don't look back. I don't want to know if anyone saw.

I walk back to the car park a different way. There's one more thing I want to see before I leave. Taking the path in front of the Templeman Library, I stop by The Senate and take in the panorama of the city at the bottom of the hill. The cathedral is clearly visible, its spire a beacon towering above the other buildings, guiding pilgrims home.

I drive into the city centre and find a space in the multi-storey car park. I stuff another rose into my handbag and walk the short distance down the High Street, turning right into the narrow side street that leads to the cathedral gate. As an alumni of the university I have free entrance to the cathedral, my graduation having taken place there some years back. But graduation memories aren't the ones that spring to mind now. This time it's all about you. Me. Us. The memories can never be anything but bittersweet now.

The cathedral is quite busy, as it is pretty much all year round, a steady stream of visitors, of pilgrims, coming to marvel, to worship, to pray, or just appreciate its magnificence. I take a deep breath and head down the left hand side of the nave, heading for the Chapel of the Holy Innocents. I'm aware my heart is beating faster, and my breathing becoming erratic. This is going to be tough. I falter at the door to the chapel, but I know this has to be done. I have to face this part of the painful process if I want to achieve any sort of closure.

Taking another deep, ragged breath I step over the threshold and am immediately overwhelmed by a torrent of memories and emotions. Taking a seat in the farthest corner of the tiny room, I try to steady my breathing and get my heart rate under control. I want to sob, but I daren't let those floodgates open. Not here. Not now. Thankfully, there are no other visitors in the chapel. I don't want to share these moments with anyone else. Anyone but you, at least.

This was always going to be the hardest part of today. This is where I'd been sitting when you died. Where I'd waited and wondered and agonised, thinking you weren't coming to me, that I'd left it too late. But you *were* coming to me, weren't you? I swallow back the lump in my throat, and blink away the tears that prick my eyes. I don't know how I can bear this. If I can bear it. Leaning forward I rest my elbows on the pew in front, resting my forehead on my hands and closing my eyes. To anyone who entered the chapel I would have looked as though I was praying. I suppose I was in my own way. Praying for the strength to get through this, to survive the onslaught of emotions.

I don't know how long I sat like that, allowing the memories to flow through me, trying to hold it together. I think I was rocking gently back and forth, almost imperceptibly, so close to losing myself to the grief. It was so easy to blame myself for what happened. If only I hadn't asked you to come to me. But I did. If I could turn back time, I would do it all differently. Even if it meant I could never be with you, at least you would still be in the world. It was my fault. And I had to live with that knowledge for the rest of my life. The pressure of my tears has become too much now and they track through my fingers down my cheeks. I wipe them away with my hands and, as I rummage in my bag for a tissue, my fingers meet the rose, almost forgotten in its depths.

I remove the flower, placing it on the pew beside me while I wipe my eyes and nose. I feel a little calmer now. The pressure has eased after opening the valve and releasing some of the tears that had built up. But am I ready to say goodbye to you, Marty? I don't think I'll ever be ready.

Chapter 37

Blame It On Love

I make that pilgrimage every year. On the anniversary of your death, the fifth of April, I buy a bunch of yellow roses and I travel my own pilgrim's way to remember you. Every year I have to come up with an excuse to be absent from my life for a day. I can't tell anyone what I'm doing any more now than I could then.

I sit in the same seat in the same chapel and quietly remember you. The sorrow I feel now is a faint echo of the agony of that day. It still hurts though, Marty. I still feel the regret, the guilt, the loss, the longing. I've never really come to terms with any of it. I've got on with my life – I had to for my daughter's sake, but the colour never really came back into my existence after the terrible darkness of losing you. I live in a world of pale greys and muted blues. I've never loved again. Not really. Nothing that didn't pale into insignificance when the light of your love shone on it. All my love was poured into my precious daughter. All I could hope was that she lived a better life than I had; a life without a great weight of regret that crushed any chance of real happiness.

After leaving the cathedral that first year, I drove up the A2 and past the spot where your car went off the road. I don't know why I put myself through it. It was impossible to stop there and leave flowers, but some masochistic impulse took me there anyway. I've driven past hundreds, possibly thousands, of times since then, but have taken to avoiding it on April fifth. My pilgrimage ends at the cathedral now.

Do I still feel responsible for your death? I don't know. I still feel every emotion under the sun where you're concerned, Marty. The feelings are just kind of diluted, like a jug of orange squash left under a dripping tap. I think about Anna from time to time, and Esme. I wonder if she looks like you, or has your mannerisms, your intelligence, your capacity to love. I did hear Anna remarried and had another child. I hoped they all had happy lives. Anna actually wrote to me, Marty. It was a few years after your death, and the letter was addressed to me at my mum's. She must have got the address from your belongings. I still have the letter. I haven't read it for a long time. There's no address or date on the letter, and it starts with just my name...

Louise,

You're probably as surprised to receive this letter as I am to be writing it. I don't know really who I'm writing it for, or why. I just felt I had to write it.

I have thought of you often since that terrible night at the hospital. You didn't have to stay with me, or comfort me – you must have been in so much pain yourself. I was, and am, grateful to you for your strength at such a horrific moment in both our lives. I don't know if I said it at the time, but I'm saying it now: Thank you.

I know I blamed you for Martin's death because he was coming to you that day. With hindsight and the healing powers of time, I know that was unfair. It was just a tragic accident. With the state of his car tyres, it could have happened anywhere, any time. In moments of clarity, I remind myself it could have been much worse. He could have had our daughter in the car. The tragedy could have been much worse.

I have wrestled with my own demons since that day, as I'm sure you must have. As painful as it is to admit, I have to accept responsibility for my own part in the tragedy. I should have let Martin go. I should have let him go years earlier, when I first found out about you. I knew he didn't love me. Yes, he cared about me, but he never loved me the way he loved you. I always knew that. He used to call out your name in his sleep. Did you know that? Can you imagine how that felt?

I was so filled with bitterness and jealousy. I didn't want you to have him. Even if he wasn't fully mine, I was determined he wouldn't be yours either. But he was yours. In every way that really mattered, he was yours. I trapped him and he stayed out of a sense of duty. He was a good man. In spite of everything that happened, I still believe that. It took a while to admit it to myself, but I know it to be true. If I had let him go, let him be with you, he would still be alive. My child would not have lost her father. I have to live with that knowledge every day. And for the part I played in this, I am truly sorry. It's not easy for me to admit that. I guess time has mellowed me and my hatred of you. I am sorry, Louise.

I have tried to bring my daughter up as Martin would have wanted; to be honest and kind and brave. She gives me great comfort in life. I'm immensely proud of her, as I know Martin would have been too. He very much lives on in her. I don't know if you can take any comfort in that fact. I hope so.

I hope you have gone on to find love and happiness in your life, Louise. I know it can't have been easy for you, because I know how *hard it was for me. I know how much you loved him, because I saw it reflected in his love for you.*

I won't write again, and I don't want a reply – you'll see I haven't included my address. I think this is just something I needed to do for my own peace of mind, and to close the door to the past. And maybe to offer you some small comfort too.

With kind regards,

Anna

I remember the immense surprise I'd felt when I got Anna's letter. Gobsmacked is probably the only word for it. Even if she'd felt those things, I never dreamed she'd put them down on paper and send them to me, the woman she'd hated with the same level of passion her husband had loved with. I was grateful to have someone to share the burden of blame. The emotional orange squash got weaker still after I received that letter.

Chapter 38

Coming Home

Christmas is approaching rapidly and I can't pretend it's not happening for much longer. I want to embrace it, as I did when Libby was little; when I wasn't on my own. As much as I have no regrets about my marriage ending, it did make celebrations like Christmas less appealing.

I force myself to decorate a tree for Libby's sake, but I could quite easily go full Grinch over the festive season. I remember a time when I took so much pleasure in shopping for the perfect presents for family and friends. I haven't quite reached the point of buying everyone humbugs, but it might only be a matter of time. This year is even worse, because it's Libby's dad's turn to have her on Christmas Day. I will see her on Christmas Eve, but it's just not the same. With everything that's going on with Laura and Nigel, I think this is a Christmas to be glossed over. I suppose I'll spend the actual day with Mum at Laura's. At least I can help make it a good one for Richard before the bombshell of his parents' looming divorce hits.

Knowing this will be Richard's last Christmas with both his parents gives me the kick up the bum I need to make it special. I know my Christmas presence can help keep a lid on the powder keg of Laura's marriage, and my peacekeeper skills will probably be tested to their limits. The combination of Mum, Laura and alcohol is a volatile one at the best of times, without the addition of Laura's fragile emotional state. I make a mental note to advise Laura against inviting Dad. With any luck, he'll be off sunning himself somewhere with my future-ex-step-mother, AKA 'The Gold Digger'. Although, that term had been amended by Charlie the last time I saw him: 'Not so much a gold digger, Lou,' he'd said, 'more of a tin digger, 'coz the gold's all gone'. I probably don't need to tell Laura not to invite our troubled and troublesome half-brother. He probably wouldn't turn up anyway.

Having someone else's problems to focus on is just the ticket, and I begin to feel more positive about the prospect, attacking my to-do list with renewed vigour. I *will* make this a good Christmas for my family, even if it kills me. Which it may still do, let's be honest. I'm seriously going to have my work cut out for me, and I think I'm going to have to do the whole thing sober. Someone needs to stay in control of the situation.

It'll be my seventeenth Christmas without you, Marty. I think about you more during the holiday season. I suppose that's only natural. All these years wasted when we should have been together. I have a little Christmas tradition: I go to the carol service at the cathedral and light a candle for you each year. It's actually quite comforting to be there for a joyous occasion. Bittersweet, really, like so much of our story. I wonder if I'll ever find someone to take your place, Marty? Is there room in my heart for anyone but you and Libby? Dangerous thought. I shake it away and return my focus to my present list. *What on earth do you buy for the woman who's about to lose everything?* I wonder, with a sigh.

Libby's due home on the sixteenth and I can't wait to spoil her. I decide to plan lots of treats for us to share and am looking at what's on at the Marlowe Theatre when the phone rings. It's Libby.

'Hello! You must be psychic – I was just thinking about you.'

'Hey, Mum. That's nice. Aren't you always thinking about me, though?' she jokes back. There's something flat about her voice though. Something's wrong.

'You okay?' I ask.

'Yeah... well, no, not really. I just wanted to check if it's okay to come home a few days earlier?'

'Yes, of course it is. Has something happened? Are you okay?' I wish I could see her face. I wish I could hug her.

'I can't talk about it on the phone. I just want to come home.' I can hear a break in her voice, and it hurts my heart.

'Why don't I drive up and collect you?'

'No, it's alright, thanks. Maybe you could pick me up from the station? I'll text you the time. It'll be on Friday afternoon sometime.'

'Okay, if you're sure. It's no trouble to drive up there though.' All I want to do is jump in the car and go to her now.

'Honestly, Mum, the train's fine. I'll see you on Friday.'

'See you Friday. I love you!'

'Love you too, Mum. Bye.'

'Bye, darling.' I hang up the phone, wondering what's happened. Well, whatever it is, all the more reason to make this the best Christmas possible, I think as I return my attention to theatre bookings and the Christmas lights trail at Bedgebury Pinetum.

The next few days pass in a busy blur of work and shopping.

I'm grateful to have a couple of weeks booked off over Christmas and the New Year. As ever, I feel for all the staff and patients who will be stuck in hospital. Libby's train gets in at five fifteen on Friday and I go in early so I can get away in time to meet her. I'm excited to have an extra weekend with my daughter, but anxious all the same about how low she'd sounded on the phone.

I'm waiting at the barriers by ten past five on Friday, and can see that Libby's train is running on time. Sure enough, the train pulls in at exactly five fifteen. My heart catches, as it always does, when I see her approaching the exit. I scan her face, trying to read what's wrong. She looks so much more tired than when she was home for my birthday, just six weeks ago. As she gets closer, I can see she's lost weight too. Libby spots me and picks up her pace, throwing herself into my arms in the tightest of hugs and promptly bursting into tears.

'I didn't know how much I needed my mum,' she squeezes the words out between sobs.

We stand like that for a minute, ignoring the sea of people parting around us. I just hold her as she sobs.

'Oh, my darling girl. You're home now. I'm here. Shh,' I try to soothe.

Eventually, the sobbing subsides and I can feel her body hiccoughing against me as she tries to control her breathing. I pull tissues out of my bag and pass them to Libby.

'Oh God, how embarrassing,' she groans, as she wipes her face and blows her nose.

'Hey! That's no way to talk about your mother!' I joke, nudging her arm. 'Let's get you home.'

Libby manages a weak smile and we walk back to the car

arm in arm. We drive the short distance home. Libby's quiet. I don't push her to make conversation. I feel the time to talk will be once we're indoors with a cuppa. Or a large gin.

'Is it okay if I go and have a bath?' Libby asks, throwing her stuff down in the hall.

'Yes, of course. I'll sort out dinner while you have a soak. Do you want a drink to take in with you?' As desperate as I am to find out what's wrong, I know I can't push her, and she'll talk to me when she's ready.

'Um… actually, I'd love a glass of wine, Mum. Have you still got that bottle of sparkling pink stuff I got you for your birthday?'

'You're in luck – I haven't had an occasion to open it since. I'll get you a glass to take up.'

With Libby soaking in the bath, I pour myself a glass of rosé and set about browning some mince for a spaghetti Bolognese. It's nice having someone to cook for, I think as I stir. I've always found cooking for one rather depressing; just a sad reminder of how lonely I am most of the time. I press play on the CD player in the kitchen. I can't actually remember what's in it, but am soon singing along to Years & Years.

'Something smells good.'

I hadn't heard Libby come in, and she puts her arms around me where I stand at the hob. I can feel the fluffy warmth of her bath robe against me.

'Feel better?' I ask her, turning as she steps away and sits down at the kitchen table. 'Dinner won't be long. Only spag Bol. Hope that's okay?'

'Mm, lovely, thanks. Probably just what I need to soak up the enormous quantity of alcohol I plan to consume,' she smiles sadly. This is not my bubbly girl, I think as I take the bottle from the fridge and top up her glass.

'Well, it's nice having someone to cook for. And drink with!' I tell her, clinking my glass against hers. 'It's lovely to have you home.'

'Thanks, Mum. It's lovely to be home.'

We eat dinner in the lounge with trays on our laps. I've lit the fire and switched on the Christmas lights, and a mixture of cinnamon and orange essential oils burns in the diffuser, making the room cosy and festive. We make small talk while we eat; Libby asks about my job and the rest of the family, and I cautiously probe her about university, not wanting to push before she's ready to talk.

With dinner finished, I leave Libby curled on the sofa while I quickly stack the plates and cutlery in the dishwasher. Grabbing the bottle of wine from the fridge, I head back to the lounge, topping up our glasses before settling myself in the armchair opposite my daughter.

We sit in silence for a while, but we both know the elephant in the room won't be silenced indefinitely. As much as I don't want to push her, I want to know what's troubling Libby. I know she's suffering and all I want to do is try to take away her pain, whatever the cause.

'Penny for them?' I finally give in.

Libby looks rueful. 'Not sure they're worth a penny. More of a huge student loan,' she says with a grim smile, staring down at her glass, swirling the pink liquid around, as if looking for answers.

'Is it to do with money then, I ask?' breaking the silence that has once again ensued.

'No, that was just my poor attempt at humour.'

I'm about to say, 'You get that from your father', in my own attempt at humour, but I stop myself. 'Your studies, then?'

'Nope, it's all good – I'm still enjoying my course.' She pauses, obviously trying to work out what to say next. 'Um… maybe I've been enjoying one module more than the others…,' she says cryptically, unable to meet my gaze.

I can feel my eyebrows knit together as I try and decipher the meaning of Libby's words. Then the penny drops. 'Oh. I see. At least I think I do,' I tell her.

Chapter 39

Doctor Love

'Oh, Mum, I've been such an idiot,' Libby says, finally meeting my eyes. 'I'm sorry. You didn't raise me to be so stupid.'

'Don't you dare say sorry!' I tell her, getting up from the armchair and seating myself next to her on the sofa. 'Do you want to talk about it?' I ask, putting my arm around her.

'Honestly? I'd rather chew my own arm off, but I think I need to.' She takes a big swig of wine before continuing. 'I suppose it started at the end of my first year when I was looking at the modules for this year. I'd seen Professor Lewins around campus, but I'd never really spoken to him. Or really looked at him, I s'pose. Then I had a meeting with him in his office and – boom – it hit me like a ton of bricks. I'm pretty sure I went the colour of beetroot. He probably thought I was a right dork.'

I can't help chuckling. 'I'm sure he didn't.'

'Well, anyway, I thought it was just a stupid crush and would go away, but... well, apparently he didn't think I was a right dork after all, and it didn't go away. It just grew. Honestly, Mum, I've never felt like this before – it was like static in the air every time he was close. And when our eyes met... shit... it was electric. God, this sounds so cheesy. I am such a dick,'

Libby groans.

'You're not a dick. Well, probably not. Can I reserve judgment until I've heard the whole story?' I smile at her.

'I'd take my word for it if I were you,' she says wryly. 'Well, you can work out what happened next. I started to find excuses to go and see him in his office, and then one day I passed an essay over to him and as he reached out to take it, our hands touched, and neither of us let go. It was weird. Time kind of stood still and then he just looked me and I melted. I'm sure you don't want the gory details. Suffice to say, he's married and I'm a dick. And I love him. And I'm a dick.' Silent tears are now running down her face, and my heart is breaking for my precious girl.

'Oh, my poor Libby,' I say, wrapping her in a tight hug. 'You're not a dick, my love. Well, maybe a tiny bit of one,' I say with a small smile, sitting back and pushing her hair away from her face.

She can't help laughing, in spite of herself. I take her face in my hands. 'You're only human, my darling girl. You're not the first woman to fall for the wrong man, and you sure as hell won't be the last. So, has he ended it?' I'm kind of assuming that's why she's so upset.

'No. I did.' The tears flow once more.

'But you still love him?'

'Yes. He didn't want us to stop seeing each other, but I couldn't handle being the other woman any longer. And I know men don't leave their wives for their girlfriends – especially ones that are twenty years younger and their students. I'm not that naïve.'

Unlike your mother, I think. 'That can't have been easy. I'm very proud of you for having that strength.'

'Thanks, Mum. It's such a relief to talk to you. I was worried you'd be disappointed in me.'

'I am disappointed, Libby, but I'm disappointed *for* you, not of you. I'm sad you've had to go through something so painful. And on your own too. But I'm glad you're able to talk to me now.'

'I just feel like an idiot. You'd never have done something that stupid. And you brought me up better than that.'

'Oh, Libby, I have done much more stupid things than have a fling with a university lecturer. Trust me, I'm in no position to judge you. We can't help who we fall for, but we can choose how we deal with the consequences, and you've shown enormous courage and strength of character in how you've handled this. Not many people your age would have handled the situation this well.'

'It just hurts like hell. I love him so much. And he never promised me anything – he never said he'd leave his wife for me. And I never asked him to. I just couldn't resist him, Mum. And he couldn't resist me.'

You made me so many promises, Marty. 'Well, I'm glad you're home now. And I'm glad you told me. Hopefully the next few weeks will help a bit. I know it's a cliché, but time does heal. And I'm here for you, whenever you need to talk or cry, or watch *Bridget Jones's Diary* and eat chocolates.'

Libby smiles. 'Thanks, Mum. Thanks for understanding. I love you so much.'

'I'll always understand. And I'll always love you. You do know you'll always be my baby, don't you? You are my favourite child.'

'And your least favourite!' Libby says with a laugh.

'Yep, and the one in between!' I finish.

'I think I'm going to have an early night, Mum, if that's alright with you. I feel absolutely wrecked one way and another.'

'Yes, of course. Your room's all ready. Just shout if you need anything.'

'I just need to sleep. For about a week.'

'Okay, I'll wake you up in time for Christmas,' I tell her.

'Night, Mum.'

'Goodnight, Libby. Sleep tight.'

I listen as Libby climbs the stairs, waiting until she's out of earshot before I start to cry. I can't bear to see my only child in so much pain, and to be unable to do anything to take that pain away. I know only too well what she's going through and how much it hurts. It's not what I wanted for her. Like mother, like daughter, though. An affair with a married man. But she's handled it so much better than I did. If only I'd had the same strength... but no, that's not a road I want to go down, and I mentally put the 'road ahead closed' signs back up.

I'm grateful Libby didn't pick up on my comment about my having done 'more stupid things'. If she'd asked, would I have been able to tell her about you, Marty? There'd be no getting those worms back in the can. I don't suppose for a minute she'd have judged me, any more than I judged her, but I still couldn't bear the thought of her knowing the half of it. I'm not ready to run the risk of her thinking less of me. Maybe that's hypocritical, but so be it. I'm just not ready for the questions that would inevitably arise. I'm not sure I could tell the whole truth.

Chapter 40

Walk the Dinosaur

I sleep fitfully after Libby's revelation, worrying about her and inevitably thinking about you, Marty. I'm still dozing when I hear Libby get up and go downstairs. I'm surprised she's up at this time, but she did go to bed very early. Hopefully it means she's slept well.

I'm still resisting the start of the day when Libby comes into my room carrying two mugs of tea. She walks round the bed and puts one on my bedside table, before going back to the empty side, putting her mug down and clambering under the duvet beside me.

'Morning, Mums,' she says brightly.

'Good morning. This is a treat. Thank you,' I say, shuffling myself and my pillows up. 'How are you feeling?'

'Not too bad, all things considered. I slept really well. I think being at home was just what I needed. Some distance,' she says thoughtfully.

'Good. That's good. What do you want to do today?'

'Ooh, I don't know. Anything you need to do?'

'I need to do some serious Christmas shopping if you're up for it?'

'You just want someone to carry the bags,' she jokes.

'And? Your point?' I love these easy exchanges with my daughter. Sometimes, just sometimes, it reminds me of how we were together, easily batting remarks back and forth, always on the same wavelength.

'Where shall we go? Canterbury? Can you face the hordes?' Libby asks.

'Sure. We can use the park and ride. Let's make a day of it – hot chocolate in the Christmas market, lunch somewhere nice and stay to see the Christmas lights.'

'Sounds perfect,' Libby agrees.

'Do you need to get something for Dad?'

'Yep. Wine and socks probably!'

'I'm sure we can do better than that.'

'Wine, socks and hankies?'

I laugh, relieved to see Libby in such good spirits. They probably won't last but, for now, all is well and I'm looking forward to our day together.

We arrive in Canterbury at about ten thirty. The park and ride car park is already almost full, and the double decker bus is packed with shoppers. It's only a five-minute ride to the city centre and soon we're in the Christmas market, queuing for hot chocolate. We wander around the stalls, blowing on our drinks and admiring the assortment of crafts and gifts. One particular stall catches my eye. It's selling handmade felted tree decorations like the ones I always put on my tree, and I can't resist having a proper look. I usually buy one or two new ones each year, and one in particular has caught my eye.

It's a giraffe. It's a beautifully made giraffe complete with a Santa hat and a scarf wrapped around its long neck. I can't help smiling at it and, of course, thinking of you. Once upon a time, you would have bought this for me had you seen it. I have to have it, despite the fact it will probably look ridiculous amongst the assortment of woodland creatures currently inhabiting the tree.

'Can you hold my cup a minute, Libby? I'm going to get a couple of these.'

'Sure. Which ones?'

'Um... the giraffe... and you choose one.'

'The giraffe? Are you sure? It won't go with your others,' Libby advises, pulling a have-you-gone-mad face.

'I know. I just really like it. Which other one shall we get?'

'Well, if we're going off-piste, it has to be the T-Rex,' she says, pointing to the dark green dinosaur, also donning a Santa hat, and with a parcel wedged between his tiny arms.

'T-Rex it is, then,' I agree, picking up both ornaments and handing them to the stallholder with a smile.

Libby hands me back my cup and links arms with me as we walk on. I'm still thinking about you. And the giraffe. Canterbury always brings you that much closer. Should I explain the giraffe thing to Libby? No, not today, not yet. But maybe... one day.

The rest of the morning passes easily and, by the time lunchtime arrives, we've accumulated quite a few bags between us.

'Well, we've definitely earned lunch,' I remark to Libby. 'What do you fancy?'

'Do you know what I *really* fancy?'

'I'm afraid to ask.'

'Burgers from Five Guys. Could you stand it?'

'Yes, of course. For you, anything, you should know that by now.'

'Yeah, I do! Still don't want to take it for granted though.'

'God, how did you get to be so mature and well-balanced, young lady? I'm quite sure I was still taking Granny completely for granted at your age.'

'Well, just goes to show you did a better job of bringing me up, doesn't it?'

I make a sort of strangled raspberry noise and grimace at her. 'I guess I must have done something right with you. Dad has to take some credit though,' I say, holding my thumb and forefinger up in front of my eyes with the tiniest of gaps between them.

Libby laughs. 'Joint effort. You both get to share the credit. Or blame. Depending on the day. And what mess I've got myself into.' She looks serious for a moment. I hope she's not going to cry. She doesn't, snapping herself out of the moment, taking my arm again and pulling me in the direction of her favourite burger joint.

'Had to pick the most expensive burger restaurant in the WORLD, didn't you,' I pretend to grumble. 'Whatever happened to the days of a Happy Meal for one ninety-nine, including a toy?'

'Sad times, eh, Mums? I might've got a Christmas T-Rex.'

We walk on laughing and thoughts of you fade once more.

Arriving at Five Guys a few minutes later, we push open the doors to find the place heaving. We look at each other and shrug: we need to eat and everywhere's probably going to be just as busy on a Saturday just before Christmas. We join the queue and prepare for a long wait.

'Keep your eyes open for a table coming free,' I tell Libby. 'Grab one if you can and I'll stay in the queue.'

'Okey dokey. Can you get me a cheeseburger, little fries and a vanilla and chocolate shake please?'

'Yep. What extras do you want on your burger?'

'Um… lettuce, tomato, mayo and ketchup I think.'

'Can't tempt you to bacon in your shake?' I ask, keeping my face as straight as possible.

'Ugh! No! Never again,' Libby says, pretending to vomit.

'Do you mean to say you've actually tried it? Did you lose a dare or something?'

'Ha! No, I actually dared Dad to try it last time he brought me here. Vanilla and bacon. Of course, he made me try it. It was kind of okay – just a regular vanilla shake, until you sucked a crunchy, salty bit of bacon up the straw.'

'Mm. sounds delightful. Did you make Dad drink it all? I bet you did!'

'Naturally!' Libby shrugs.

'Poor Dad.'

Libby suddenly darts off. 'Table!' she cries in explanation, leaving me alone in the queue. I work out what I want from the menu above the counter and then wait patiently, trying to remember it all. It's hard when thoughts of Libby and her dad and you are all vying for my attention.

Eventually, I collect our order and head to the table Libby managed to secure.

'Yum,' she says, opening the bag and sorting out its contents between us.

'I'm sharing your fries,' I tell her.

'What did you get?'

'Same as you, actually. Well, almost. Same burger, but my shake's vanilla and coffee. No bacon.'

'Chicken.'

'Nope. No chicken either,' I say as I unwrap my burger and take a bite. 'Oh, that's so good. What a brilliant idea of mine to come here.'

'Er… excuse me! This was my idea,' Libby pretends to look put out.

'Yeah, yeah,' is all I can say as I take another bite of the amazing burger.

We're both quiet for a while as we tuck into our food. I'm only forced to speak when Libby starts to dip the remaining fries in her milkshake.

'Good god, what are you doing?' I pull a face to express my distaste.

'What?! Don't knock it 'til you've tried it,' she throws back.

I immediately pick up a chip and dunk it in her shake, popping it into my mouth before I can chicken out. It's revolting.

'Mm, yum…' I say, pulling a face that says the opposite. 'That is truly disgusting. Although it reminds me of something…'

'I know, right! I still haven't worked out what that is.'

'I think I can live without finding out,' I tell her, taking a good glug of my own drink to take the taste away. I watch as my beautiful daughter continues to eat fries dipped in shake.

'I love you, Libby Grace,' I announce out of the blue.

Libby pulls a face that suggests I've lost it. 'Love you too, Mums. You feeling okay?'

'Never better,' I tell her, smiling. And I do love her. So very much. More than I've ever loved anyone. More than I loved you, Marty? Yes, maybe. This girl, this daughter of mine, is everything to me. You would have loved her too. And she would have loved you.

We hit the shops with renewed vigour again after lunch, and have soon ticked off pretty much everything from our lists. It's starting to get dark and we take a slow stroll back down the High Street towards the park and ride bus stop outside Fenwick, enjoying the orange and white Christmas lights along the way.

'Ooh!' I say, giving Libby a nudge as we're about to pass Abode. 'Do you fancy a quick cocktail before we go home?'

'Sure,' she replies, with a shrug.

We head inside the hotel and turn right into the bar, delighted to find it not too busy and a free table for two by the window. Dumping bags and shrugging off our coats, we check out the cocktail menu.

'Espresso Martini for me,' Libby says.

'Good choice. I think I'll try an Amaretto Sour. And hope you can't taste the egg white.'

Soon we're sipping our drinks and enjoying the relaxed ambience of the place.

'It's really nice here, Mum,' Libby says, looking around.

'It's lovely, isn't it? The food is amazing, too. Wonderful place for a special occasion. Maybe we can come for your birthday?'

'Definitely. Just us, though. Not with the whole family. Granny and Auntie Laura would ruin it by complaining – even if everything was perfect – and, as much as I love Grandad, it's bloody hard work smiling sweetly and not rising to some of his less tactful remarks.' Libby rolls her eyes and pretends she's throttling someone. My father, presumably.

I can't help laughing. 'Just us sounds perfect.' It's the first time Libby's said anything like that about the more difficult members of the family. She's always been incredibly sweet and tolerant: a peacekeeper, like me. 'I have to say, you do a very good job of keeping Grandad under control when you're around, and we're all very grateful.' I raise my glass in a toast and Libby clinks hers against it.

'What are we toasting to?' she asks.

'Hmm... to... you, my beautiful girl, and to the mending of broken hearts. May they come back even stronger!'

Libby groans. 'No, not to me. To you, the best mum I ever had!' She grins.

'Cheeky! How about, to a peaceful Christmas and a New Year full of good health and happiness?'

'And cocktails!' Libby adds. 'You do realise there's bugger all chance of a peaceful Christmas with Granny and Auntie Laura in the same place, though, don't you? Just saying.'

My turn to groan. 'I know. Just got to get through it. And all without the aid of a safety net.'

It's been the perfect end to a delightful day. We finish our drinks, load ourselves back up and head out once more, calling thank you to the barman as we go. And it's a tired, but happy, pair who arrive home some forty or so minutes later.

Chapter 41

One Day

That evening, Libby and I change into pyjamas and plan a girlie night in. Neither of us is very hungry after our enormous burgers, so I round up a selection of snacks and mix generous gins before we settle ourselves on the sofa. I've left the choice of film up to Libby. My money's on *Dirty Dancing* which is her all-time favourite. And secretly mine, too.

'So, what are we watching? Mr. Swayze's biceps?' I ask, wriggling myself down into the sofa cushions.

'Nope. Been meaning to watch this one for absolutely ages – I know you loved the book. We are watching *One Day*,' Libby replies, hitting play on the remote control.

'Oh lordy, hope you've got tissues at the ready then. I cried reading the book.'

'Yep. I know. Me too,' Libby admits, placing a newly opened box of tissues between us.

I can't help chuckling, but I really don't know if this is a good idea. This is a story that somehow always reminded me of you, and of us. And with Libby's fragile emotional state... I sigh. 'Well, if you're sure? Don't say I didn't warn you.'

Just under two hours later, we are a pair of snotty messes, having blubbed our way through the film and used most of the box of tissues which now lie in a heap on the floor. I feel absolutely drained.

'I needed that,' Libby says. 'I needed a good cry.' She actually sounds as though she feels better for it.

'That's one expression I could never get my head around – "a good cry". Complete oxymoron if you ask me. All I end up with is a rotten headache. Not to mention the puffy eyes and face like a blotchy frog.'

Libby laughs. 'No! It's cathartic – it's a release. All that pent-up emotion. Better out than in.'

'Hmm. We'll have to agree to disagree on that point, I think. Probably shouldn't have been drinking gin either – mother's ruin. It's certainly ruined me. Between that and the film, I feel shattered.'

Libby reaches her arms around me in a hug. 'Aw! I'm sorry, Mums. You can choose the next film.'

'Great, thanks. Can we just watch something full-on action then, please? Zero emotions, thank you very much.'

'Ha! Okay, or we could have the best of both worlds… a Christmas action film…'

'Don't start, my girl. *Die Hard* is NOT a Christmas film. I don't care what your father says.'

Libby laughs. 'I do love to wind him up with that every year. But I'm with you. Just because it's set at Christmas, does *not* make it a Christmas movie.' Libby nods solemnly.

'Amen to that. Right, I need a glass of water before I do anything else. Want anything?' I ask, pushing myself up from the sofa, and consciously trying not to make that old person noise as I do so.

Libby asks for water too. I leave her in charge of selecting a film and head to the kitchen. I don't know how long I stand there at the sink. I know I drifted off to thoughts of you and, eventually, Libby calling me from the lounge broke through my subconscious.

'Thought you'd got lost,' she says as I hand her a glass of water moments later.

'Sorry. Drifted off,' I explain.

'Where to? Anywhere nice?'

'What? Oh. No. Not really. More someone than somewhere.' I realise what I've said. Too late. Libby's jumped on it.

'Ooh! And who might this someone be? Have you met someone, Mum? Are you seeing someone? Spill!'

'What? No, no. Just someone I knew a long time ago.' I hope she won't push for details.

'How long ago? Before Dad, obviously.'

'Yes, long before Dad. I was even younger than you are now.'

'Not your first husband?' Libby's still pushing for more.

'No, not Steve. Even before him.'

Libby looks puzzled. 'But wasn't Steve your first serious boyfriend?'

'Yes, yes, he was.' I hesitate. 'This was someone who was just a friend.'

'Well, he obviously meant a lot to you if you still think of him now. Are you still in touch? Ooh, can I find him on Facebook?'

I wish she'd stop pushing.

'Um… no… he's not on Facebook.'

'But everyone's on Facebook, Mum. Even Dad has an account. Although he doesn't really post anything.'

'No. He died, Libby.' I can feel tears threatening.

'Oh! I'm so sorry, Mum.' Libby places her hand over mine and gives it a squeeze. I can feel her eyes on my face, trying to read what's there.

'This person meant a lot to you, huh?' She always was perceptive. 'What was his name?'

'Martin. His name was Martin. Marty.' It's the first time I've ever spoken his name to Libby.

'Marty,' she echoes. 'You've never mentioned him before.'

It's a strange feeling, hearing your name come out of her mouth. I've kept you secret for so long.

'No, maybe not. I guess after he died, it was too painful to talk about him.'

'What happened to him? He can't have been very old.'

'No, he wasn't. He was in a car accident.'

'Jesus. How awful, for you, and for his family.'

His family. 'It was. But of course it was much worse for his family – his mum, and his wife and daughters. It was a terrible tragedy.'

'That's so sad. How many daughters did he have?'

'Two. Two daughters.' It's getting harder and harder to hold back the tears.

'Poor things, losing their dad like that. I can't imagine what my life would've been like without Dad. I know he can be a bit of a dick sometimes, but he's still my dad.'

'Yes, and he loves you very much, Libby. Never forget that.' I'm hoping that she'll stop asking about you now. No such luck.

'So, Marty... how did you know him then?'

'He was just a friend – we met at a party when I was fourteen. He was friends with Auntie Laura's boyfriend at the time. We used to hang out – until he went off to university and I met Steve.' There, that should satisfy her.

'Didn't you keep in touch after he went to uni?'

'I suppose we exchanged a few letters… but Steve was the jealous type, so…' Closing the door on the conversation, I hoped.

But she's like a dog with a bone. 'But he obviously meant a lot to you. Did you ever see him again after that?'

Why won't she stop? 'Um… I guess, a few times, over the years…'

'It's strange you never mentioned him before. Like you kept him secret or something.'

'Well, after he died, I suppose there was no reason to speak about him.' I shrug, trying to shake her off.

'I s'pose. So, Auntie Laura knew him too?'

'Well, yes, a bit, not very well.' The last thing I need is you asking Laura about Marty. She's the one person, apart from Anna of course, who knew the truth about my relationship with you, Marty. The abridged version at least. 'It's ancient history, anyway. He just popped into my head for some reason this evening. Right, what film are we watching next?' Please, please, please, let it go, Libby.

She shrugs, and I know she's going to drop the subject. For now, at least.

She grins at me and presses play. The opening credits for *Die Hard* hit the screen.

Chapter 42

Human

I wake the next morning, Sunday, feeling a little muzzy-headed. Too much alcohol and not enough water. I lie in bed staring at nothing, trying to summon up the energy to get up and make a cup of tea. We'd gone to bed at about midnight, after sharing the tightest of hugs.

'Thank you for a lovely day,' Libby had said, kissing me on the cheek.

'Oh, you're welcome, it was my pleasure. It has been lovely, hasn't it?'

'Really lovely. And I've hardly thought about you-know-who, which is a bonus.'

I pull a face that says I-don't-know-what-you're-talking-about, and flip my hands out, palms up. 'It's okay, you can think about Father Christmas. I'm reliably informed you're still on his nice list.' I wink at her.

Libby harrumphs. 'I doubt that very much after having a very naughty affair with my married tutor!'

'That doesn't make you a bad person, Libby. It makes you human, like the rest of us. With all our faults and frailties. We're none of us perfect.' I can't help thinking about Nigel and his six-year affair. He's the perfect example of a good and decent man who just wanted some love and affection in his life, but people would be shocked if they found out. He's the last person you would expect to have an affair. What do they say? It's always the quiet ones? I wonder for a second about confiding in Libby about Nigel and Laura's marriage, but decide against it. The last thing she needs is any more emotional baggage to lug around, and I know she would feel sad, especially for her cousin, Richard.

Finally, dehydration wins and I drag my tired body out of bed and head downstairs, stretching and yawning as I go. I pop my head in on Libby as I pass her room, and find her sleeping soundly, her long brown hair spread out across her pillow. I smile to myself and hope she's dreaming happy dreams.

Armed with a cup of tea, I head for the lounge, opening the curtains before I curl up in my favourite armchair. Again, my body quickly reminds me I can't sit like that anymore and I grumble some rude words as I straighten out my legs, pulling the footrest closer. More and more I'm aware of the aging process, and it scares me. More than anything, I hate the idea of facing old age on my own. I don't want to be a burden to Libby – I want her to go off and have a wonderful life.

As an afterthought, I get up and switch the Christmas tree lights on. There's a squirrel on the top, and an abundance of foxes, mice, owls and other woodland critters adorning its branches. And then, front and centre, where Libby hung them last night, are the giraffe and the Tyrannosaurus Rex. I can't help chuckling at the sight of them. They should look totally out of place, but somehow they fit right in. I give the giraffe a little nudge. 'This one's for you, Marty.'

I know there are no guarantees in life, I think to myself

as I sit back down, but I'm pretty sure we'd have been happy together, Marty. Wouldn't we? We'll never know now. Maybe it wouldn't have worked though? Maybe it was the illicit unavailability that made our love so intense, so all-consuming. What if the reality couldn't match up to the fantasy, and the thrill of the chase was actually what made it so appealing? Always wanting what you can't have, and then not actually wanting it when you get it. Would you have ended up resenting me for missing out on seeing your daughter every day? Would the guilt of taking you away from her have eaten away at me? I sigh. This is pointless speculation.

I push you to the back of my mind again, and try to focus on the day ahead and on what I need to get done. I must admit, I'm feeling quite weary, and would quite happily have a day of pottering at home. I will just have to wait and see what Libby's plans are when she wakes up. If she wants to go out, I will rally these old bones, I think with a sigh.

It's not long before I hear the creak of Libby moving around upstairs. A couple of minutes later, I hear her jogging down the stairs. She comes to find me.

'Morning, Mums.' She flops down on to the sofa.

Good morning. How's you? Sleep okay?'

'Yep. Like the dead. It's so quiet here compared to the shared house at uni.'

'Good. Didn't think you'd be up for a while yet.' It's about nine fifteen by my reckoning.

'Phone woke me. Well, text, actually.' She stretches her arms and upper body.

'Oh?' I hope it wasn't the tutor, and he at least had the decency to honour her decision and leave her alone.

'Mm. Richard – wants to know if I'm free for a catch up today. Bit odd, really, but…' she shrugs.

'That's nice though,' I say, while thinking it is definitely a bit odd. Although the two cousins have always been close, and firm friends, it's still unusual for him to ask to meet up just the two of them. 'Maybe he wants help choosing presents for his mum and dad. I can certainly recommend your Christmas shopping companion skills. Excellent bag carrying. Ten out of ten, would use again.'

Libby laughs. 'Yeah, maybe. Anyway, can I borrow the car? As long as you haven't got plans, that is? I said I'd pick him up about eleven.'

'Yes, of course. I'm looking forward to a day of pottering here. Maybe write a few cards, wrap some presents.'

'Great. Right, I'm making coffee before I do anything else. Want one?'

'Yes, please. Feeling decidedly lacklustre this morning,' I say, silently wishing someone could plug me in and turn my lights on.

'Can't shop like you used to, eh?' Libby sympathises.

'Nope. I literally do drop now. And need a day off to recover. Getting older is no joke, young lady. I'll soon be needing one of those old people chairs that tips you up.'

'Fight it, Mums. Age is only a number.'

'Easy for you to say. My number is getting decidedly large.'

'Rubbish. You could live another fifty years. Look at Great Granny – she was ninety-nine.'

The prospect of another fifty years, with mind and body deteriorating at a rate of knots makes my heart sink. 'Well, when you have to put me in a home, please don't put me in the same one as Auntie Laura, will you? Although she might have mellowed by then, I suppose.'

'Deal. Right. Coffee.' Libby leaves the room, and me to my thoughts. They're not happy ones. Everything at the moment makes me feel old and sad and lonely. So very lonely. I put my now empty mug on the table and massage my temples before running my fingers through my hair. I think idly about getting it cut shorter in the new year. And getting rid of my jeans, especially the skinny ones. And buying more sensible skirts. Isn't that what women my age do?

'Not gonna happen,' I mutter, as Libby comes back in bearing two steaming mugs of coffee.

'What are you mumbling about?' she asks as she hands me one of them.

'What? Oh! Nothing. Just turning into a mad old woman. Take no notice,' I reply, shaking my head.

'You're not mad and you're not old. Well… maybe a bit mad,' she winks. 'But that's wholly un-age-related. That's just your genes.'

'Don't mention jeans,' I grumble.

Libby looks puzzled.

'The denim variety,' I clarify. 'I was just thinking maybe it's time to ditch them and start to grow old gracefully.'

'Frumpily, more like,' Libby harrumphs. 'You still look great in your jeans. And there is no law that says you have to turn into Granny.'

'Bless you, my child,' I say, blowing her a kiss. 'That is just what I needed to hear this morning. I will carry on tucking my perimenopausal muffin-top into my skinny jeans for a bit longer.'

Libby laughs. 'Honestly, Mum, I don't know what you're worried about. You look great. No way do you look fifty.'

'That means a lot – thank you. I will put off the elasticated waistbands and the blue rinse a little longer.'

'You need to get back out on the dating scene. When's the last time you went on a date?'

'Ooh, I don't know… 1989?' I say, not wanting to admit to Libby or to myself how long it's been.

'Seriously, Mum, you should join a dating site or a Meetup group or something. I can help with your profile.'

I'm torn between being uncomfortable talking about my love-life (or lack thereof) with my daughter, and being thrilled our relationship has reached such maturity. My daughter is fast becoming my best friend.

'God! It all just sounds terrifying, Libby. Maybe in the New Year…?' I say, hoping that will satisfy her.

'I will be nagging you,' she says sternly.

'Lordy. Okay, I promise to give it some thought. I do need to make changes though – you're right. As usual, oh wise one.' The child has rather become the parent, or the equal at least. I'm so proud of this young woman. 'Anyway, enough of me, how are you feeling about things today?'

'It's strange, actually. I thought I'd be in bits over Robson, but I feel alright. It's really helped putting some distance between us. I feel sort of… empowered, I think. Making the decision to end it and taking back the control, you know?'

I marvel again at the strength and sense demonstrated by my daughter. 'Makes sense. I wish I'd had half your maturity when I was younger. In fact, I wish I did now,' I say, laughing. 'You, my dear daughter, have become the responsible adult in this relationship.'

'Hate to tell you this, Mum, I always have been,' she says solemnly.

'How very dare you?' I reply in mock indignation. 'Actually, though, you're not wrong. Do you remember the time you answered the phone to Grandad and asked if he wanted to speak to a responsible adult, because there was only me there?'

Libby laughs. 'Yes! Grandad failed to see the humour, as usual.'

'I honestly look at your grandparents sometimes and think I must have been adopted,' I say, shaking my head. 'I'm really not sure I have anything in common with either of them. Grandad's lack of a sense of humour being a prime example.'

'And Granny's fashion-sense. I know what you mean though. You're nothing like Auntie Laura, either. I definitely take after you, don't I? Looks-wise especially.'

'Yes, I think you do. Sorry about that,' I joke.

'Nothing to be sorry about. I'm actually very happy with the way I look.'

'Well, I will take that as a huge compliment, although I think you are better than me in every way. You're certainly more emotionally mature and grounded than I ever was. And you seem happy in your skin. I don't think I've ever really been completely happy with who I am. Maybe next year I need to learn self-acceptance?'

'You do. You should see yourself as others do, Mum – a kind, strong, beautiful woman who makes the world a better place just by being in it. Surely you know how much people love being around you? Jeez, all those boy-friends I had at school had massive crushes on you.'

'No! Don't be daft. They all flocked round you like bees to a honeypot.'

'Nope. You were most definitely the honeypot, Mum. Did you really not realise?' Libby laughs. 'Today you'd be called a MILF.'

'Well, I'm stunned. Probably just as well I didn't realise back then. Might've been tempted,' I say, winking at Libby.

'Ew! Honestly, though, Mum, you and Dad did a great job bringing me up, even if I do say so myself. I'm happy being me.'

'I'm glad.' I smile, hoping she doesn't pick up on the slight sadness in that smile. 'All I ever want is for you to be happy, Libby.' And all I ever want is for you to love and respect me. I worry the day will come when that might not be the case.

We sit quietly for a while, sipping our coffee.

'Right, I'm going to jump in the shower,' Libby eventually breaks the silence. 'Go and see what that cousin of mine wants.'

'Mm… curious. Hope he's okay.' I can't help a worrying thought intruding, knowing what I do about his parents. 'Will you be home for dinner?'

'Probably. I'll let you know if not. Need anything while I'm out and about?'

'I don't think so. Just go and enjoy yourself. And give Richard my love.'

'Will do.' She disappears off and I'm left alone with my thoughts again, which is not good. I shake them away and push my aching body up from the chair, muttering under my breath again. Picking up my two mugs I head to the kitchen and turn on some music, hoping the songs will replace the thoughts crowding into my head, like passengers in a packed tube station. Eventually, someone's going to fall onto the track.

Chapter 43

Christmas Rappin'

Libby texts to say she'll be home by six, so the only thing I have to do is plan something for dinner. The rest of the day is mine for the taking. I'm torn between lazing on the sofa watching rubbish on the television, or tackling the present wrapping. It's too close to call, so I compromise and set up a wrapping station on the dining table with my laptop showing the latest Scandi-noir series on iPlayer.

It takes all of thirty seconds to realise what a stupid idea that is. It's impossible to follow the subtitles and wrap presents at the same time. I then spend ages trying to find something else to watch, eventually settling on a fairly mindless comedy starring Rebel Wilson which shouldn't require too much effort to follow.

I actually quite enjoy gift-wrapping, and sadly do derive pleasure from neat folds and lines. When things are in regular-shaped boxes that is. Then there's the triangular, metal Toblerone tin. It's not even just a triangle, but has the corners sort of rounded off too. I give it my best shot. Nothing is pleasing about any of it. It's proving impossible to make it look good and there is a growing pile of wasted wrapping paper on the floor next to me. I've already sworn several times and am rapidly losing my patience. One last try. Maybe use a little less paper, might make the folds a bit easier. Oh my effing God.

'Sod it!' I discard yet another load of scrunched up paper in disgust, open the tin and begin eating the Toblerone. Problem solved. I will replace them with something more appropriately shaped.

The day passes quickly, with one mindless comedy after another, and a growing pile of wrapped presents on one side of the table, and of Toblerone wrappers on the other. *Just eating the evidence, eh, Lou?* I say to myself. By four o'clock the sky's grown dark and I get up and stretch before heading round the house to close curtains and switch on lights. I missed lunch altogether, unless you count the mountain of chocolates.

I'm feeling bad now I didn't shop for a roast dinner for Libby, but I know she won't mind. It'll be something bunged in the oven with chips probably. I've been wondering on and off all day what Richard wanted to see her about. I guess I'll find out soon enough.

Soon enough arrives at about five forty, when I hear Libby's key in the door, followed by a shouted, 'Hi, I'm home!' from the hall.

'Hello! I'm in the dining room,' I call out to her, quickly checking there are no secrets visible.

I look up as she comes in a few seconds later, still unwrapping a scarf from around her neck, her cheeks and nose rosy from the cold.

'Hi, Mums. Ooh, Toblerone,' she exclaims, helping herself to one from the accursed tin.

'Sorry, I've eaten all the white ones,' I confess, guiltily.

'Let me guess... someone's Christmas present, wrapping

nightmare. Give up and eat the evidence?' Libby says, laughing.

'You know me so well.'

Still laughing, she says, 'Well, it's what I would've done too.'

'Like mother like daughter, eh?'

'Yep! Dad, on the other hand, would just have stuffed the tin in a gift bag.'

'Probably very sensible. Gift bags always feel like a bit of a cop out though, like taking the easy way out. Apart from bottle bags, of course, they're perfectly acceptable.'

Libby reaches out and takes another chocolate.

'So, tell me about your day? What did Richard want to see you about? Tell me everything.'

Still munching on the chocolate, Libby sits back in her chair and pulls a face that says she has much to tell, and of a dramatic nature.

'Oh God, Mum. You're not going to believe it! But first, you have to promise not to say ANYTHING to ANYONE. Seriously, Richard asked me not to tell ANYONE.' She pauses. 'I'm sure he didn't mean you, though.' She shrugs. Another pause for dramatic effect. 'Sooo... ooh... not really sure how to say this...'

'Just spit it out! I'm dying here. Please tell me he hasn't got a girl pregnant?'

'God, no! Richard? Can you imagine? He's way too sensible.'

I thought that about his father too, I think to myself.

'No, it's about Auntie Laura and Uncle Nigel. Richard thinks they might be getting a divorce,' Libby says, watching for my reaction.

I pull what I hope is a suitably shocked face. 'No! Why would he think that?'

'Well,' Libby says, clearly rather enjoying her role as gossip-monger, 'Richard apparently heard Auntie Laura and Uncle Nigel "having words" as he put it. He said they're both rubbish at whispering and he picked up on something about not saying anything until after "his exams". Then, later that night he said it looked as though Auntie Laura had been crying. He asked her if she was alright and she brushed it off, but he said something's definitely up. He said his dad seems really stressed too and there's a strange atmosphere in the house.'

'Oh dear.' I'm weighing up in my mind whether or not to disclose what I know to Libby. 'Is Richard okay?'

'Yes, he's fine. You know Richard, he's very self-contained – takes things as they come and just gets on with it, doesn't he?'

'So he wasn't upset?'

'No, not really. We talked about what if they did get divorced and how that made him feel. But he was quite matter of fact about it. Pretty much said he'd be fine with it as long as both his parents were okay.'

'He always has been very mature. Very grounded.'

'I know, right? And he said he'd hate them to stay together for his sake.'

This is, of course, exactly what Nigel and Laura are planning to do. But, based on what Libby's just told me, maybe it's not the way to go. 'What did you advise Richard?'

'Well, I didn't really. Wasn't sure what to say, to be honest. I mean, obviously I told him about when you and Dad split up and what it was like for me, but you made sure it was all very amicable. I said I'd've hated it if you and Dad stayed together for me too. I think parents don't realise that actually their kids do want them to be happy. I told him I was here for him

– anytime he needed someone to talk to, stuff like that. But actual, constructive advice, I didn't know what to say.'

'No... difficult... I'm glad he felt able to confide in you though, Libby. It's important he has someone to talk to. I know he's a bit of a loner, and I don't suppose boys talk to their friends about this sort of stuff, do they?'

'No, probably not. I did force him into a hug when I dropped him off. It was like cuddling an ironing board.'

I laugh. 'Bless him, he's done all his growing vertically so far, hasn't he? Needs to fill out a bit now.'

'What do you think I should do?'

'Just be there for him; keep in touch – check in with him from time to time. I think that's all you can do.'

Libby looks thoughtful. 'Yeah, I guess so. What about Auntie Laura and Uncle Nigel?'

I decide in that instant to confide in Libby. 'Okay, my turn to tell you not to say anything to anyone,' I meet her gaze and try to convey the seriousness of my words with my eyes. 'Auntie Laura and Uncle Nigel are having problems and they have been talking about separating after Richard's through his 'A' levels.'

'Crap,' Libby interjects.

'Well, yes, it's sad. It's sad when any marriage breaks down.' I'm still wondering how much to tell her. A part of me wants to see how she reacts to the fact of an extramarital affair. I know she was sleeping with her tutor, but she herself was single at the time. I want to see if it changes how she sees Nigel, someone she's always liked and respected. I guess, ultimately, this is about me and you, Marty. I want to know if she'll think less of me. I'm having my own internal battle about whether to tell her or not. It's not really my secret to tell, but now that Richard has involved her… I'm torn. Am I being selfish if I use Nigel's situation for my own fact-gathering? I wonder. Libby is my daughter at the end of the day – isn't it my duty to protect her from things like this? I sigh and press my hands into my tired eyes.

I can feel Libby's eyes on me, reading me. She knows me too well.

'What aren't you telling me, Mum?' she asks.

'It's not really for me to say, love.'

'But if it affects Richard? I want to know. I'm old enough to understand.'

'I know you are, Libby. It's just… oh… God. Okay, there is more to it. Uncle Nigel came to see me not so long ago. Like Richard, he needed someone to talk to. It turns out he's been unhappy for quite some time and he'd reached the point where he really didn't want to stay married any longer.'

Libby shrugs, quite matter-of-factly. 'It happens. People fall out of love, marriages end. It's no-one's fault. Plus, Auntie Laura must be a nightmare to live with.' She pauses and looks up at me. 'Sorry, Mum, I know she's your sister, but…'

'No apology needed. You're right, she can be an absolute nightmare. To be honest, I don't know how Nigel's put up with her for this long. As much as I love my sister, I don't always like her.'

'So, what's the biggie? They should just tell Richard they don't love each other anymore and separate.'

'I wish it was that easy, Libby. Ending a marriage is never easy, especially where kids are involved. We parents are very good at the whole guilt thing, and we would rather suffer in silence than turn our kids' lives upside down. I never wanted you to come from a broken home. I wanted to break the cycle started by my parents.'

'I get that. But kids just need love and honesty. We pick up on the bad vibes and it's got to be better to have two happy parents living apart than living a lie all together?'

'You're absolutely right, Libby. But parents don't always get it right. We think our children need protecting from the truth. We make bad decisions. Wrong decisions. We're only human.'

'But they shouldn't stay together just for Richard. He doesn't want that.'

'No, I know. But it's going to be scary as hell for Auntie Laura to be on her own after all these years. Nigel's all she's known for most of her adult life.'

'Surely better to be on her own than with someone who doesn't want to be with her anymore? And, I daresay it won't be a picnic for Uncle Nigel either.'

'No, but he's got…' I realise what I'm about to say, and stop myself.

Nothing escapes my sharp girl though. 'He's got what?'

'Well… his job, for one thing. Laura's job has been taking care of Nigel, Richard and the house.'

'And? What else aren't you telling me?' She's determined to force the truth from me.

'Okay, Libby, but this goes no further than this room. Uncle Nigel has been seeing another woman.' There, it's out.

She raises her eyebrows but doesn't look particularly shocked. 'Oh! I see. Does Auntie Laura know?'

'No! And she mustn't find out. If anyone's going to tell her, it has to be Nigel.'

'Is he still seeing this other woman? Is it anyone we know?'

'Yes, he says he loves her. It's Karen, his secretary.'

'God, that's a bit of a cliché! I've met her though. She's nice. Always thought she was very devoted to Uncle Nigel in a spinster-of-the-parish sort of way. Has it been going on for long?'

'Six years. Almost.'

'Shit! The sly old dog!' Libby seems almost impressed.

'Libby! It's not something to be proud of.'

'No, I know, but blimey, Mum, life's too short to spend it with the wrong person. They should just rip the band aid off and get on with their lives.'

'Just stop for a moment and think about how that news would affect Laura? She would feel a total fool. Bad enough to know your husband doesn't love you anymore, but…'

Libby wrinkles her nose. 'I s'pose so. I just think it's sad that people aren't living their true lives. Auntie Laura would get over it in time. And she'd love all the drama that came with it.'

'I'm not so sure she would. You know how important appearances are to her.'

'Well, I still think they need to tell Richard and separate sooner rather than later.'

'I think you're probably right, and I will talk to Laura. Ultimately though, it's between her and Nigel. All we can do is be there to support them.'

Libby looks thoughtful. 'Imagine being in Karen's shoes… being in love with a man she can't have for all this time. That must have been awful. She must've been really lonely. Don't you think that's sad?'

Libby is venturing into forbidden territory and my heart skips a beat as I know only too well how awful, how sad and lonely it is to be the other woman. I put my hands to my mouth to conceal the deep breath I have to take to compose myself.

'Yes, I do. I think it must be terribly sad. And she must really love him to live what basically amounts to half a life.'

'I guess we really can't help who we fall in love with.'

'No, I guess we can't,' I agree.

'I think if you find someone you love you should do everything you can to be with them.'

'Do you? That's a very idealistic thing to say. It's not always that easy.' I'm loathe to bring up her own recent history as an example. I don't have to.

'I know what you're thinking. What about me with Professor Plum in the library with the candlestick? But that was different. I knew he didn't love me enough to give up what he already had to be with me. What we had wasn't... real. I mean it was real, the feelings were real – for me especially – but the reality was he wasn't going to leave his wife over a fling with one of his students. It could only ever be temporary. But it sounds as though what Uncle Nigel and Karen have IS real, and it's really sad if they can't be together. Besides, even Auntie Laura deserves the chance to find someone who really loves her and wants to be with her.'

'Goodness, how did you get to be so wise, young lady? I think you've got your head screwed on tighter than I have mine.'

'Maybe that's what I inherited from Dad? His everything's black and white attitude.'

I swallow and say, 'Yes, maybe.' Not like you and I, Marty, always lost in the grey, searching for one another. Time to change the subject. 'Right, cup of tea? And I need to find something for dinner.'

I get up from the dining table and head out of the room, squeezing Libby's shoulder and leaning over to kiss her head as I go. 'Love you.'

Chapter 44

Ice Cream Girl

Libby and I give the Scandi-noir another go after a gourmet supper of fish finger sandwiches. White bread, butter and ketchup, naturally. I push away any thoughts of failed parenthood as we both tuck in, enjoying every finger-licking morsel.

'Not exactly a Sunday roast. Sorry about that,' I say as I take Libby's empty plate.

'I am not complaining, trust me. Haven't had fish finger sarnies for ages, and you make the best ones.'

'Well, that's very kind of you to say so,' I reply, taking a bow. 'Ice cream?'

'Yes! Please. Tell me you have Dulce de Leche or Pralines and Cream?' Libby puts her hands together in prayer.

'Er… is the Pope Catholic? Of course I do. I have both. Which would you prefer?'

'I have to choose?' Libby says, pretending to look outraged.

I laugh, and head to the kitchen with the empty plates, returning a couple of minutes later with both tubs of ice cream wrapped in tea-towels and two spoons. I hold them both out to Libby. 'Pick one, then we'll swap at half time.'

The next couple of hours pass in quiet contentment, as we concentrate on both ice-cream and subtitles. After two episodes, Libby stretches and yawns.

'That's me done, I'm afraid, Mums. Gonna have a bath and do some reading in bed.'

'Okey dokey, lovely. Take some water up, won't you?'

'Yep. Night night. Love you!'

'Love you too. Night night, sleep tight.' Sleep tight. I've been saying this to her since she was a little girl. I'm not sure when I stopped saying 'Hope the bugs don't bite', as my mum had to me and Laura. I'm left wondering about it as Libby heads off upstairs. Is this what happens with family traditions and customs? They become diluted over time, until they become altered, something new, or abandoned altogether. I wonder what Libby will say to her children in the future? You flash into my head, unbidden, Marty. Are you just reminding me you'll never know what your daughters say to their future children? You haven't been able to impart family traditions to your girls. Has your absence changed them? I wonder. Have they grown into the same young women they would have been had you been present in their lives?

Suddenly, I'm overcome with tiredness and melancholy. Putting you back in your box, I pick up my phone and text Laura.

Hey, Sis. How are you doing? Hanging in there I hope? X

I know I probably won't have to wait long for a reply, and I just sit and let my mind drift. It doesn't get far.

Hello, Lou. Honestly, I don't know how I feel. Angry, sad, scared, relieved. Take your pick. X

Understandable. I think you're entitled to be all of those things! Let's meet up for coffee and a chat. Sending hugs. Xx

OK, I'll check my diary and get back to you. X

She doesn't ask how I am, but that's okay. As far as my family's concerned, I'm always okay. Because that's the persona I present to them. That's my gift to them: Lou's okay, so that's one less thing to worry about. It's just easier for everyone that way. Besides, I don't want to invite the inevitable questions that will arise if I let them see how sad I am a lot of the time. They don't need to know I'm held together by string and Sellotape, like a badly wrapped tin of Toblerone.

I can feel myself sinking lower into this mood. I know I can't allow myself to drop deeper. I recognise the pattern. It's not a pretty symmetrical one, but a page of black scribbles made by someone holding a thick black crayon far too tightly, and pressing hard into the paper as they drag the black stick back and forth. They're probably a patient in a psychiatric hospital. It's the drawing equivalent of a scream, but with none of Munch's obviousness.

Forcing myself up, I pick up the two now-empty ice cream tubs and head to the kitchen to clear up. Action is required to snap this thought-chain, accompanied, as ever, by mood-altering music. Well, it's either that or drugs, I think wryly.

I take my time clearing up, singing along to Heart 80s. Very hard to think and sing at the same time in my experience.

'Kyrie eleison, down the road that I must travel/Kyrie eleison, through the darkness of the night/Kyrie eleison, where I'm going, will you follow? Kyrie eleison, on a highway in the light...' I bellow out, completely forgetting I'm not on my own in the house.

I'm standing at the sink, with my back to the room, as the next chorus comes on, and I realise another voice has joined in, just before I feel Libby's arms go around my waist. We stand like that, both belting out the rest of the song, with a few la-la-las where lyrics escape us. The song finishes and we both laugh.

'Love that song,' Libby says.

'Me too. I'm always surprised you know the lyrics to so many songs from the eighties.'

'Well, you played them constantly when I was growing up, so…' Libby shrugs. 'Some of my earliest memories are associated with music from your yoof, Mum.'

She sits down at the kitchen table. She's pink from the bath and wearing pyjamas and dressing gown. Fluffy slippers complete the ensemble and she looks so young, her face free of any make-up and her long hair scrunched up in a messy bun. I dry my hands and sit at the table with her.

'So, how are you feeling about everything?'

'I'm not going to lie, Mum, I miss him. And I absolutely hate the thought of never being with him again. It's not going to be easy getting through the rest of his module.'

'Could you switch to something else? Or is it too late?'

'I probably could… but… not without having a good reason, I s'pose. Can hardly tell the truth, can I? Besides, I really love his course. And it's going to be key to what I do next – I think I'll probably do my dissertation on it. I just have to grit my teeth and get on with it.'

I marvel again at my daughter's stoic acceptance of the situation. I'm not sure I'd be handling the situation half as well as she seems to be. 'What is the course on?' I haven't wanted to delve too deeply into Professor Lewins before now.

'Genes and behaviour. You know, nature versus nurture stuff. It's really interesting. Next semester we'll be looking at ourselves – everything from inherited physical characteristics to whether as babies we're like blank slates to be written on by upbringing and experience, or if genetics make us a certain way.'

'Oh, okay, yes, that is an interesting field.' I know how inadequate my answer is.

'I'll apologise now – I'll probably have to ask you and Dad loads of questions.'

'Um, yes, of course. You know we'll both give you all the help we can.'

'Thanks, Mums. Right, I'm going back upstairs. Fascinating article on Nativism to get through. Could you keep your caterwauling down to a dull roar?' She grins at me and gets up, blowing a kiss as she goes.

'Rude!' I call after her as she goes, and immediately joining in with the Go West song that's playing:

'Don't look dooooooooowwwwwwnnnnnnn, girl…' I wail, turning the lyric into a howl.

I can just make out Libby's laughter as she walks up the stairs. I stop singing and put my face in my hands, trying to block out the black dog who's just appeared in the corner of the room. If I refuse to acknowledge him, maybe he'll go away.

A beep from my mobile alerts me to a text message, and I eagerly seize the distraction. I expect it's from Laura. It is.

I can do any lunchtime except Wednesday this week, and Monday or Tuesday evenings. Let me know what suits. X

I'm fully aware I need to speak to Laura sooner rather than later, and I'm keen to get a difficult conversation out of the way.

Shall we do tomorrow lunchtime? Hospital at half twelve? X

OK, see you then. X

See you then, Night night. X. I add two more words as a sort of afterthought: *Sleep tight.*

I feel as though a great weight is resting on me as I drag myself up to bed a short while later, and I can feel the black dog plodding up the stairs behind me. He takes up his position in the corner of my bedroom. I can feel his eyes on me, watching, waiting, wondering if it's time to clamber up onto the bed and sit on my chest. I get changed for bed and clean my teeth, checking in on Libby who's fallen asleep with a book open on her tummy. I tiptoe into her room, remove the book and turn out the bedside lamp. Touching my fingers to my lips, I transfer a kiss to her head. 'Sleep tight.'

Back in my room, I sit on the side of the bed. I sit like that for a while, just staring into space. Wondering. Is today the day? I slide open the drawer of my bedside cabinet and look at the box of medication sitting there, sticking out under a packet of dental harps. I apply pressure above my eyes, trying to ease the ache behind them. 'No,' I say quietly, pushing the drawer shut. Climbing under the covers, I reach for the Peter Robinson thriller I'm about halfway through and try to escape into its pages. After a few pages of nice straightforward murder, my eyes grow heavy and I put the book to one side, turn out the lamp and welcome sleep.

Chapter 45

Honest

The next morning, I leave Libby sleeping and head to work. I've left her a note on the kitchen table: 'Have a good day, whatever you decide to do. Seeing Auntie Laura at lunchtime. Be home about five forty. Mum xx'. She had mentioned trying to catch up with an old school friend, and she's more than capable of entertaining herself anyway. One more week of work, then two lovely complaint-free weeks off. I can't wait. Although I am slightly concerned about the direction my mental state is going in, and all that time to think might actually be dangerous. I'll just have to keep busy.

It hasn't escaped me today is December sixteenth, either – the date you said you'd always be in our chapel, hoping I'd show up. It's a key date for me still, and one that is never without pain and remembrance. Thankfully, the morning at work is relatively uneventful and I conclude people are too busy running round getting ready for Christmas to write complaint letters about the NHS. I can't help but chuckle at one particularly seasonal complaint I've received about a doctor whose hands were too cold. Apparently it was "like being examined by Frosty the Snowman". I'm longing to write back along the lines of asking Santa to bring the doctor in question some woolly mittens. Lunchtime comes around pretty quickly, and I head out to meet Laura in reception.

She walks in through the double doors just as I arrive, and we exchange hellos and a brief hug. She looks pale and tired.

'Right, let's go and brave the canteen. I've heard good things about the chilli.' When I say good things, really I mean no-one's sent a complaint letter about it, and no-one's died. Yet.

Laura smiles weakly and we set off down the long corridor.

Five minutes later we're settled at a corner table with plates of chilli and rice and glasses of water. I tentatively try a mouthful.

'It's edible,' I tell Laura. She probably doesn't realise this is high praise indeed. She also doesn't look as though she feels like eating it, edible or not, and proceeds to push the food around with her fork.

'So, what's happening at home?' I ask gently.

Laura sighs. 'It's awful. Trying to pretend nothing's wrong. Nigel feels like a stranger to me. Honestly, Lou, I don't know if I can keep up the pretence until after Richard's exams. I feel like I'm either going to burst into tears or scream at any moment.'

'It can't be easy.'

'It's like lying in bed with a stranger. We sleep on the far sides of the mattress, turned away from each other. I can hardly sleep for worrying I'll roll over onto his side and accidentally touch him. Knowing he doesn't love me...' Laura looks as though she's going to cry, but she somehow manages to hold it together.

'Well, there is a reason I wanted to see you, actually, other than just to see how you're coping.'

Laura stops the food-pushing and looks at me expectantly. There is so much pain and sorrow in her eyes. It almost reduces me to tears.

'Okay, before I start, you must know I was told this in confidence and I'm only sharing it with you because I think it's important for you, Nigel and Richard as a family. Important for what you do next.'

'Okay.' Laura scrunches up her eyes in confusion.

'Libby met up with Richard yesterday – at his instigation.' I pause, weighing up my words. 'I'm just going to say it, Laura: Richard overheard you and Nigel talking and he picked up enough to start wondering if you're getting divorced.'

Laura puts her hand to her mouth, fighting tears again.

I reach out and put my hand over hers. 'It's okay. He's okay. The thing is, he told Libby he hates the idea of you two staying together for his sake. He'd much rather you were honest with him about it all.'

Laura doesn't say anything. I think it's taking everything she has to hold herself together. I squeeze her hand. 'I know it's hard, but it's all going to be okay, I promise.'

'What do I do, Lou? Tell me what to do.'

'Well, I think you need to talk to Nigel again – make sure Richard's out though. Tell him what I've told you and then make a plan to tell Richard together. The most important thing is to present a united front, make sure Richard knows it's a joint decision and that you'll both be there for him, none of it's his fault, and so on. Although, Richard's so sensible, I don't think it'll be a problem. He'd much rather you were happy apart than miserable together. Especially under the misguided notion that it's better for him.'

'Happy apart… not sure that'll be the case,' Laura says sadly, picking up on my words.

'I know. No-one's saying it'll be easy, but better than carrying on as you are now. At least when Richard knows, you can start the process of grieving and moving forward. It has to be better than living under this sort of strain for another six months.' I give her hand another squeeze and take a mouthful of food, conscious that I still need to eat and that my lunchtime isn't long.

Laura doesn't say anything, but I can see she's processing what I've told her.

'I don't think you should let on to Richard you know about his meeting with Libby. I think it's important he trusts her – he might need a friend going forward; someone he can confide in. She only told me because she was worried about him. And you and Nigel, of course.'

Laura thinks about this for a few moments. Her thought process seems slow, deliberate, almost as if she's been drugged. 'Yes, of course, you're right,' she says eventually. 'I'm glad he felt he could talk to Libby. And I'm grateful for her intervention.' She pauses. 'I still dread the idea of telling him though.' A lonely tear trickles down her cheek.

'I know. I do understand. I remember going through it with Libby. But at least you know it won't come as a complete shock to him, and that he's actually okay with the idea. He just wants you both to be happy.'

'He'll be okay, won't he?'

'Yes! He really will. He'll be absolutely fine. I promise.'

'God. How did it come to this, Lou? All I've ever wanted is to give my child a stable, happy home and stay married to one man all my life. How has this happened? Am I just like Mum and Dad after all? Destined to repeat history?'

I shake my head. 'You can't think like that, Laura. I

understand, though. I felt the same. But it's not a failure. It's just life. Messy, real, uncontrollable life. It happens whether we want it to or not. All we can control is how we react to it.'

'I just want Richard to be alright. Ultimately, that's all I really care about.'

'And he will be. He really will be fine.' I smile at her. The furrow between her brows seems to have relaxed a little, and she doesn't seem to be quite so tightly wound. I'm relieved I've told her and she's taken it well. She still hasn't eaten any of her lunch. 'Do you want something different to eat?' I ask her. 'A muffin or something, just to keep you going?'

'No. No. Thank you. I'm really not hungry.'

'Are you sure? It's no bother.'

'Honestly, I'll have something later.'

'Okay. Will you be alright?' I'm conscious I have to get back to my desk, but I need to know Laura's okay first.

'Yes, I'll be fine. Thank you, Lou. Honestly, I appreciate today. I think it'll help. I'll speak to Nigel...' she drifts off.

'Well, you know where I am. If you need anything, just shout.'

We finish up at the table and I offer to walk Laura out to her car.

'No need, really. I'm going to nip into the Ladies on the way out anyway.'

We say our goodbyes, and exchange a longer hug than I can ever remember sharing with my oft-times prickly sister. It makes me sad it's taken something like this to bring us closer together.

The rest of the work day is uneventful, just the usual round of gripes about the waiting times in Accident and Emergency, and the rudeness of the receptionists. You try doing their job, I felt like saying, knowing what they had to put up with on a daily basis. When I pack up just after five, it's nice to know I won't be going home to a cold and empty house.

It's my turn to call out, 'Hi, I'm home!' a short while later, and I'm greeted by Libby's voice from the kitchen and lovely cooking smells. 'Something smells good,' I call as I hang up my coat and slip my shoes off in the hall. That something also smells suspiciously familiar.

'Chilli con carne,' comes the reply, as I walk into the kitchen.

I can't help laughing.

'What?' Libby asks. 'What's so funny about chilli?'

'Nothing. Nothing at all. Chilli is extremely serious,' I reply, with the straightest face I can muster.

'Mad woman.'

'Always was, always will be. No escaping it. It's in our DNA,' I wink at her.

'God help me!' Libby says. 'Let's hope nurture wins out over nature in my dissertation.'

'Indeed. I'm fighting the metamorphosis into Granny. Not sure how well that's going, to be honest. Sorry. You have my permission to stick me in a home for delinquent old ladies and forget about me.' I sit at the kitchen table and put my feet up on the chair opposite. 'Well, I must say it's very nice to come home to someone cooking for me. Thank you.' I don't feel the need to tell her I had chilli for lunch, and spoil her kind act.

'No worries. You haven't got any rice left though, so are jacket wedges okay instead?'

'Absolutely. Yum. So, what did you get up to today?'

Libby tips a bag of frozen potato wedges onto a baking tray

and slides it into the oven before answering. She leans back against the sink, fox oven gloves still on her hands. 'I met up with Sarah – we had a coffee and mooched round a few shops. That was nice. Did a bit of uni reading. Not a lot else. Oh, and spoke to Dad. Told him I'll be grilling you both for my dissertation.' She pauses. 'I'd rather he didn't know about my little... er... dalliance with the good, or not so good, professor.'

'Of course. He certainly won't hear it from me,' I reassure her.

'Thanks, Mums. Not my finest hour, I know.'

I shake my head. 'Maybe not, but the way you're handling it is incredibly mature. I'm really proud of you.'

Libby makes an "aw shucks" gesture with the oven glove and we both laugh. 'How about you? How was your day? Did you see Auntie Laura?'

'Yes, I did. She's going to speak to Uncle Nigel and I think they're going to tell Richard sooner rather than later.'

'That's good, then. Was Auntie Laura okay?'

'Yes, in the circumstances. She's under a lot of strain.'

'Yeah. I wonder when they'll tell him. Crap time of year to share this sort of news. Although I don't s'pose there's ever a good time?'

'No. Indeed. I was thinking about that too. They don't want to ruin Christmas but, equally, they don't want this Christmas to be a big fat pretence either.'

'My big, fat fake Christmas.'

'Hmm. And if they wait until after Christmas, that kind of ruins the New Year. Tricky. If it was me, I think I'd do it as soon as possible, but agree to make it as good a Christmas as possible. I'm sure it will be less awkward for Nigel and Laura once it's out in the open and they can stop the pretence.'

'I think I agree. Where will Uncle Nigel go? He can hardly move in with Karen, can he?'

'No. I'm not sure to be honest. I'm sure he's thought about it though – he can afford to get a little flat or something for now. I'm pretty sure they have little or no mortgage left on the house.'

'I kind of wish I could be at theirs on Christmas Day now – you know, for Richard's sake. Help make it a good one. Still, he'll have his mad old aunt there, won't he?' she winks at me.

I pretend to look confused. 'Has Laura got a sister I don't know about then?' I ask, all innocence.

Libby just laughs, and turns her attention back to dinner, which we eat in front of the TV again, ticking off another couple of episodes of the Scandinavian drama. And then it's my turn to opt for a bath and reading in bed. Just before I sink into a hot bath, I text Laura to let her know I'm thinking of her and hoping she's okay. I sleep fitfully that night, my mind so full of family, of faces, of complicated human relationships. I need to speak to Libby's Dad, Alan. I can't keep putting it off.

Chapter 46

Vertigo

Another day at the hospital, and another day nearer the Christmas holiday. It's a strange place to be working in the run up to Christmas. There's a mixture of excitement and sadness in the air. The staff make a special effort to cheer up the children's ward, and a steady stream of carol singers appear around the hospital. As always, Father Christmas will be visiting the sick children and handing out the many gifts that are always so generously donated. The cheerier (by that I mean, newer and therefore less disillusioned) staff dress up and decorate their uniforms, and I've seen some mistletoe hanging in the staff room. I can't remember the last time I had someone to kiss under the mistletoe.

As I close up my office for the day, calling out my goodbyes to the other admin staff, I think about what Libby said: that I should join a dating site. The more I think about it though, the more I hate the idea. Besides, there's just too much going on with the family at the moment. I don't have the energy to devote to finding someone for me. Maybe when Laura's in a better place. Or when hell freezes over. It's pointless, Marty. Because no-one matches up to you.

My phone pings with a text message just as I reach my car.

I get in before checking it. It's from Laura.

Spoke to Nigel at lunchtime today. We're going to tell Richard tonight. Nigel will stay until after Christmas, but move into the spare room. We're going to be a family for Christmas and then he'll move out in the New Year. There's never going to be a good time, but this feels like the best option. Wish me luck. X

Good luck! I'll be thinking of you all. I think you're doing the right thing. Here if you need me. Xx She's doing exactly what I would have done. Good job, Laura.

I don't start the engine straight away. I put my hands on the steering wheel and rest my head on them. I feel an unutterable sadness wash over me and suddenly burst into tears. Not quiet, restrained tears, but proper full-on sobbing, the kind I haven't let myself give in to for a long time. They feel necessary somehow. And they do feel like a release, in spite of my protestations to Libby that crying makes me feel worse. That's still true. I do feel rubbish when the sobbing subsides, but I also feel as though some sort of cathartic release has happened too. I don't even really know what I was crying for, whether it was for Laura and her family, or because another year has passed without you, Marty. Or because secrets have a way of coming out eventually and I was utterly, utterly terrified of losing the only person who really mattered to me.

Ferreting around in my bag, I pull out a packet of tissues and wipe my face, checking the damage in the mirror. There's no disguising the blotchy mess, and nothing except time is going to remedy it. There's no way I can hide this from Libby when I get home, so I spend the drive thinking up a convincing cover story.

Libby's in the lounge when I get home. She spots my patchy

red face as soon as I walked in the room.

'Oh my God, Mum! What's happened? Are you okay?'

I wave my hand dismissively. 'I'm absolutely fine. Just came over all emotional for some reason. I think I was already feeling a bit teary-eyed over the children's ward, and then Auntie Laura texted to say they're telling Richard tonight. It just all hit me at once I think.'

'Oh! Bless you. You're such a softie.' Libby gets up and hugs me. I want to cling on to her, never let her go. I can feel the lump in my throat return and tears threaten once more. I give myself a mental shake, and let her go, hoping my voice doesn't wobble and give me away.

'Anyway, how was your day, oh daughter of mine? Get up to any mischief?' I flop into the armchair.

'Sadly not. But it was productive. Got quite a bit of work done on my next essay. And read some interesting studies on twins and adopted siblings.'

'Well, that all sounds very productive indeed. Unlike the rest of my evening, I fear. Now I've sat down, I don't think I'm going to be getting back up.' I lean my head back and close my eyes.

'Well, that's okay, isn't it? There's nothing you need to do, is there?'

'No, I suppose not. Except feed you. You know, make some pretence at being a responsible parent.'

'Good grief! I'm more than capable of feeding myself.'

'Oh, I know. It just feels like I should look after you when you're home. But, let's face it, you're actually the better cook.'

'True that. Even if you did laugh at my chilli yesterday.'

'I wasn't laughing AT your chilli.'

'Yeah, yeah. Whatever.' She pretends to turn away in a huff.

I can't help laughing again at the easy banter between us; but at the same time, I'm filled with dread at the possibility of losing it.

Between us, we cobble together some pasta and salad. While we're eating, Libby gets a text from her friend, Sarah, asking if she fancies going down the pub.

'Do you mind, Mum?' she asks, looking up from her mobile.

'No! Of course I don't mind. Go out and have fun. I won't feel so guilty sitting on my bum doing nothing with no witness.'

After dinner, Libby gets changed and heads out. Before I can chicken out, I text her dad.

Hi, don't suppose you're free? Need to talk about Libby.

I wondered when I'd hear from you. Free tonight. Where and when?

Libby's out, so can you come here? 7.30?

Fine. See you soon.

The knot that's been growing in my guts pulls tighter still and a wave of nausea hits me. I feel like a little boat being tossed about on a stormy sea, desperately trying to moor, its ropes being wrenched from the posts, constantly at risk of being set adrift. I literally feel all at sea. I wouldn't normally invite Alan to my house, my sanctuary, but I don't want to risk running in to Libby if we meet in town. It's always been amicable between me and Alan anyway. I'm really hoping Laura and Nigel can manage the same for Richard. But right now, I have to think about my own family, and let Laura and Nigel get on with their own problems.

The doorbell rings at exactly seven thirty, and I open the door to my ex-husband. He seems shorter. And rounder. He looks as serious as I feel.

'Hi, thanks for coming. Can I get you a drink?' I usher him into the lounge.

'Got any Scotch? I have a feeling I'm going to need it.'

'You and me both. Won't be a sec.' I head off to pour the drinks, on the rocks (aptly) for me, straight up for Mr. Black and White. Heading back into the lounge, I hand Alan his drink and sit down opposite him. 'Cheers.'

He lifts his glass and nods, before taking a sip. I do the same and wince slightly as I feel the burn on my throat. One of us needs to start the conversation but Alan looks as reluctant as me, not at all his usual straight-up self. We sit there in silence for a while, each looking lost in thought.

'So…' In the end we both start to speak at exactly the same moment.

'You first,' Alan says.

'Thanks. I think. I don't really know how to start this conversation.'

'I know. I always hoped we'd never have to have it.'

'I know. I just don't see how we can avoid it now though. I can't bear the thought of having to tell Libby lie upon lie otherwise.'

'No. It's going to be hard enough confessing to this one, however good the intentions were to start with, all those years ago.'

'Why did she have to choose to study bloody psychology at university anyway?' I grumble.

'Well, she did, and now we have to deal with this, Lou. As much as I don't want to, we really don't have a choice, do we?'

I shake my head. 'No. There's no way we can lie when she

questions us for her nature versus nurture study.' I take another sip of my drink.

'So, how? When? How do we tackle this?'

'I think we need to tell her together, don't you? Present a united front.'

Alan nods. He looks worried. I can't remember him ever looking so close to breaking. He hunches over his glass and looks at the floor. When he looks back up, there are tears streaming down his face. 'I'm scared, Lou. I'm so scared of losing her!'

I spring out of my seat and go to sit by him on the sofa, forgetting he's my ex-husband. Right now, he's just a human being in distress. I wrap my arms around him and hold him close as he cries.

'I know. Me too. I'm terrified. I've never been so scared in my whole life. We just have to pray she understands.'

Alan pulls away and sits back. I reach for the box of tissues on the side table and pass a handful to him. I wait while he blows his nose and regains his composure.

'Sorry,' Alan says, clearly a little embarrassed at breaking down.

'God, don't say sorry. I blubbed my eyes out in the car earlier. Had to tell Libby that Coco the Clown upset me on the children's ward.'

Alan looks at me as if I'm mad, then just shakes his head. 'Okay, so when are we doing this? Shall we ruin Christmas or the New Year?'

Libby's "big fat fake Christmas" comment comes back to me, and I realise we shouldn't delay telling her, however much we want to.

'I think sooner rather than later, don't you?'

'Yep, I guess. Get it over with.'

Alan and I talked for a little while longer, deciding what we we're going to say to Libby, and discussing where we should meet.

'Do you think it should be somewhere neutral?' Alan asked.

'Like Switzerland?' A picture of Libby munching on Toblerone flits into my head.

'Constructive as ever, Louise. Seriously, I don't know what's best.'

'No, I know, I'm sorry. I don't think we can do it anywhere public – that wouldn't be fair to Libby. If there's going to be a scene, it should be at home. Are you happy to come here?' Alan still lives in our former marital home, and I don't really think that's the right place for this conversation.

'Yes, of course. When?'

'Tomorrow evening? Does that work for you?'

'Yes, that's fine.'

Alan had finished his drink and gone by nine. I left Libby a note on the kitchen table and went up to bed early, hating myself for my cowardice, but totally unable to face her just yet. I knew I wouldn't be able to sleep, and I just lay there in the dark, worrying and wondering what the next evening would bring, tossing and turning, the little boat getting no respite from the storm at sea.

Chapter 47

Don't Leave Me This Way

I'm up and out while Libby still sleeps the following morning. I don't even stop for breakfast, opting to grab something at work rather than run the risk of seeing her. I feel nauseous constantly and am not sure how I'm going to get through the day.

I force down a coffee and a blueberry muffin at my desk and try to focus on dealing with my emails. I find myself staring unseeing at the screen most of the time, and have to reread everything umpteen times before anything sinks in. I'm grateful things are relatively quiet in the run up to Christmas.

Somehow I make it through to five o'clock. As much as I'm glad the work day is over, I dread going home. I'd texted Libby mid-morning to say I'd planned dinner for us this evening to ensure she didn't make other plans. The feeling of nausea is worse than ever as I drive home. I really don't know if I can do this. I stop for fish and chips on the way home. The last thing I feel like doing is cooking.

Arriving home a short while later, I find the downstairs rooms in darkness but I can hear music drifting down the stairs. I flick on the hall light and call out.

'Libby! Dinner! Come and get it.' Hoping she'll hear me

over the music, I go round closing curtains and switching on lights, stopping beside the Christmas tree and giving the giraffe a nudge. 'Wish me luck, Marty. I'm gonna need it.'

There's still no sign of Libby when I pad back through to the kitchen, so I jog up the stairs to her room, knocking on the door and calling out again, 'Libby, dinner,' before putting my head round the door. She looks up from the bed, where she's tapping away on her laptop and singing along with the music. She looks so young and beautiful, and my heart swells with love for her.

'Oh, hi, Mum. Sorry. Be right down.'

I just smile at her, not sure I can squeeze a word out.

I listen to Libby chat happily about her day while we eat our cod and chips. I take in every word she utters, and absorb every nuance, appreciate every gesture. I enjoy the feeling of normality; a mother and daughter talking about their day, as I try desperately not to think about what comes next.

'It's a fascinating area of study... what makes us who we are? Are we products of our environments or the embodiment of our genes? It's definitely what I want to do for my dissertation, I've decided.' Libby looks happy and excited as she talks about her studies. I think my heart will break.

'That's great, darling. Um... changing the subject a bit... er... Dad's coming round later.'

'Grandad?' she groans. 'God, do you mean to say you kept me here under false pretences tonight?'

'Um... no, not Grandad, your Dad,' I correct.

Libby frowns. 'My Dad? Why on earth is he coming here? Has he ever even been to your house before?'

'No, I know it's unusual, but... um... there's something we

274

want to talk to you about, together.'

Libby shrugs, seeming to accept this fact. 'Okay.'

We finish dinner and I head to the kitchen to deal with the few dishes, leaving Libby in the lounge. It's not long before the doorbell goes.

'I'll get it!' I shout. I open the door to find a grim-faced Alan standing there.

'Reinforcements,' he says, holding a bottle of wine aloft.

'Come in. Libby's in the lounge,' I tell him, taking the proffered bottle.

Alan shrugs off his coat and hangs it over the bannisters. 'Been dreading this all day,' he says. 'Scratch that, I've been dreading this for nineteen years,' he adds, grim-faced.

'I know. Me too. We just have to get through it. Thanks for being with me on this.'

'Of course. Where else would I be?'

'Well, it is kind of my mess – you could've told me to deal with it myself.'

'It's not just your mess, Lou. We agreed that nearly two decades ago.'

'Well, anyway, I'm glad you're here, Alan, and I'm sorry it's come to this.' I get three wine glasses from the cupboard and we go into the lounge together.

Libby looks up as we enter the room and her face lights up at the sight of her dad. 'Dad! Hi!' she says, uncurling her legs and getting up to hug him. 'What on earth are you doing here? It's like seeing a teacher out of school!' she laughs.

Alan smiles at her. He looks as though he can't speak. My heart constricts, and I distract the two of them, busying myself with the wine, and jabbering on about God knows what. Soon we're all seated and Libby is looking at us expectantly. I think I might actually vomit.

She looks from one to the other. 'Well, are you going to tell me what this is all about? Or just sit there like a pair of waxwork dummies?'

I take a deep breath. Alan and I agreed that I would start the conversation. It seemed only fair when we were discussing it last night. Now I'm not so sure I'm up to the task. Alan reaches over and gives my hand a squeeze. This, of course, does not escape Libby's attention.

'Holy cow! Now I know something's going on,' she says, only half joking.

One more deep breath. 'Libby…' I begin, 'before we tell you what this is about, please remember Dad and I both love you more than anything in this world. You literally mean the world to us.' Another deep breath. I can see Libby processing my words. She looks confused.

'Shit. Please tell me one of you's not dying?'

'No! No, we're both fine, I promise you.'

Libby looks relieved. 'Thank God for that! Well, nothing could be worse than that, so spit it out.'

'I wish it was that easy, Libby, really I do. Okay, here goes… When Dad came into my life, Libby, I already had you.' I pause, watching her face, waiting for the words to sink in. Her furrowed brows tighten and the colour drains from her face.

'I don't understand… what are you saying? Are you saying that Dad's not really my dad?'

I nod, trying desperately not to give in to tears. 'To all intents and purposes, Libby, he is your Dad and he's always loved you as his own. But, he's not your biological father. I'm sorry.' I look over at Alan to see tears streaming down his face.

Libby still looks confused. 'But I've seen my birth certificate. It's got Dad's name on. How...?'

'We had Dad added later – it only had me on when your birth was first registered. As far as everyone's concerned, Dad really is your Dad. And he always has been, Libby. No man could've been a better father or loved you more. When we met, he fell as much in love with you as he did with me, and we agreed you should be his...' I'm struggling to find the words.

Alan comes to my rescue. 'It's not all your Mum's fault, Libby. I made her promise not to tell you the truth. I so desperately wanted you to be mine, to give you a happy, secure life. I, we, never wanted to hurt you. I'm sorry.' Tears continue to stream down his face.

Libby's head is shaking from side to side as she tries to deny the words entry to her brain. A painful silence fills the room, until Libby breaks it.

'So, if Dad, sorry, Alan's not my real father, who the hell is?' She sounds eerily calm now, her distress teetering on the verge of anger.

'Remember the friend I told you about? The night we watched *One Day*?'

Libby stops to think for a moment. 'Martin? The guy you said you were just friends with? Wow. Really, Mum? Christ! Is he even really dead?'

Her words and the look on her face are like slaps to my own. 'Yes,' I tell her, 'he died when you were little. When I met Dad, it seemed like the perfect solution. We only ever wanted to do the best for you.'

I can see Libby's mind still working on overdrive. 'Wait, you said this Martin was married. Had… two…? daughters. Am I one of those daughters? Or…?'

I nod my head. 'Martin was the love of my life, and he would have loved you so very much. He was on his way to me when he died. I was going to tell him about you and we were going to be a family.'

'So, he didn't even know about me? What the hell, Mum?' she shakes her head angrily.

'It was complicated, Libby. He was married… and… how can I make you understand? I didn't want him to have to choose between his children. If he came to me, it had to be because he wanted me, not out of some sense of duty. It would've killed him to have to choose between you.'

'Well, it did kill him in the end, didn't it?' she says sharply, wanting to wound with her words. 'You're basically telling me my whole life is a lie?'

'No!' Alan and I say in unison.

'No, Libby, not a lie. You were raised by two people who loved you and wanted the best for you. That's not a lie,' I insist.

'I can't deal with this,' Libby exclaims, jumping up. She runs from the room, with Alan and I following suit. 'Please, Libby, please!'

'No. Just leave me alone,' she shouts, pulling on her boots and grabbing keys from the hall table. Unable to stop her, she slams out of the house. Only when she gets in my car do we realise she's taken the car keys.

'Oh God, Alan. She shouldn't be driving!' I'm stricken with terror at the thought of her behind the wheel of a car in the state she's in. A horrific flashback to the night you died bursts in my brain. 'I can't lose her, Alan! I can't lose Libby too!' My panic is Alan's cue to compose himself and take control.

'Shh! She just needs some time, Lou. She'll be okay. She's a sensible girl. She just needs some time to take it all in. She'll be back.'

I've collapsed on the bottom stair and am sobbing uncontrollably, words stammering out incomprehensibly through tears and snot. Alan fetches the tissues and tries to talk me down.

'Come on, Lou. You have to pull yourself together. When Libby gets back, she's going to have questions, and you need to be in a fit state to answer them. Come on. Blow your nose. And breathe!'

After a while, I manage to get control over my emotions sufficiently to get up from the stairs and we go and sit in the kitchen. Alan gets me a glass of water.

'You always were an ugly crier,' he says, with a half-smile. 'But still the most beautiful woman I've ever met.'

I don't know whether to laugh or slap him, but I'm grateful to this man I'd raised my daughter with. 'Where do you think she's gone?'

'Honestly? I don't know. But I'm sure she'll be fine when she calms down enough to think it through. That girl has a streak of compassion a mile wide, like her mother.'

'And her father,' I whisper, thinking of you, Marty. I'm so sorry I never told you I was pregnant. It somehow seemed wrong to force you to choose between your daughters. I thought I was doing the right thing, keeping Libby a secret until I knew you were coming to me for the right reasons. It wasn't easy keeping her existence from you. So many times, I almost broke and confessed to you. So often over the years I have wished I handled things differently. If I'd told you about Libby, you wouldn't have been on the road on that fateful rainy April day. I have lived with regret and loss and guilt for so long, Marty. And now I fear I've lost the one good thing to come out of you and me: our daughter.

'I've texted her.' Alan's words break through my thoughts.

'What? Has she replied?'

'No, not yet. But I've told her I'm not going anywhere, and we'll both be right here to answer any questions she has. And that we both love her.'

'Thank you. Thanks, Alan. I'm glad you're here. I'm so sorry.'

'Shut up, Lou. We made these decisions together. And they were made for good reasons. Libby'll understand. Eventually,' he adds.

'God, I hope so. What if she hates me? I couldn't bear it. I literally couldn't bear it, Alan. She's the only thing that's kept me going all these years.'

'I know. She won't hate you. She could never hate you.'

'I'm not so sure. Her face… she was so angry. So hurt.'

'Yes, but it's all raw right now. Give her some time.'

I shake my head, unsure if we can get through this and come out whole the other end.

We sit in silence. I don't know how much times passes. Eventually, there's a beep from Alan's phone.

'Is it Libby?'

'Yes, she says she's staying at your mother's tonight and she'll talk to us both tomorrow.'

'Christ! Why on earth did she go to my bloody mother? If anyone can throw petrol on troubled waters!'

'She might surprise you. She's actually a wise old bird

underneath it all.'

'Wise old bird? Well, she certainly bloody well knows how to ruffle my feathers. Should we call her?'

'Your mum? No, I think we just have to respect Libby's wishes tonight. Are you going to be okay?'

'No. Yes. God, I don't know. I'm terrified, Alan.'

'I know. Me too. But there's nothing more that we can do tonight. I'm working from home tomorrow, so can be around when Libby's ready to talk. It'll be okay.'

'I'm never going to be able to sleep. I'll have to phone in sick tomorrow. Libby's more important than that poxy job.'

'Just get through the night as best you can, and I'll speak to you in the morning. Um... can I ask... are you still on the antidepressants? The ones that help you sleep?'

I shake my head, embarrassed at the mention of my mental health. 'No, but I still have some.'

'Maybe you should take one tonight?' Alan suggests.

'Maybe.'

'Right, I'm going to go. If you're sure you're going to be okay? I can ring Laura if you want? Maybe she could come and stay?' Alan thinks about what he's just said and backtracks. 'On second thoughts, Laura's probably not the right person to have around at a time like this.'

'Shit. Laura. Oh God, Alan, she and Nigel are getting divorced – they were telling Richard last night. And I've been so preoccupied I haven't even checked to see if they're all okay.'

'Er... I think you're forgiven! You've had other things on your mind. Worry about it tomorrow. Right now, you need to rest. I'll see myself out. Try not to worry.'

'Easier said than done. Thanks, Alan. Speak to you in the morning. If you hear from Libby, please let me know, won't you? Any time.'

'Of course. Night, Lou.'

'Night, Alan. Thank you.'

Chapter 48

Don't Dream It's Over

It is the longest and blackest of nights. I lie in bed because I don't know what else to do. The only time I can ever remember feeling this lost and alone, this hopeless, was the night you died, Marty. It was too late then. I pray it's not too late now. At least I know where Libby is, and that she's safe. I can only hope my mother is not further alienating my daughter from me. I wonder how much Libby has told her, if anything, about the situation. I suppose she will have told her at least some of it to explain her unexpected arrival at her grandmother's.

The hours tick by slowly. I think I doze intermittently, but my brain won't switch off completely to allow sleep to claim me. Feverish thoughts of you and Libby vie for my attention, until they all become a jumbled mass. I finally give up at about six and get up, pulling on my dressing gown and slippers and plodding downstairs. I feel absolutely wretched and, seeing my reflection in the hall mirror, I look it too. I make a cup of tea and go and sit in the lounge, shivering a little as the house is still warming up. I pull a fleecy throw from the back of the sofa and wrap it around me, cupping my chilled hands around the mug and staring into space. I'm too tired even to think coherently. I'm just a mess of worry and what ifs.

I'm so very tired and I can feel my head lolling. I put my mug on the table and allow my head to lean back. I'll just close my eyes for a minute...

I don't hear the key in the lock, or the front door opening. Or closing. I don't hear the sounds of boots being removed or footsteps along the hall. I don't even feel the weight of someone sitting down on the sofa next to me. Then I hear Libby's voice in my dream:

'Mum. Mum, wake up.' She shakes my arm. It feels real. I want it to be real. I feel like I've been drugged as I try and prise myself from sleep. My eyes are too heavy to open. 'Mum, wake up. It's me.' Another shake. I manage to open my eyes. I'm worried if I'm waking from a dream, I'll have lost her all over again.

But she's here. My Libby is here. I promptly burst into tears and throw my arms around her. 'Oh my God, I thought I'd lost you. I thought you hated me, Libby. I'm so, so sorry. For everything.'

Libby's crying too. 'I could never hate you, Mum. But it was a lot to take in last night and I didn't know what to do with it all. I needed some space to... process, I suppose. I didn't want to react before I had a chance to think about things with a bit of time and distance.'

'We never meant to hurt you, you must know that?'

'Yes, I know. And I do understand. Sort of. I do have a million things buzzing around my head though, and lots of questions.'

'Of course you do. And I will tell you everything and answer all your questions. Have you spoken to Dad? Does he know you're alright?'

'I texted him to let him know I'm okay and that I was coming back here. Said we'll catch up later.'

'He'll be so relieved. He loves you, Libby. We both love you so much.'

'I know you do. I never doubted that, but it was a hell of a shock. It knocked me sideways for a minute there!' My girl, trying to make light of it.

'I'm sorry.' I don't know what else to say.

'You don't have to keep saying you're sorry, Mum. I know you would never hurt me intentionally.'

'God, you don't know how relieved I am, Libby. That honestly was the worst night of my life.'

'That'll teach you to be honest with me in the future then, eh?' I can't believe she's smiling and cracking jokes. Again I marvel at her resilience and strength of character.

I smile weakly. 'I was so worried when you left last night. I couldn't think where you would go. You couldn't go to Auntie Laura's with everything that's going on there. Was Granny okay?'

'Actually, Granny was really rather marvellous. I said we'd fallen out about something and I needed some time to cool down. She didn't push me for information or anything. She just made me hot chocolate and we played Scrabble until bedtime. Oh, and she knows about Auntie Laura's situation. Apparently, they're all okay after the big reveal to Richard. Jeez, it's been quite a week for our family, hasn't it?'

'That's good - I'm glad. Did you manage to get any sleep?'

'A bit. Mostly I just lay and thought about everything. I was thinking about why you chose to tell me now and then it hit me – it was because of my uni work wasn't it?'

'Yes, that was the catalyst...'

'And you didn't want to lie to me when I asked you questions.'

'No, neither of us wanted to lie to you, Libby.'

'Would you ever have told me if I hadn't been studying psychology?'

'Honestly? I don't know. I promised Dad it would stay our secret when you were a baby. He hated the thought of you knowing he wasn't your biological father. And you were so young when he came into our lives – it made sense at the time. You'd never known any other father, and with Martin gone...'

'I get it. I'm not saying I'm okay with it all yet, but I think I understand why you did what you did.'

'I'm so sor...' I start to apologise again.

'Don't say it!' Libby puts her finger to my lips. She's quiet for a moment. 'I do want to know all about my real dad though, about Martin. Was he really the love of your life?'

'Yes, Marty really was the love of my life. He was my soul-mate. And I'm happy to tell you everything. He would've been so proud of you, Libby. I wish things had been different, of course, but I'm glad you have Alan.'

She pauses again. 'The thing I'm struggling with most, if I'm honest, is the fact I have a half-sister out there somewhere. She doesn't know about me, does she?'

I shake my head. 'No, love, she doesn't. As far as I know she doesn't know about me, either; about my relationship with her dad. Her mum protected his memory. And she was very little when he died, too.'

Libby sits quietly, clearly lost in thought. I sense I should just wait.

'Then I want to protect his memory, too. Part of me would

love to meet her but it would be selfish of me to turn her life upside down and ruin her memory of her father, our father.'

I squeeze her hand, rendered speechless once again by her maturity.

'Tell me about Marty, Mum. Tell me about my father. I want to know everything.'

'Well, it all started with a small, plastic giraffe…'

THE END

Acknowledgements

Thank you for reading *A Giraffe Thing*. I really hope you enjoyed reading it as much as I enjoyed writing it. Writing is a solitary profession at the best of times, and the pandemic we were living through when I wrote this book meant this was even more the case. There's one person without whom I could not have got through and out the other side. His name is Gwynne Morgan and he means the world to me. My bubble buddy. Thank you. I owe you a debt of gratitude I can never repay – thanks for putting up with me.

My grateful thanks go to James Essinger at The Conrad Press for his continued support and guidance, and to Karla Harris for her careful proofreading. To the brilliant and talented Charlotte Mouncey for her inspired cover design and typesetting, despite the challenges I threw at her!

My love and thanks also go to Kathy Matthews for her friendship and support, in good times and bad. I'd be lost with you, Kathy!

This book is dedicated to an incredibly special man who sadly passed away while I was writing it. Graham Norgate: uncle, husband, father, grandfather, and all-round awesome human being. Taken too soon, but he leaves a wonderful legacy in his home town of Beccles.

And last, but never least, I give thanks for my son, Sam, who continues to astound me and fills me with immeasurable pride. Always.